PERFECT PARTNERS

by

Maggie Cummings

2019

PERFECT PARTNERS

ISBN 13: 978-1-63555-363-5

THIS TRADE PAPERBACK ORIGINAL IS PUBLISHED BY
BOLD STROKES BOOKS, INC.
P.O. BOX 249
VALLEY FALLS, NY 12185

FIRST EDITION: FEBRUARY 2019

CREDITS
EDITOR: RUTH STERNGLANTZ
PRODUCTION DESIGN: STACIA SEAMAN
COVER DESIGN BY SHERI (HINDSIGHTGRAPHICS@GMAIL.COM)

Praise for Maggie Cummings

Against All Odds

"This story tugged at my heartstrings, and it hit all the right notes for me because these wonderful authors allowed me to peep into the hearts and minds of the characters. The vivid descriptions of Peyton, Tory, and the perpetrator's personalities allowed me to have a deeper understanding of what makes them tick, and I was able to form a clear picture of them in my mind."—*The Lesbian Review*

"*Against All Odds* is equal parts thriller and romance; the balance between action and love, fast and slow pace makes this novel a very entertaining read."—*Lez Review Books*

Definite Possibility

"I enjoyed this book, well written with well-developed characters, including some familiar faces from the previous book in the series. The leads had good chemistry and the angst level was just right. It was an enjoyable read for a quiet afternoon."—*Melina Bickard, Librarian, Waterloo Library (UK)*

"[T]wo parallel romances give a quick pace to the book with more drama and romance...But what I really liked is that the story goes beyond both romances and is a tale of friendship, family and love. Overall, a heartwarming and feel-good story with a bit of drama on the side."—*Lez Review Books*

Totally Worth It

"This book was absolutely delightful...A sweet story about love and friendship."—*My Fiction Nook*

"[I]t was...really nice reading about people going through the same transitory period in their lives that I, and many other twenty-somethings, also are...By the end of the book, I was a little jealous that I didn't live in Bay West like the characters. Needless to say, I was pretty pleased when I found out that this was going to be a series because Bay West has so much potential given the setting and the diverse cast of characters already in play. After a very solid first novel, I can't wait to see where Cummings takes us next."—*Read All About Queer Lit*

By the Author

Totally Worth It

Serious Potential

Definite Possibility

Against All Odds
(with Kris Bryant and M. Ullrich)

Perfect Partners

Acknowledgments

Once again, my sincerest thanks to Rad and Sandy for giving me the opportunity to be part of such a wonderful company and community. To the entire team at Bold Strokes Books, thank you for everything you do. It is an honor to be part of something so special.

Writing can be such a solitary venture, and yet this book felt like a team effort. I have so many wonderful people in my life, and I am grateful to be so fortunate. Immeasurable thanks to Kat, Caleb, and Abby for always believing in me, encouraging me, and supporting me every step of the way. A special shout out to Abby, who helped me name every single dog in this book, and to my own pup, Zach, who sat next to me (or on my laptop) for continued inspiration throughout.

I would be lost without my BSB family. My most heartfelt thanks to my amazing editor, Ruth Sternglantz, who has boundless wisdom, patience, guidance, and enthusiasm and has the uncanny ability to deliver each at the perfect moment. Huge hugs to Kris, Megan, and Aurora for always pushing me, believing in me, keeping me laughing and smiling, and for being great friends and amazing people.

Finally, and perhaps most importantly, I'd like to especially thank Captain John Kerwick and the MTA Police K-9 division for affording me the opportunity to spend time at their training facility, ask a thousand questions, and observe the dogs and their handlers at work. Without these officers, human and canine alike, this book would not have been possible. Thank you for all you do, every day. Stay safe.

I would be remiss if I didn't mention my extended family: Stu, Ron, Dottie and the Kerns—you. You! Thank you all for your support. Always.

For Bernie Bal, my hero

CHAPTER ONE

E yes on me."
        Sara resisted the urge to look at the car approaching up the long gravel drive. It was important to set a good example, and damned if she was going to sacrifice progress for a lost driver. Her voice was just above a whisper, the tone gentle but firm. "I know it's hard, but you've got to stay focused." Her eyes were fixed and steady and she spoke with a balance of confidence and affection. "We're going to see who's lost in just one…more…second," she said, dragging out the sentence to test her student's patience.

Sweet brown eyes locked with hers in a stare so sincere it melted her right on the spot. Sara smiled and watched as Chase's eyebrows furrowed hopefully, his jaw dropping open with a heavy pant as he sought approval for his deft adherence to her instruction. Sara knew he wanted to run to the car and investigate, and she could hardly blame him. It was barely seven in the morning, the campus quiet, save a few earlybirds like herself. It was still hours away from real activity at the training facility.

Chase held his position, and proud of his progress, Sara rewarded him with a tender scratch between the ears. "You're a good boy," she said. The dog relished the attention, seeming almost to smile at her touch. She rubbed under his chin softly, holding his face as she spoke. "Now don't go getting your hopes up," she said playfully. "It's just going to be another desperate soul in need of help because their GPS can't hold a signal in these woods. We still have work to do. But let's see what's up." She patted his head. "Go," she commanded as she dropped the lead and peered over her shoulder, surprised to see an NYPD cruiser making its way up the hill. The patrol car was moving at a glacial pace, the driver almost making the turn into the visitors' lot but then redirecting at the last minute, seeming uncertain where to go. Finally, the car came to a complete stop in the middle of the road. "What could this be about?" Sara asked herself under her breath as she racked her brain to remember the day's schedule.

Even though curiosity was killing her, Sara took her time walking over to the vehicle, using the opportunity to watch the dog's approach. He circled the marked car once, sniffing at it continuously. When the door opened, a female driver emerged, and Chase wasted no time tracing his nose up and down her legs before putting his front paws up on the vinyl seat and poking his head inside to get a good whiff. Sara smiled at his perfect instincts.

"Don't worry, he won't hurt you," she called across the short distance.

"Can I pet him?" the stranger asked.

"Sure."

Sara studied the woman's body language and smiled when she dropped to both knees and showered the dog with affection, talking directly to him. Most people freaked at the mere thought of a German shepherd barreling toward them. But this woman showed no fear. Dog people—she couldn't help but have a weakness for them. Her guard dropped immediately.

"Can I help you?" Sara asked as she got closer.

"I hope so." The woman stood up and brushed dirt off the knees of her dark blue BDUs. She straightened her shoulders and nudged her chin upright, as if presenting herself for inspection. Her dark brown eyes were bright and hopeful as she spoke. "I'm looking for Miss Wright," she said emphatically, her voice a mix of excitement and anticipation, and Sara couldn't keep her coy grin under control. "Oh my God," the officer added, realizing what she'd said right away. "That's not what I meant. I mean, it is, but not like that." She shook her head and bit her lower lip, her cheeks dimpling at her unintentional play on words. "Wright with a *W*," she corrected, adding a delightful self-deprecating eye roll.

Sara dove in to save her. "Happens all the time." At thirty-four years old, she'd endured enough *Miss Right* jokes to last a lifetime. These days, she ignored such comments, the pun mostly coming from men—but sometimes women—deliberate and pathetic in their weak attempts to use her surname to their advantage. But this moment felt entirely different than those interactions. Whether it was the result of a boring weekend spent in solitude or an insufficient amount of caffeine for her brain to function properly at this early hour, she wasn't sure. Perhaps it was simply the source. An adorable, dog-loving brunette in full police gear was enough to make anyone swoon, right? Whatever the reason, she felt herself fighting the urge to flirt, and she stopped herself from telling the cute officer to look no further. Blinking the thought away, she composed herself and cleared her throat, trading her unexpected desire for professionalism. "I'm Sara Wright."

"Oh, good." The woman let out a deep breath in relief. "Isabel Marquez." She touched her own chest before thrusting her hand toward Sara. Sara accepted the greeting, shaking the woman's hand even though—despite the introduction—Sara had no idea what she was doing at the training facility. Isabel must've read the confusion in her expression. "From the NYPD," she said, seeming confidently optimistic saying the name of her police department might jog Sara's memory.

Sara was still clueless. "Sorry," she offered, furrowing her brows in a kind of apology. "Are you here for a class or something?"

"Yes. Well, sort of." Isabel stroked the dog's head as she spoke. "I was just assigned to the K-9 class. The one for explosive detection dogs."

Now Sara was full-on confused. The K-9 explosives class started in a week and she'd had the roster for months. There were no female NYPD officers registered, of that she was sure. She had the breakdown of prospective handlers committed to memory. There were eight federal agents, two cops from small local police departments, two sheriff's officers from Florida, and one cop from the NYPD. Sara couldn't quite recall his name, but she remembered his pedigree—a ten-year vet who'd be getting his first canine partner.

"Are you sure you're in that class?" she asked. "Maybe you're assigned to a different training location."

"I'm pretty sure I'm in the right spot," Isabel responded quickly. "This is the Northeast Regional Training Facility at Overton?" The wind whipped her long brown hair in her face and she tried to tuck it behind her ears, looking anxious as she shook her head. "The guy from my job who was slated to be here…his wife got sick. Cancer, I heard. He had to back out at the last minute."

This was news to Sara. Her head spun as she tried to figure out how a complete switch had gone down without her knowledge or input.

"Anyway, I'm here in his place." Isabel's voice rattled, her nerves clearly escalating. "My boss told me you'd know I was coming." She licked her lips repeatedly. "I feel like kind of a jerk right now, seeing you clearly had no idea." Her hair blew in her face again and she huffed, trying in vain to hold it back with one hand. "I was putting my hair up when I pulled in here and I hit a pothole. I dropped my clip." She sounded flustered. "Excuse me for just a second."

She kneeled on the front seat, bending over as she searched the floorboard with both hands. Sara waited, trying to divert her eyes from Isabel's behind perfectly outlined in the uniform cargo-style pants.

Finding her clip, Isabel planted herself in the driver's seat and stole a glance in the rearview as she pulled her hair off her face. Grabbing a folder from the console, she attempted to stand but the wind had other plans, railing against the open door, pushing it into her with force enough to knock her back into the seat. "Jesus." She grasped the door frame for balance.

"Are you okay?" Sara stifled a laugh as she reached forward to help her.

"I'm fine. Sorry." Isabel waved her off. She stood up and closed the door behind her, leaning on it as she opened her manila folder. Immediately, the top page blew out. She stomped on it, smashing it into the ground.

"Nice reflexes," Sara said with a chuckle.

"Except now it's a mess." Isabel reached down and dusted the dirt and gravel off the top page of her application. "I'm a mess." She shook her head at herself. "I'm not usually a disaster. I swear."

"You're fine. Relax." Sara hoped her smile showed her sentiment was real.

Pointing to a yellow Post-it on the inside of the folder, Isabel leaned toward her and in the breeze Sara caught a hint of her lovely light scent.

"It says here to report to Sara Wright," Isabel said. "There was another name in here somewhere." Her eyes scanned quickly. "There it is. Special Agent John Dixon."

"Now that makes sense." Sara nodded. "John's in charge of the program. I just run the dogs. So odd you were told to find me." She frowned, brushing it off. "Anyhow, John—that's Agent Dixon—he's inside. Come on, I'll take you."

Glancing down at the dog who was nudging her hand for attention, Isabel asked, "Does this sweetie get to come too?"

"This is Chase. And absolutely he gets to come with."

"Chase," Isabel repeated. "That's a cool name. Because he likes to run after squirrels and stuff?" she asked, her eyes wide, before she added an enthusiastic, "Oh, wait"—she popped her head up—"it's because he'll chase the perps, right?"

Sara smiled. "Actually he's named after a cop. All our dogs are named for heroes who've made the ultimate sacrifice in the line of duty." She stroked Chase's head. "This guy is named for one of yours. An NYPD officer—Sebastian Chaiskovanich."

"Of course," Isabel's voice dropped and she diverted her eyes. "Everyone called him Chase. Because no one could pronounce his name."

"Did you know him?"

"Hardly." She chewed her lower lip. "He was in transit division, though. Like me. I worked with him a few times. Nice guy." She covered half her face with one hand. "I'm an idiot. Saying Chase's name was cool."

"How would you know?" Sara offered, letting her off the hook right away. She studied Isabel for a brief second. Dark brown hair, almost black. Long, thick, and full of body even pulled up away from her face. Eyes to match. Expressive and rich, an exquisite brown, their hue darker than any she'd seen, framed by incredible lashes. They were plain yet captivating and Sara felt herself getting lost in them. Her sincerity was also appealing. Even in this moment it was apparent she felt awful at minimizing her colleague's death, however inadvertently.

Sara longed to break the tension, make Isabel feel better about the exchange, about the whole morning.

As though she was reading her thoughts Isabel muttered, "I want a do-over on this whole day."

"You're being too hard on yourself." She reached down to pet Chase and her hand brushed over Isabel's, the touch sending an unexpected chill up her forearm. "Come on," she said. "Let's get you squared away. I'll introduce you to John. There's a pile of paperwork to complete before class starts on Monday."

With an outstretched hand for Sara to lead the way, Isabel said, "I'll follow you." Sara watched her turn and fall in step next to her and Chase, the spirit of her early morning smile beginning to return. Sara hated to deflate her again.

"Just one thing, Isabel," she said.

"Please, call me Izzy."

"Sure, Izzy." Sara bit the inside of her cheek in an attempt to conceal her grin. "You should probably park your car." She hunched her shoulders and squinted, making a playful *eek* face.

"I hate this day." Izzy looked at the sky in defeat, but her voice was bright.

"Nah, don't hate. This is a good day. K-9 is the best and we're going to have fun for the next twelve weeks."

Sara's positive outlook was rewarded with a dimpled smile, so she pushed it as she walked ahead of the car with Chase. "One last thing, Izzy."

"Anything. I will literally do anything to redeem myself right now."

"We're going to walk up to the building. Me and Chase." She ticked her head toward the dog. "Try not to run us over, okay?" She scrunched her nose up and smiled, so Izzy would know she was teasing. Flirting with recruits wasn't something she ever did, but Izzy needed a pick-me-up, and goddamn it, Sara wanted to give it to her.

Izzy's cheeks flushed with embarrassment, but she smiled big as she slipped into the driver's seat. Right out of nowhere, Sara felt her heart pound in response.

CHAPTER TWO

After she'd made the requisite introduction, Sara beelined to her small office, burying herself in admin. There was curriculum to be finalized, upcoming certifications to be scheduled, canine health records needing review and filing. All tasks that could wait. Truth be told, she needed to regroup. Start by pulling herself together and shaking free the impact five minutes with Izzy Marquez had made. Damn if that woman hadn't gotten her blood pumping in all the right ways.

Two cups of strong coffee later and she'd forgiven herself the fleeting distraction. Rationalizing her behavior as the result of too much alone time and not enough extracurricular activity, she'd resigned to make some changes. Go out more, perhaps start dating even. There were apps and meet-ups, a whole world of social opportunities out there. Her behavior this morning signaled her body longed for something more than work even if her brain was slow to realize it. She adored her job, loved working with the dogs and with their human counterparts. Still, she needed an outlet and she never mixed business with pleasure. Not anymore, anyway. She was not about to break her cardinal rule simply because Izzy Marquez had dreamy eyes and a slamming body. Nope, she was more mature than that.

Considering that truth, she probably should have stayed with John and sat in on Izzy's interview. Of course she would have been welcome. John kept her up to speed on every minute detail of the program. There wasn't a light bulb that got changed in the kennels without her knowledge. It was partly why her ignorance about Izzy's eleventh-hour admission to the program had her reeling. Sure there'd been changes before. Substitutions. This wasn't the first time someone backed out last minute. But vacancies were supposed to go to a person already on an agency's wait list. A candidate who'd been previously cleared and backgrounded.

Something didn't add up. There were procedures and protocols, and even the political appointees were required to meet them. She stood up from her desk ready to get some answers.

"Got a minute for me?" she asked, knocking on the open door to John Dixon's office.

"For you? Always." He moved a stack of files aside, the action signaling she had his full attention. "Come. Sit." He gestured at the chair across from him as he swiveled back and forth behind his desk. Sara passed the chair, walking over to the window to watch the dogs exercising outside. "I'm going to guess this visit is about our new student," he said. "Isabel Marquez."

"It is," she responded, hoping to God her voice came out without cracking. "I do have a couple of questions."

"Don't know that I have answers," he said. "But I'll tell you whatever I can." She watched him pull the top folder from the pile. "You met her this morning. What did you think?"

Sara's head was all over the place. Mostly she thought she wanted to run her finger over Izzy's full lips, rip her uniform off, kiss her senseless. She thought about the odds Izzy dated women. She thought about what it might be like to work as her mentor, become friends, maybe more. *What did she think?* Nothing appropriate, that was for sure, but that wasn't what her boss was asking.

She blinked hard, pushing the illicit images of Izzy down, and snapped into work mode. This was her job and John was seeking her input. She paused for a long moment to consider the question objectively, still conflicted. On the one hand, Izzy was sweet and seemed innocent, but she had also circumvented the program's thorough system of checks and balances. Plus, she made Sara's pulse race enough to prompt her into reevaluating her social life. The whole interaction left her thoroughly unsettled.

"I don't know." It was the most honest response she could muster, but it felt inadequate. She focused her attention on the crew of dogs and instructors working and playing in the open field. "She was nice, I guess. A little ditzy. But nice."

"Ditzy?"

She cocked her head to the side. "Scattered is maybe a better word."

"Hmm." John frowned. "I didn't get that impression from her." He drummed a pencil against his desk considering her words. "It was probably nerves. You can be very intimidating."

"Intimidating? Me?" Her reputation for being stoic and chill way preceded her.

"I'm kidding." He let out a brusque laugh. "But that was worth saying just for the reaction." He ran his hands through his thick black hair. "I'm sure she's just excited. You know how newbies are."

That was an understatement. Handlers were always excited to get a new canine partner. But first-timers were a breed of their own. They brought with them a level of excitement and energy that was unparalleled. Perhaps that was the vibe she'd been feeding off all morning. Unbridled anticipation, nothing more. But could picking up on Izzy's eager passion for her new assignment have been enough to give Sara goose bumps during their exchange? She reined herself back for the millionth time.

Casting her eyes at the file in front of her boss she said, "Level with me, John. What's the story here?"

He laughed out a breath as he leaned back in his chair. "Damned if I know."

"Well, what's it say in her application packet?" Sara asked.

"That she's a model officer with a stellar record. An active cop on a tough beat. She works transit patrol. A lot of arrests, no disciplinary actions."

Sara waited to hear the unofficial reason Izzy had bypassed procedure and slipped into the program. John answered her unspoken question with two upward palms and an empty shrug.

"You don't know or you won't tell me?"

He chuckled at her candor. "Believe it or not, there's things that are even above my pay grade."

She furrowed her brow, confused and disheartened by his answer.

"I know when to ask questions and when not to," he explained.

"So that's it? She has a decent record so doors just open for her?" She crossed her arms and shook her head. "Something's missing. It doesn't add up."

"I understand your frustration." He hitched one shoulder up. "I don't know what to tell you." Empathy was present in his tone and on his face.

"Hey, I don't blame you," she said. "And I'm not trying to sabotage her, either. Honest."

"Oh, God, I know that," he blurted.

"I just—" She cut herself off and let out a long sigh. "I worry about political favors. They never work."

"That's not true." His response was friendly even as it challenged her theory. "Some cops and agents do just fine. Regardless of how they get here." His raised eyebrows indicated he was implying a message deeper than what was on the surface.

Sara knew what he was getting at but she ignored him, wanting to make her own point. "In the beginning, sure." She leaned forward. "When it's all new and exciting. Cut to a few years later, sometimes a few months later," she reminded him, "after they realize it's not just fun and games. When they see the commitment required—endless training, getting called out all hours of the day and night. This is a lifetime gig. You have to want it." She rolled her neck, shaking her hair off her shoulders. "I don't know why I'm preaching to you," she said, making an effort to get her emotions under control. "I'm just frustrated. I hate cheating the dogs. It's not fair to them."

"Look, I know how you feel." He opened his drawer and pulled out an accordion file filled with loose papers. "You're not the only one who believes in what we do here." He looked out the glass wall of his office and gave a small wave to a trainer walking by with one of the new dogs. "This program means the world to me too." He leaned forward and handed the unwieldy file to her. "Take a look before you make up your mind."

"The class starts in a week. I've been studying profiles for months. It's a little late for what you're asking."

They had an informal routine: after the candidates were selected and interviewed and all their references checked, Sara reviewed their files. Even though her technical title was consultant, not agent, she still carried a top-secret clearance and she used it to assess each member of an incoming class. Her focus was geared at figuring out how the officers and dogs would play off each other. But she provided a fresh perspective, and having civilian insight had at times proved invaluable.

John shook his head. "For once, I'm not asking for your opinion. This is a done deal." He picked up a paper clip and bent it between his fingers. "But I still think looking through that file will be helpful. And it might relax you."

"What would relax me is knowing she'd been vetted properly. And believing she's legitimately invested in the program." Sara was surprised at the tension audible in her voice. "This is a federal facility last time I checked. Or is her hook so big she gets to skip all that?"

"I know how important this program is to you." Sara opened her mouth to speak, but John stopped her. "It is to me too. You know that." He gestured to the red accordion folder he'd given her. "That's why I did some digging."

"Wait." Sara finally comprehended what he was saying. She looked at the file in her hands. "You did her background?"

"I made some calls. Poked around a little. My notes are in there." Her surprise must have showed, because he continued. "I'm not just going to push cops through the program. No matter who they are or how they might be connected, politically." He rubbed his big hands together. "We've worked too hard for that. The reason this training site, our training site, is the country's best is because we care." He pursed his lips to cover his emotion. "And because we have you. Nobody I've ever worked with has insight and skill like you do. I saw it when you were a kid."

She breezed past his compliment. "Stop it. We all give a hundred and forty percent every day."

"That's my point." He shifted forward in his seat. "I value my program. And my staff. I'm not interested in wasting time and money on an officer who's going to wash out in a few months." He leaned all the way back, his seat reclining a little as he hooked his fingers behind his head. "I don't think that's the case with Officer Marquez."

Sara nodded, considering his words.

"Just give her a chance, Sara." He smiled at her. "Don't make me remind you that sometimes relaxing the rules a little can lead to great things."

"Yeah, yeah," she said. She looked away, hating that she knew she blushed when he brought up the past.

"You know it's not so long ago I convinced my boss to hire a nineteen-year-old kid, with zero law enforcement experience, no technical canine training, a girl who had no desire to be a federal agent, by the way, to come on staff and train police dogs and their handlers." He was full-on grinning. "You"—he pointed right at her—"better than anyone, should understand sometimes amazing things happen when you take a chance."

She returned his smile. "That was fifteen years ago, by the way. I've since been fully certified in every area of canine-handler training."

"I know. I would go on record that you are the best trainer in the country. Maybe the world. No one can do what you do." His pride was evident, his smile almost boyish, and she knew it signaled a zinger was headed her way. "You're still not an agent, though." He thrust his finger in the air in playful challenge.

"Never gonna happen. I told you that from the beginning. You can't hold it over me forever." She shook her head in support of her defense. "I'm only interested in the dogs. No guns for me. Stop fake-threatening you're going to cut me loose over it."

They laughed together at today's version of their constant battle before John turned serious. "I am sorry it played out this way. But I do have confidence Officer Marquez will work out okay. I don't have too much to base it on, but she seems like a good kid to me. And I have an excellent track record for hunches paying off." He winked and his expression was so optimistic, Sara couldn't help but be swayed by his instincts. She felt her stress over the course of events melt away.

"How long have you known?"

"About Marquez?"

Sara nodded. As close as they were, John was still her boss and he didn't owe her an explanation. She knew he'd be frank with her anyway.

"A couple of days." He reached for the mangled paper clip and started twisting it again. "This was a direct order from the very top."

Sara eyed him curiously. "The New York City Police Commissioner?" she asked in disbelief.

"No," he corrected. "On the federal side, I mean. Our bosses." He rubbed his mustache stoically. "Word came down from the Homeland Security executive branch. Specifically, the Director of Training," he added.

"Nicole?"

"I didn't speak to her directly." He dropped his gaze. "A woman on her staff called and said this was a priority." He cleared his throat, a nervous habit she was familiar with. "I'm sorry, Sara. Up until this conversation...I just figured you were in the loop." He made brief eye contact. "I know you and Nicole still talk."

Sara's head spun at the mention of her ex. As John laid out the details, Sara let herself get lost in her past. Nicole Vaughn was so woven into the fabric of her life, it was hard to parse out the appropriate qualifier for her. They were ex-girlfriends; that was true. But they were also friends and colleagues, and recently, they'd slept together for the first time in years. It had happened randomly, the culmination of a business trip to Washington, DC, that resulted in dinner at Nicole's apartment. It involved too much wine and too many glorified memories, but there had been no fallout. They still spoke frequently, but conversation about their tryst never surfaced.

Come to think of it, they had talked just last week. The thought that Nicole had known at that time and not said anything annoyed her on the spot. They were always open and honest with each other. It was the main reason they'd been able to survive the transition from romantic to platonic and back again seamlessly over the last decade. She swallowed her irritation at the mild deceit, keeping her composure as she focused on John, still talking away.

"Anyway, have a look in there." He gestured toward his secret file. "And here, take this too," he said, handing over the official application packet. "Let me know if you have any questions."

"Sure thing, boss man." She reached for the application folder and studied Izzy's police ID photo stapled to the edge. Her hair was pulled back in a tight bun, her expression no-nonsense. Inexplicably Sara's heart warmed at the super-serious image of the bubbly, flustered woman she'd met hours ago.

"Oh, Sara." John moved quickly, making his chair creak with the sudden movement. "There's something I need. I almost forgot." He tapped one finger on his desk. "Officer Marquez still needs a home visit." He twisted his mouth to the side as he spoke. "Her only day off this week is Friday. But I just found out I have a meeting scheduled in Manhattan. Will you do it for me?"

The home visit was a formality that existed to ensure the handler had a home appropriate for a dog. It was ridiculous and outdated and Sara couldn't recall a time when a candidate didn't make the cut as the result of their housing situation. And with these circumstances—where the candidate was fast-tracked through the process—it could no doubt be glossed over. But seeing where and how a person lived provided an opportunity to get a real sense of their personality, and right off she knew John was throwing her a bone. She loved him for it.

"Sure, I can take care of it."

"Great." He shuffled some papers on his desk. "I have her sergeant's number here somewhere." Pulling a sticky note off his laptop, he smiled in success. "Here it is. I'll notify Marquez through him. I owe him a call anyway," he said to himself. "Friday at eleven work for you?"

"Perfect."

"Great. I'll set it up." He reached for his glasses, sliding them on. "Hey, Sara," he said, looking out over the bifocal frames. "This is going to be good. I can feel it."

Sure, it was going to be completely fine, Sara mused, as she strolled back to her office. She just needed to get her libido in check, focus on a new class, finish prepping the dogs, and stop fantasizing about the new handler. Piece of cake.

CHAPTER THREE

"What did I get myself into?" Izzy muffled the complaint into the fluff of her pillow. Facedown, sprawled on her queen-size bed, she searched for the energy to get up, get dressed, and make coffee.

Her phone buzzed next to her and she checked the screen. Her sister. She answered it with, "I am a complete idiot."

"According to whom?" Elena responded, not missing a beat.

"Me, mostly," Izzy said through a loud yawn.

"Oh my God, were you sleeping?"

"I'm up." Izzy glanced at the clock. Ten forty-five. "I'm up," she repeated, throwing back the covers so it felt true. "In my defense, I didn't get home until four in the morning."

"Out searching for the woman of your dreams?"

"I wish. I was working overtime," she answered, scooting out of bed and grabbing a pair of cozy pajama pants to throw on over her panties. Spring weather still eluded New York's Lower Hudson Valley region and her house harbored a chill leftover from the endless winter. She reached for a hoodie to cover the loose ribbed tank she'd slept in but decided against it at the last minute. Something about the cool air felt like a wake-up call, and she embraced it.

"Overtime's good, right?"

Her sister's question was rhetorical but she answered anyway. "It is," she said, her voice trailing as she padded down the hall, the benefit of those extra shifts on display in her newly remodeled kitchen. Holding the phone between her chin and her shoulder, she reached for the Café Bustelo and milk from the fridge.

"So why are you an idiot?" Her sister cut to the chase.

Fuck, why couldn't she keep her mouth shut? Now she had to explain her predicament without including any of the backstory. She hated lying, especially to Elena. Izzy closed her eyes and concentrated. The best way to convey her situation without revealing the specific event that had led to her new assignment and stay honest was to be as vague as possible.

"I just overdid it this time. I put in for an assignment and I'm in way over my head."

"Wait a second. Are you going to be a hotshot detective? Like Olivia Benson?"

"No." Izzy huffed out a breath, wondering if she should explain the processes of the Detective Bureau. "It doesn't really work like that." She shook her head even though her sister couldn't see her. "Becoming a detective is a promotion, not an assignment."

It was also something she wasn't remotely interested in. It was a truth no one seemed to understand. Once or twice she'd tried to explain her decision to avoid the detective route, but it never resonated. Her friends and family were swayed by the portrayal of TV detectives decked out in designer suits finding murderers and rapists, or cracking terrorists with unrivaled interrogation skills.

Izzy wanted no part of it. She loved being in uniform. Interacting with the public on the daily had been her draw to join the police department from the outset, and she'd yet to be let down. She hated standing still, and her patrol beat kept her busy with something new every day. She was never confined to desk work, always roaming about, deterring trouble and keeping safe the people and the city she loved. There was no way to make the transit division sound sexy or satisfying, so she didn't try. Her reward was the feeling that came with making a small difference in regular people's lives. Giving directions to a confused tourist, helping an old lady hail a cab, stopping pickpockets and purse-snatchers at Grand Central Terminal. There was little glory, but damn, doing good felt good.

"Tell me about the assignment," her sister said, interrupting her faraway thoughts.

Izzy blew out a deep breath as she scooped coffee grounds into the filter. "Where to start?" She did some mental editing on the spot. "The long and short of it is"—she paused, choosing her words carefully—"I helped with a situation at work." She tried to sound nonchalant as she continued. "It's one of those things that would usually result in some kind of merit award." And a shit-ton of press. "But it's sort of on the down low, so instead of a public commendation, I was asked if there was a special unit I wanted to go to."

Her sister's silence told her she wasn't following. Elena's confusion was warranted—she was being purposely cryptic. Izzy couldn't very well reveal that last week she'd delivered a teenager's baby in the middle of the night in the bathroom of Grand Central Terminal. Or that the teenager was the daughter of a high-profile ultraconservative senator. In fact, her ability to keep it confidential was how she'd landed the coveted K-9 post.

"Well, are you going to tell me or what?"

"Um…"

"The assignment, Izzy. I'm dying over here."

"Oh, that." She lit a burner to heat some milk for her coffee. "I'm going to K-9."

"K-9?" Elena sounded skeptical. "That's the dog cops, right?"

"Yep," Izzy answered, feeling her initial excitement rush to the surface.

"That's great, Iz. You always wanted a dog." She heard her sister's other line ringing in the background. "But why are you upset about it? It's a good thing. It's what you asked for, you said."

Standing on tiptoe, Izzy stretched to grab her favorite oversized mug. "I know." She gave it a quick rinse even though it was clean. "The thing is…well, it's less that I asked to go there…" Shaking out the excess water, she twisted the empty cup in her hand and reached for a paper towel to wipe it dry. "More like I was questioned about my dream job." Filling her mug, she took in the rich, bold aroma as it wafted toward her. God, she loved coffee. "It was this whole to-do, this meeting I was part of. Anyway, I gave my answer—K-9—but I didn't think it was a real question. I expected it was more of a hypothetical, you know?"

"Well, who cares?" Her sister was all support even if she didn't understand the situation. "And it's a reward you earned." She loved how even absent the facts, her sister was on her side. "So what are you worried about?"

"Well, aside from the fact that I jumped the waiting list and have no actual qualifications—"

"I highly doubt that."

"No, for real. I totally cut the line."

"Please, people call in favors all the time. No matter what line of work you're in."

"Elena, I'm pretty sure there's an extensive background check that I completely bypassed."

"Izzy, you're the most straitlaced person I know. Not an issue. Next."

"How about this"—she said triumphantly, expecting to stump her sister—"the requirement to even be considered for the unit is at least five years of service. Technically, I'm not even eligible."

She could hear her sister mentally counting backward. "You're twenty-seven. And you started right out of college. That's twenty-two. Are you trying to tell me you're short a few months?"

"Three, to be exact." She added the warm milk to her coffee and stirred it together.

"Izzy, quit panicking. You're a good cop. And a great person. And I'm sure everyone at your job knows it. And you wouldn't have been selected if you weren't the best candidate. Trust me. I'm your older sister. I know things."

Izzy huffed out her skepticism. "Thanks, Elena," she said. She couldn't fault her sister for being supportive.

"What is it you're not telling me?" Elena typed at the speed of light in the background. "I can tell you're still freaking out. Talk to me."

"You're at work and I know you're busy."

"I'm talking to my stressed-out baby sister. Way more important than the nonsense happening here."

A paralegal at the United States Attorney's office, Izzy knew none of Elena's work qualified as nonsense. She appreciated her sister's time and attention, so she got to the point.

Still mortified, Izzy covered her face as she spoke. "I made an ass of myself in front of the main instructor."

"I'll be the judge of that. Specifics, please."

"Pft." She let her mind drift back to Monday morning, unsure where to begin. "I just did some weird things. Really weird." She cringed, thinking about it for the first time in four days. "I showed up super early and didn't know where to go." She rubbed her finger along the handle of a teaspoon on the counter. "So, the instructor, she came over to help me and I acted like a boob."

Her sister laughed. "Really? Or are you exaggerating?"

"Let's see." Izzy tapped her chin in mock thought as she made fun of herself while she listed the details. "My hair was going crazy in the wind because I dropped my clip while I was driving. Like, it was completely covering my face while I was trying to be all serious and professional." She paused to let the image sink in. "Then I fell on my butt into the car because the wind knocked me over."

"You are tiny," her sister piped up.

"I'm not that tiny." She eyed her coffee but didn't take a sip. "Wait, there's more."

"I'm listening."

"Did I mention I forgot to park my car?" She didn't give Elena a chance to respond before elaborating with dramatic flair. "Like, I was just going to leave it, just walk away." She fanned her hand in the air, a testament to her perceived ambivalence. "It was running, by the way, in the middle of the street. And I was going to leave it there." She covered her eyes, embarrassed all over again. "And if all that wasn't enough...I asked her if she was Miss Right."

"Wait, what?" Elena laughed outright, her question slipping in through her hysterics.

Izzy groaned. "It's her name, but…" She shook her head, reliving her humiliation at the series of events. "Forget it. It was mortifying. Trust me."

"Did she say anything? The instructor?"

"No. She was nice about it." Izzy hugged herself, partially for comfort, but also for protection from the chill. She debated a sweatshirt as she responded. "Doesn't change the fact that I was a buffoon."

"Is she pretty?" Her sister singsonged out the question, her voice lilting as high as it could go.

Izzy swallowed hard and bit her lower lip, remembering the image of Sara in the field. Tall and fit, with honey-brown hair that spilled from her black skully down past her shoulders. Eyes that were light brown, maybe hazel. Soft lips she'd done her best to avoid staring at. She could still picture her sauntering over in perfectly fitted jeans and a worn-out maroon hoodie barely zipped. Her expression was all confidence and charm, practically oozing sex appeal as she closed the distance between them. Even now, Izzy felt a flutter of excitement race through her body. Pretty didn't do Sara Wright justice.

"My God, Elena." She knew she sounded as helpless as she'd felt four days earlier. She hung her head as she let out a pathetic sigh, not even trying to hide it. "She's gorgeous."

"Aw," her sister teased. "Look at you. All smitten."

"I'm not." Izzy laughed out her denial but Elena had her pegged.

"Nice try." Elena's tone told her she didn't believe her for a second. "Sorry, Iz, I should get going. We're not done here," she added. "Prepare to be grilled at Mommy and Daddy's tomorrow night. You're coming to dinner, right?"

"Wouldn't miss it." She adored the Marquez weekly gatherings, and it meant the world that her family coordinated around her fluctuating schedule.

"See you mañana," Elena finished, and the line went quiet on the other end.

Izzy sipped her coffee and smiled. Her sister could make her feel better about anything even if she didn't provide any real solutions. Suddenly it felt like everything would be okay. It would all be fine, she thought with a reassuring nod. Monday was a fresh start, a chance to make a brand-new impression, and she was going to nail it.

She was lost in her fantasy, a successful do-over where she didn't act like a bumbling idiot, when her doorbell rang, bringing her back to reality. She glanced at the clock on the microwave. Who would be at her house at eleven o'clock on a Friday morning? No one she'd invited, that was for sure. And whether it was a religious missionary or a salesperson didn't matter. Uninvited solicitors were a nuisance, regardless the cause. She marched to her front door and ripped it open, ready to dole out her standard lecture on common courtesy.

"You know, if I came to your house," she started, before making direct eye contact with Sara Wright. She stopped midsentence, frozen still in the open doorway, her mouth agape. On cue, the breeze swirled by, sending goose bumps up her forearms and under her thin shirt.

"It would be *so* weird if you came to my house." Sara crinkled her eyebrows and offered a small grin. She tilted her head dramatically to the side. "I'm going to go ahead and guess you did not get the message I was coming to do your home inspection."

Izzy racked her brain, trying to remember the details of her back and forth with Sergeant Smith. There had been a slew of changes regarding the appointment, but last she'd heard, Agent Dixon had a conflict today. When there'd been no mention of an alternate visit planned for the weekend, she'd assumed it was something that would be ironed out during the first week of training.

"I can come back," Sara said, cutting through the silence. "We'll reschedule. It's not a big deal." Her shrug was pleasant. "Clearly you have a house. The rest is pretty much self-explanatory. If I have any questions, I'll find you during class."

"No, no, no." Izzy waved her off. "You're here. Come in. Please."

Sara looked past her. "I hate to interrupt if you're busy."

"Not at all." Izzy stepped to the side, giving Sara access and closing her eyes as she got a full whiff of Sara's musky scent when she passed. "I just need to change," she said, backing away. "Give me one second. Make yourself comfortable."

Less than a minute later Izzy returned, having switched out her PJ pants for leggings, a bulky fire department sweatshirt she'd swiped from her brother covering her tank. "Sorry about that," she said, pulling her hair up in a loose bun. "Can I interest you in coffee? It's fresh."

"No, thank you. I feel pretty terrible that I surprised you." Sara sat down at a tall kitchen stool and unzipped her light jacket. "It seems the universe is messing with us." Sara raised her eyebrows. "First I don't know you've been added to the roster. Now *you* have no idea I'm stopping by," she said in a kind of disbelief, a tiny pensive laugh coupling her thought.

Izzy didn't even feel bad when a loud harrumph escaped her. "I'm pretty sure the universe wants me to look like an ass." She added a smile so Sara would know she wasn't really bothered. She took a sip of her lukewarm coffee. "Despite all of our interactions to date, I'm actually a fairly responsible person." She looked around, silently thanking God she was a neat freak. At least her place was spotless.

"No doubt." Sara's voice was serious and she nodded at the iPad she'd set on the kitchen island. "Actually, by all accounts you are extremely levelheaded, dependable, and honest. Your supervisors and colleagues have nothing but good things to say about you."

"Yes!" Izzy whispered out the faux cheer, making fists with both hands for emphasis. "The payoffs are working." She looked over and saw Sara's smile reach all the way to her eyes. It made her relax on the spot. She dumped her tepid coffee in the sink and poured a fresh refill from the carafe. "Are you sure you don't want coffee?" Izzy grabbed a second mug. "I mean, how else am I supposed to bribe you for a good score on this part of the process?"

"Good point." Sara narrowed her eyes. "Better make it light and sweet, then, if you want an A."

"Done." Izzy reached for a spoon as she stirred in some sugar. "For real, though, how does this go? Do I give you a tour? Answer questions?" She placed the coffee in front of Sara and watched as she took the first sip. She was even sexy when she swallowed.

Sara raised her mug. "Thank you for this." She opened the tablet cover and punched in her passcode. "Like I said before, this is just a formality. Part of certification stipulates the handler having a home suitable for a dog. Whatever that means." Her expression suggested she thought it useless. "There's no real guidelines. So long as there's no meth lab in your basement, I'd say you're in the clear."

Izzy played along. "Don't even have a basement." She punctuated the statement with a definitive nod.

"Excellent." Sara pretended to make a note as she spoke. "No meth lab. Check." She winked when she looked up, and Izzy almost choked. Thankfully Sara didn't seem to notice as she took in the décor of Izzy's modest house. "Your home is lovely. I didn't know Hartsdale had so much undeveloped land."

Izzy followed Sara's gaze to the pine trees out the living room window. "Yeah, I was super lucky. This house was a foreclosure, so I got it for a steal. It was a mess in here." She gestured around the open plan living space. "My dad and brother helped me gut it and renovate."

"Is all that property yours?" Sara asked, still focused on the land outside.

"It is. Come." Izzy gestured with a small wave, leading the way to the back door. "Those woods mark the perimeter of Daley Park. It's what won me over." She stepped out on the deck, holding the door for Sara to follow. "That and being the last house on a dead-end block. I love the privacy. Having unlimited access to the park trails practically in my backyard is a home run. Sometimes I feel like I could hike the woods for hours. It's heaven to me." She felt suddenly exposed and a little dorky and wondered if she'd sounded like a complete dud. "I'm just a fan of peace and quiet," she added, hoping her honesty counted for something.

"You're preaching to the choir." Sara looked at the expansive yard edged by the line of trees that framed the property. "You could put a kennel out here," she said in a low voice. "There's so much room."

Izzy couldn't mask her confusion. "But I thought the dog would live in the house with me?"

"He will." Sara looked right at her. "Sorry, I was more thinking out loud." She shook her head at herself. "By all means, your dog will live with you, with your family. Inside," she added. "It's just nice for them to have a space of their own. A place to decompress, I guess." She turned around and touched the exterior siding gently, before looking out over the lawn again. "It's really nice out here. A lot of space." She made brief eye contact. "There's room, if you wanted to put one up. That's all. It's not a requirement or anything."

"I want to do whatever is best for the dog. It sounds like you think I should have one."

Sara leaned toward her slightly, their shoulders almost touching, as she nudged into Izzy's personal space. "I think I'm just jealous," she whispered. "I always wanted to be able to put up a kennel, but never had the yard for it."

"Do you live around here?" Izzy asked. Even though she was curious, the fact that she'd said it out loud caught her by surprise. "You're probably up closer to the facility," she said, before stopping her runaway mouth. "I'm sorry." She mentally slapped herself. "It's none of my business."

Sara's smile was warm and forgiving. "My living situation is a long story."

Izzy took the cue. "Fair enough," she answered with a nod.

"It's not that I won't tell you. It's just…complicated." She tapped the railing next to her. "Complicated and boring." Her answer was accompanied with half a laugh. "The short version is that I live in Phoenicia."

"All the way upstate?" Izzy couldn't conceal her surprise. "That must be some commute for you."

Sara shook her head almost like she couldn't believe it herself. "Yeah, well, anyway…" She seemed at a loss for words as she glanced down at Izzy's bare feet. "We should go back in. I'm sure you're freezing."

Izzy opened the door, still calculating the distance from the training facility in Overton to Phoenicia. It had to be fifty miles easily. But then, who was she kidding? She trekked to Midtown Manhattan daily for work and had willingly given up taking over her grandparents' awesome rent-controlled apartment on Columbus and Ninety-Sixth Street in exchange for the quiet life in Westchester County. At times her commute was well over an hour, and she wouldn't change a thing. She adored her neighborhood, and her house was her pride and joy. She knew it showed when she gave Sara the nickel tour.

Even though Sara didn't ask, Izzy provided details on the remodeling of her bathroom and all the bedrooms, only wincing a little at the sight of her disheveled duvet piled high on her unmade bed before guiding them back to the kitchen.

"You live alone, I assume?"

Sara's question seemed out of the blue and Izzy knew surprise showed on her face.

"Sorry, I'm not trying to pry into your personal life." Sara gestured with her iPad. "That is actually one of the questions I'm required to ask." She opened the tablet and pulled up an electronic form. "There's a place where I need to list everyone who lives in the home."

"It's just me," Izzy replied, feeling suddenly self-conscious. A thought occurred to her and she decided not to hold back. "What if I started dating someone? Do I have to report that?"

"No, nothing like that." Sara scrolled down the page. "I don't even know why it's on here. Although"—she chewed her lip as she typed into the template—"if you do have a boyfriend, or girlfriend, or whatever, I would advise having your dog meet that person sooner rather than later. This way there's a clear understanding of the dynamics right off."

That was odd. There were a lot of ways to get that message across without implying that Izzy might date women. Holy fuck, was Sara subtly inquiring about her preference? Izzy felt her heart pound out of control at the possibility, and she forced herself to remain calm. She did not need a repeat of her behavior the other day, and she might be dead wrong anyway. She took a long swallow of her drink, using the action as a cover to gain her composure. She had no qualms about being truthful. In fact, she never hid her sexuality. With a lifetime of support from her family and friends, there was no need. The trick right now was to reveal her status without looking like she had an agenda. Might as well just come right out with it.

"I haven't had a boyfriend since seventh grade, so that's a nonissue." She sighed. "Although, truthfully, I haven't had much luck in the girlfriend department lately either." Rubbing her chin thoughtfully, Izzy looked up to the ceiling, feigning concern before smiling big. "Eh, no worries. I'll find the right woman one of these days."

"I'm sure you will." Sara snapped her iPad closed and returned the smile. "If I see a decent prospect I'll be sure to send her your way." She hopped off the kitchen stool. "Unless of course"—her eyebrows wagged in playful challenge—"I decide to scoop her up for myself first."

Game on. Izzy swallowed her excitement and ignored the throbbing she felt at Sara's revelation. In truth, she'd been confident they were on the same page in that realm anyway. Izzy's gaydar was impeccable. But what had been half speculation, half hope was now confirmed. And they were flirting. Weren't they?

Either way, Izzy avoided eye contact, tipping her head to the floor in light laughter at Sara's joke. It was cute and clever and her hazel eyes sparkled when she delivered the punch line. It was entirely possible she was making way too much of all this. The fact they were both gay meant nothing in the grand scheme of things. This was law enforcement, after all. In Izzy's estimation forty percent of the women on the force were lesbians, and that was her conservative estimate.

But even as she told herself it was no biggie, new excitement and fear raced to the surface, and neither had a damn thing to do with the fact she knew nothing about being a dog handler.

CHAPTER FOUR

Focus. Focus. Focus.

Sara looked in her small bathroom mirror, continuing her mental pep talk. The next twelve weeks would be governed by focus. Starting today. Well, focus and avoidance. She laughed at the loophole she added.

It seemed harsh, her rigid self-imposed rules. But Friday had proven she needed stern parameters. One-time flirting could be excused, brushed off, explained away. Twice, however, was the start of a pattern, and she needed to remain professional. No matter how attractive Izzy Marquez might be. Nope. She had a job to do. One she rocked on a daily basis. She only needed to stay on point and maybe make a concerted effort to avoid Izzy. This way there'd be no temptation to get lost in her sweet brown eyes, her quick wit, her bright smile.

It was a solid plan and she high-fived herself for sticking to it this morning, choosing to hang out in her on-campus dorm suite in lieu of attending the first morning of class. It was a sacrifice for sure, but a worthwhile one if it kept her head in the game.

When she couldn't stall any longer, Sara zipped across the grounds, scrolling social media on her phone as she half rehearsed her upcoming spiel in her head, at the same time wondering how the a.m. session had gone. She loved the first day of class, so much excitement and enthusiasm, the energy in the room always off the charts. She minimized her news feed, opting to check Twitter for the latest on what was really happening in the world.

"Where have you been hiding out?"

Even from a distance, she registered the voice right away. Izzy. Here she was, all smiles, strolling toward her in dark blue uniform pants, her hands stuffed in the pouch pocket of her NYPD hoodie. Best laid plans, she thought.

"No joke," Izzy said, as she got closer. "The staff spent half the morning talking about you. Wondering where you were."

Sara shook her head. "I told John I had a few things to take care of this morning." She sighed. "Guess he forgot."

They stopped to talk facing each other and were standing halfway in front of a six-foot wall, part of the agility course for agent recruits training on the north side of campus.

"What are you doing over here?" Sara wondered out loud.

Izzy's smile was coy. "Looking for you."

Sara could only guess at what her expression revealed, but it must have been a certain amount of alarm because Izzy backpedaled immediately. "No, really, I was just exploring a little." She seemed embarrassed and toed a rock with her boot. Sara felt horrible and wanted to save her, but she had to stay strong. Izzy's voice evened out as she explained, "The instructors mentioned how big this place is and that there's a whole other side where federal agents and recruits train." She bent over and picked a bright yellow dandelion. "I finished lunch early. It's beautiful out. I was curious."

Sara bladed her body and pointed to a building in the distance. "That's the main academic building over there. There's at least one class in session right now. I forget the host agency." She nodded at the dorms behind them. "Right here's federal housing. Both for recruits and some of your classmates too. There's several folks from out of town this time around." She held a hand above her eyes to block the sun. "We're kind of standing in the middle of the obstacle course as we speak." She reached for Izzy's arm and guided her several steps to the side. "That's better. You never know when one of these lunatics is going to fly over that wall," she added with a smile.

Izzy nodded at Sara's laptop case hanging by her side, the strap crossing her chest. "Do you teach classes over here too?"

It was a valid question, considering their current location. "No. I'm strictly part of the K-9 crew." She slid her phone into the side pocket of her tan pants. "I was coming from the dorms. Sometimes I stay here instead of going back and forth home."

"That's pretty awesome."

"It's not a bad perk, that's for sure."

"Must be nice to have an option like that."

"Yeah, I use it a lot lately. Saves me a ton of time in the car." She looked off to the side, pondering her recent schedule. "For regular staff like me it's not free, but the price is minimal and it's deducted right from my paycheck. I barely feel it."

"Sounds like a good deal."

"You might qualify, if you're interested. I think there's a distance requirement, but I can check what it is for you."

Izzy shook her off. "Nah, I'm only a half-hour drive and I like being home."

"You do have a great house." She shoved her hands in her pockets matter-of-factly. "It's better for the dog anyway. Once you're partnered up. It's good for them to get adjusted as quickly as possible."

"Do we take them home right away?"

"Not right away, but soon. Typically, by the end of the second week, beginning of the third." Sara pulled out her phone and checked the time. "I'll go over all the details this afternoon in class," she said, nodding in the direction Izzy had come from. "We should probably head that way."

Izzy fell in step beside her and Sara couldn't help but enjoy her company even if it did fly in the face of her newly instituted restrictions. They talked easily as they strolled the worn path winding through the secluded campus. Sara filled in the history and layout of Overton's secluded campus, trying hard not to stare at Izzy's delicate fingers gently spinning the dandelion. The conversation moved to the morning session she'd skipped, and Sara inquired about Izzy's initial impressions of the school, the other instructors, and her classmates.

"John was my favorite. Agent Dixon," Izzy corrected herself.

"It's obvious how much he loves his job." She touched the flowery part of the weed with her palm delicately. "He was almost glowing when he talked about the dogs."

"The bomb dog classes are his favorite." Sara looked up at a turkey vulture hovering in the distance. "Mine too. The dogs are just…amazing. So smart." Her mind drifted to her dogs in action. Sniffing and searching airports, buildings, backpacks. The impact of their detection and deterrence was immeasurable. She knew it firsthand. "Nothing against narcotics dogs or patrol K-9s," she said as they reached the building. "I love all my dogs. But bomb dogs are special." She reached for the black handle and pulled it back, using her foot to chock the door open.

Izzy made eye contact as Sara held the door ajar. "He said you'd say that." Her smile was serious, as though she wanted to ask a question but thought better of it, and she accepted Sara's chivalry as she entered the first set of double doors. "I wasn't kidding when I said everyone talked about you today." Izzy pulled open the interior door, returning the favor as Sara passed through. "You're something of a legend here."

"I don't know about that," Sara responded, but she could feel a mix of emotion swirling inside.

"Sure sounded like it. A million different certifications. An expert in this, that, and the other." Izzy frowned. "Sorry I haven't got a handle on the terminology yet." She stopped walking. "He also said you've been doing this since you were nineteen. Is that true?"

"You're making me feel old." Sara added a slight laugh, but when she thought about it, those early years did feel like forever ago.

"Stop. That's not what I'm saying. I just meant it's impressive. That's all."

Sara shrugged good-naturedly. "Meh."

"I thought I heard someone say you've been here fifteen years." Izzy drew a circle on the tile floor with her boot. "Is that right?"

Sara couldn't hold back her smile. "Isabel Marquez, are you trying to figure out how old I am?"

When Izzy puckered her full lips, her cheeks rose high and

round on her face. She was positively adorable. She looked right at Sara and shrugged, owning her guilt and coupling it with delightful charm. "I might be."

Sara opened her mouth to speak, even though she wasn't sure what she was going to say.

Izzy interrupted her. "Hold that thought." Her eyes shifted beyond Sara. "I think you're about to be summoned."

At that exact moment, John's booming voice came from the other end of the hall. "There you are," he bellowed, breaking into a jog down the open corridor.

"See you in class." Izzy backed away before giving a small wave as she turned toward the main classroom.

John was talking a mile a minute as he reached her, but Sara barely heard any of it, her mind still focused on Izzy. So much for thinking she could employ some kind of mental judo to overcome her temptation. A little deflated at her own failure, she flopped into her office chair half listening to John as he followed behind her. She needed a plan B, and quick, because the slope was slippery as hell and she was already losing her footing.

❖

For fifteen solid minutes Izzy listened to Jen, a sheriff's deputy from Miami, as she kept the conversation moving between a few students gathered in a circle near her desk along the wall of windows. The conversation was light and breezy, a continuation of the getting to know each other niceties that monopolized lunch. It was tame and boring but Izzy was happy for the distraction, because even as she gave her attention over to the chatter, her eyes were glued to the clock in anticipation of Sara's arrival.

She hated that she was allowing her attention to be divided at what could be—what should be—a defining moment in her career. K-9 was an exciting and challenging unit. It required commitment and drive, and despite her last-minute appointment, she absolutely knew she belonged here.

On the spot she cringed, considering for the first time that

Sara surely knew she'd skirted the standard red tape to get into the program. And here she'd spent the last two exchanges practically chatting her up. What the hell was she doing? She didn't want Sara to think that she was the kind of person who cozied up to rank for brownie points. In fact, that description didn't fit her at all. She wasn't cutesy, she didn't flirt. Not at work, anyway. Which made their spirited banter all the more confusing. It was like something came over her each time she saw Sara, clearing all rational thought from her mind and allowing her libido to take over. Was it all her? Their back and forth was so seamless, the details of how it had gone down were fuzzy.

Whatever the case, it was going to end right now. Izzy was dedicated, and professional, and a kick-ass worker. She was going to be the best canine handler in this class. She completed her internal cheer with a firm nod and a loud crack of her knuckles, stealing the attention of her small group. She clenched her teeth in silent apology but was spared the need for an explanation as Sara entered into the room.

"Good afternoon, everybody." Sara's voice was light and professional as she waited for everyone to find their seats. Izzy followed suit, not even allowing herself to look up as she slid into her chair. She could do this.

"My name is Sara Wright. I'm the lead canine instructor for the program." Sara paced the front of the room smoothly, pausing to set a thick binder on the edge of the metal desk in the corner. "I understand you all may have heard a little about me from the other instructors this morning." She glanced up, and Izzy could swear the hint of a smile showed when Sara's gorgeous eyes met hers.

"Anyway, just to fill in some blanks," she started. "I'm not a cop. Or an agent. Or anything like that." She rocked back and forth on her toes. "Technically speaking, I'm a consultant. I mention this because in the past, once or twice, people have been put off by that fact."

She looked out the window, and Izzy couldn't help but wonder how many times she'd been challenged over the years. Cops could be real dicks about some things, and that sounded just like the type of thing they'd get territorial over.

"I have been working with dogs, specifically K-9s, my whole adult life. I've been all over the country. All over the world, actually. This program"—she nodded resolutely—"is the best I've ever seen." She wore a satisfied expression as she highlighted the statistics. "Our facility is state of the art, our staff, top notch," she added, not even trying to mask the pride in her voice. "Working here is my honor, but it's also my passion." Her face lit up as she spoke, the truth of her words evident in her body language.

"They always have me speak last because I'm the final line of defense between you and the dogs." As if on cue, a series of loud barks erupted in the distance, making Sara look toward the sound in dramatic disbelief. "Even they know," she added wistfully, shaking her head and garnering a small chuckle from the class. "Anyway, just a couple more things before we take you out to meet them."

Izzy picked up her pen to take notes but found herself entranced in Sara's sweet voice as she brought everyone up to speed. The staff had already been working for weeks, ensuring all the dogs were properly imprinted to recognize the components of bomb making chemicals and reinforcing their obedience training. Looking inside her binder, she detailed the pedigree of the animals—a mix of German and Dutch shepherds and several hybrids, German shepherd–Belgian Malinois combinations. Sara held the dogs in obvious esteem, making a point to mention the intelligence, high drive, and sweet disposition of each canine.

For a long second Sara paused, and Izzy wondered if she'd lost her train of thought.

"I just want to make sure I have your attention," she said before continuing. "This is an explosive detection class." She waited and Izzy felt the room get heavy. "I don't need to tell you how important your role is in this. I mean that on the grandest scale." She cast her eyes down, almost seeming indebted to the thirteen officers in the room for their future service. "To that end, we give you the best dogs. That's the truth."

Her tone was deathly serious and the entire class seemed to still as they listened.

"I can't tell you how to do your job. Patrol the city, or the subway, or the airport, make arrests. I wouldn't dare." She shook her head. "My job is to send you out there prepared, trained, and ready to do what you do best." She held up one finger. "I'm going to do that by teaching you and your partner to understand each other." Lifting a second finger, she added, "And making sure you respect each other." She shrugged. "It's that simple." She brought her hands together in front of her body. "There are some people out there who will tell you it's got to be this way or that." She frowned. "Not me. I don't believe there's only one way that's right. The bottom line is all the methods and techniques can be taught and practiced over and over. But if there's not genuine affection and understanding between you and your dog, none of it matters. Those two things—love and respect—they're the building blocks of trust. When it's all said and done, you can strip everything else away—all the training in the world isn't worth a damn. Trust is what makes perfect partners."

Izzy's heart drummed in her chest. Full of inspiration, she was ready to bolt out the door and spring into action. She wasn't alone. Without even looking around, she could feel the momentum bouncing around the room. Sara was no fool—she could obviously sense their anticipation—and she clapped her hands once before she said, "All right. Enough talking. Let's go have some fun."

Izzy closed her blank notebook as Sara gave last-minute instructions while they got ready to go outside, reminding the class that it was still the first day and cautioning against getting too attached to a specific dog. Assignments would be made soon enough. For now, they should focus on throwing a ball, playing tug, giving basic obedience commands, and allowing time for everyone to adjust, dogs and humans alike.

Regardless of Sara's warning, Izzy was thrilled when Chase ended up her partner right away. He looked up at her and did a tiny little jump, just enough so the top of his head came in contact with her palm as she gripped the end of his leash.

"I know," she said, giving him a small rub. "I remember you too." She headed to a spot where some dog toys were set up. Before selecting one, she knelt in front of him, so he could see her face at his eye level. "I'm Izzy." She gave him a good scratch between his ears and petted his face with both hands. "You are a handsome boy." It was the truth, even if she was biased. Where the majority of the dogs had the traditional tan and black saddling associated with shepherds and shepherd mixes, Chase's coat had an almost reddish overtone to it, a mottled mix of dark and light browns and blacks, rinsed with an auburn wash. Perfectly proportioned black-tipped ears and eyes rich with emotion complemented his muscled square frame.

He sat patiently, allowing Izzy to drown him in affection, before he leaned in and licked her cheek. "Yeah, I missed you too, buddy," she said with a smile.

She stood and selected a thick rope and offered it to him. Even though she knew he was strong, the sheer force of his bite on the knotted end threw her off balance. She had to use all her strength to hold on to it and keep from face-planting.

"Let him win." Sara's voice surprised her even if it shouldn't have. Izzy turned and Sara was closer than she realized. In two steps, Sara was right next to her, her musky scent preceding her by a mere fraction of a second. "I see you two found each other."

"Yeah, it just kind of worked out that way." It was the truth, and Izzy hoped Sara believed her.

"Don't worry about setting up a hierarchy just yet," Sara said, looking between Izzy and Chase. "Today is just about playing." She stuffed her hands in the pockets of the sweatshirt that covered her staff polo. "We'll shift things around so everyone will get the opportunity to work with different dogs. Outside of basic obedience commands, it doesn't make sense to set up too many parameters at this point."

Izzy nodded in response, disheartened at the thought of working with another dog. It was foolish, her instant attachment, but she'd be lying to herself if she denied it. Chase nudged at her with the rope, and she steadied her footing before she reached for the end of it.

"There's no shame in going for a different toy. I don't want to see you get hurt." Izzy heard judgment in Sara's tone and the slight put-down hurt her feelings. She looked up to gauge the intent behind the comment, but Sara's attention had shifted to another team working a few yards away. "Excuse me," she mumbled, already walking off.

For the rest of the afternoon Izzy fought the insecure feelings Sara's statement brought to the surface. She followed her advice anyway, trading out the rope for a heavy plastic ball on a thick string, which Chase seemed to like just fine. But before the session ended, she picked up the rope again. Getting a good handle on it, she held it out in front of her. Chase took the bait and clenched it in his jaw, tugging her forward gently.

"That's it, buddy." She wrestled back and forth, keeping her arm nice and loose, which enabled her to control the activity. After a few seconds she let go, and he spun in a happy circle, bowing down and placing the rope at her feet.

"Again?" she asked, witnessing his openmouthed pant, his giant pink tongue hanging out to one side, a smiling snout if ever she saw one. "Sit," she ordered, the command taking her by surprise.

Scampering into place, Chase set himself squarely in front of her, his butt glued to the ground. "Good boy." She heard her voice pitch higher than usual as she praised him. "Let's do this," she said, picking up the rope and repeating the exercise. She let him win every time, and after each round, she made him sit and stay until she was ready to go again. She commended him for his good manners and rubbed his soft gorgeous head.

After countless repetitions of the game, she decided to mix it up. As they sparred, she stepped back but didn't let go. "Chase," she said, stilling to get his attention. "Drop it," she ordered. He looked at her, still clutching tightly as he tilted his head. "Enough. Drop it. Now." Her voice was strong and even. "Drop it," she repeated.

When he let go, Izzy fell to her knees and hugged him. "Yes. Good boy! What a good, good boy you are." She had no clue if he understood her at all or if he simply released the rope out of sheer boredom. It didn't matter. He clearly knew she was pleased with his actions, and he returned her affection with an overzealous series of kisses to her face. She finished the day goopy and slobbered on. She couldn't wait to do it all again tomorrow.

Chapter Five

Remember something. This is a game to them. The dogs will pick it up faster than you."

Izzy could listen to Sara talk all day. Her eyes twinkled and her voice brimmed with excitement over the job she clearly adored. Every day after lunch, Sara came in and addressed the class, dropping tidbits and pointers, lightening the mood after the morning classroom instruction which had invariably centered on improvised explosive devices, suicide bombers, and active shooters. Necessary training for sure, but heavy as hell.

"Your dog's whole existence is based on pleasing you," Sara continued. "And on chewing." Izzy chuckled with the rest of her cohorts. "In all seriousness, these pups will work all day for their tennis ball or their rawhide. It's just who they are. They want to work and they want to play. It's an amazing combination." She tucked a loose strand of hair behind her ear, and Izzy spotted a dark red scratch on the back of Sara's hand poking out from the long-sleeved T-shirt she wore for layering.

The injury hadn't been there yesterday. Izzy would know. Not that she'd spent any one-on-one time with Sara since Monday afternoon's chastising of her play session with Chase. In fact, she'd seen Sara only peripherally in the last few days. Talking with the other instructors, working with her classmates. It almost seemed like Sara was avoiding her. The thought made her stomach turn, and even though it didn't make sense at all, Izzy couldn't help being aware every time Sara checked in on her colleagues.

Izzy seemed relegated to getting Sara's attention as part of the group only. It was frustrating, but perhaps she was overthinking it. Either way, right now Sara was front and center, and Izzy capitalized on it, studying her instructor from head to toe. Her hair was pulled up, save the few layers that wouldn't stay back, and she wore a dark blue golf shirt with the DHS logo over the left breast and sneakers in lieu of boots today.

Sure, Izzy was ogling, but she was also listening. She even took a note here and there. There was no harm in it, she rationalized. It was a glorious sunny Friday, she was on her way to surviving the first week without making a fool of herself or failing out, and she believed a small reward was in order. Staring at the sexy instructor in tight tactical pants ten feet away seemed as harmless as it was satisfying. A win all around.

Her day scored a second boon when Chase bounded toward her the second she stepped outside. He did a happy dance when he reached her, topping it off with a controlled leap touching his head to her hand, an expression of his obvious joy at seeing her. Both yesterday and the day before, the staff had paired off teams as they'd started the first organized exercises. After the structured partnerings of the last two days, Chase appeared to be taking matters into his own hands this afternoon. She greeted him with an upbeat hello and some good neck scratches. She'd missed him too, but rather than dwell on it, she got right to work. Starting with some basics, Izzy ordered him to sit, stay, and heel. Just a few simple commands to find their groove before they started drilling as a team.

"I can't stress enough how important it is to work with some of the other dogs." Sara's voice behind them startled her.

"Hi." Izzy righted herself and stood beside Chase, her fingers touching the baby soft down of his left ear. "I spent yesterday with Jax and the day before split up between Tempe, Dodger, and Sammy. I'm getting around. Promise." She didn't want to be disrespectful, but she also didn't understand why she should apologize for having a connection with Chase.

Sara shifted her weight to one hip and crossed her arms as she backed away, looking dismayed at Izzy's response.

Izzy bent down to Chase. "We made it, bud. Rock on," she whispered in quiet support, leading him to play for a few minutes before the staff called everyone to order for some rudimentary agility drills.

A few cycles in, Sara stopped the action. She looked up and down the line, cocking her head back and forth. Signaling Gilmartin, Reyes, and Hayes—the team of trainers—to meet her in the center, the staff conducted an impromptu meeting while the group waited with their dogs on the sidelines. Every few seconds the instructors glanced over. Izzy felt all eyes on her and wondered if she was being paranoid.

Before she could assess the possibility, Sara broke off from the group. "We're going to try a few changes, gang," she said to the class. Taking two paces closer, she looked at the far end. "Let's have Sammy up here. Come here, Sammy." Izzy saw her classmate Mark frown as he let go of the lead, allowing Sammy to trot over to Sara. "Good girl, Sammy," Sara said, picking the leash up and handing it off to Agent Gilmartin. Izzy felt her heart pound in anticipation when Sara looked right at her. "We're going to switch you with Chase. Chase, come."

Chase looked up at Izzy, his eyes as expressive as ever. He was looking for guidance, seeking her permission, waiting for her command. God, she loved him so much already. Meeting his stare, she smiled reassuringly. "Go ahead, Chase. Go," she ordered sweetly, before shifting her gaze to Sara, boring her eyes right through her, not even attempting to hide her feelings about the move.

Izzy held her tongue and for the remainder of the day she worked with Sammy, a lovely shepherd mix who was smart as a whip and eager to please. But she missed her boy and she knew the feeling was mutual.

At three o'clock when her classmates were en route to their families or had retired to their campus dorm rooms, Izzy knocked on Sara's half-open office door.

"Yep," Sara said in response to the interruption, still facing her computer. She swung her chair halfway around, and her expression changed on the spot. "Hey," she said, her tone full of surprise at Izzy's presence. "Izzy, hi."

Izzy leaned into the room, but most of her body stayed in the hallway. She shifted her backpack higher on her shoulder. "I was hoping I could talk to you for a minute." She knew her voice betrayed her anxiety, and she prayed her nerve would hold up.

"Of course." Sara's voice was soft and welcoming and she waved her in pleasantly. "Come in, please."

"I know it's not my place to question your decisions or anything," she started. "And I don't want you to think I'm challenging you or being difficult." Izzy worried her lower lip repeatedly, knowing it would be raw by evening. "The thing I'm trying to understand is... why?" Even though she'd practiced in her head, she knew her pitch was coming out as a pathetic whine.

Sara leaned all the way forward, resting her arms across her pristine desk. "About Chase, you mean?"

"Yes." Izzy looked up at the large ceiling tiles, wanting to keep her composure. "It's just..." She searched her mind for the best argument. "We seem to get each other. I thought that would matter."

Sara's smile was warm and understanding. "It does, Izzy."

"Why don't you want us to be partners, then?" She heard the desperation in her defensiveness.

"It's not that I don't want you to be partners." Sara's gentle frown bordered on apologetic. "I know you two work well together. But there are other factors to consider." She moved her chair the tiniest bit away, and Izzy inched to the edge of her own seat in response.

"We have a connection. We click, me and Chase. I don't know how to describe it."

She saw Sara's smile reach her eyes. "I know you do. It's sweet." Sara nodded. "You have the makings of a very strong handler, Izzy. You'll pair well with any dog here. I think Sammy is a good fit for you. She's a great dog."

Izzy slumped in her seat and folded her arms across her chest like a petulant child. "So is Chase." She crossed one leg over the other in defiance. "Mark is pissed too. He's been bonding with Sammy all week."

Sara laughed out loud. "Where is he? Or are you the designated rep for this arbitration?" Her tone said she wasn't mad, but it bothered Izzy to think she wasn't being taken seriously.

"I don't know," she said with a flippant shrug. "I guess he doesn't have the balls I do." She let out a heavy breath, collecting herself. "I'm sorry." Rubbing her neck with both hands, she added, "I'm just fired up about this. And honestly, I don't get it." She pitched forward in her seat. "The very first day, you said trust was key. Chase trusts me, I can feel it. What could be more important than that?" She knew she was begging but felt justified.

"You're right," Sara acknowledged, appearing stoically sound in her decision. She rubbed her lips methodically with the tip of her index finger as though she was making sure to select her words with care.

"Izzy, I can see you're taking this personally. And you shouldn't. Honestly." Sara dropped her hand away from her face and she appeared to almost frown in commiseration. "You do make an excellent point." Her words seemed to signal a kind of half-hearted agreement. "Having trust and good click, as you put it, is important."

Izzy couldn't help but notice that the words were optimistic but the shrug that accompanied them was positively defeatist.

"Unfortunately, there are some logistical factors to consider as well," Sara finished.

Izzy racked her brain but came up with nothing. "What does that even mean?"

"The long and short of it"—Sara raised her palms in a kind of surrender—"Chase is a big dog. You are a petite woman." She picked up a stray shred of paper with the pad of her index finger and flicked it into the wastepaper bin behind her. "It's not an optimal match. I'm sorry."

Izzy closed her eyes and shook her head, trying to make sense of what she was hearing. "I don't get it," she admitted. "I can't have him because I'm petite? That makes no sense."

"It's not that simple." Sara rose from her chair and came around to the front of her desk, leaning against it as she spoke. "Chase is one of the bigger dogs in the class. And I know you've been working with him a lot in the very structured, very organized environment we've created for this class for the first week." She crossed her arms. "Chase is strong. Left to his own devices he wants to go after rabbits, squirrels." She rolled her eyes. "Chipmunks, forget it. They're his kryptonite."

"But you just said you thought I had it in me to be a good handler." It came out like a plea but she couldn't stop herself.

"You are a good handler." When Sara looked at her, Izzy felt the sincerity of her words. "Which is why I don't want you to get hurt by pairing you with a dog that outweighs you, especially while you are both still learning."

Sara's voice was soft and Izzy was touched by the sentiment in her tone. But even though she was moved by the concern, she rushed past it, still fighting for what she wanted.

"He won't hurt me."

"Not on purpose, of course not." Sara paused and pinched the bridge of her nose as though she was giving it some thought. "Izzy," she said, waiting a beat until Izzy made direct eye contact. "Chase weighs eighty pounds." She brought her hands to her face and pressed both of her temples. "There are times when you will be required to carry him. If he gets hurt, God forbid," she said with a heavy sigh. "Even if he just needs a boost to get into an SUV or the bed of a truck. That's on you." She gripped the edge of her desk and drummed her fingertips underneath. "I need to be confident you can safely do that. I'm not trying to hurt your feelings or your ego, but you're tiny. I'm just not sure you'd be able to do it."

It took Izzy less that a second to consider Sara's explanation. She clapped her hands against the arms of the chair with gusto. "I can do it." She stood quickly. "Let's go—I'll do it right now."

She was ready to bolt but Sara's hands on her forearms stopped her. "Whoa. Hold on." They were in each other's personal space and their eyes locked for a second. Sara dropped her hands to her sides, her gaze shifting to the floor. Izzy used the moment to telegraph her confidence.

"I can do it. I can lift him. I'm a thousand percent sure of it and I want to show you."

"I do love your enthusiasm," Sara said through a shy laugh, still avoiding eye contact. "Look—I'll give it some thought over the weekend." Her expression was earnest, and standing so close, Izzy noticed a spray of light freckles just beneath her eyes. "It's Friday afternoon. I'm sure you have weekend plans. Go home and try not to dwell on this. We'll talk about it Monday."

Izzy's shrug was playfully optimistic. "I have no plans tonight." She rested one hand on the textured frame of the Glock 9 mm holstered on her gun belt, placing the other on her handcuff case on the other side of her duty rig, getting close to a battle stance. "Let's do this," she said. "Unless I'm keeping you from something," she added as an afterthought.

"I'm sitting at my computer on a Friday afternoon working on next month's certification schedule." She half laughed at herself. "You're not keeping me from anything."

"All right, then." Izzy started for the door but Sara stopped her once more. This time she reached out, applying the gentlest touch to her forearm, making the tiny hairs stand on end.

"You don't have to do this," Sara said. "We'll figure something out."

Izzy's head was in a million places at once and she thought she might be winning her instructor over, but she wasn't sure and she wanted Sara to be confident in her decision. She pressed on. "It's obvious how much this matters." She willed herself to look at Sara's eyes, even though her beautiful mouth was so close. "I appreciate you seeing me and listening to my opinion." She rubbed her palms against her gear. "And I know this won't set anything in stone. You still have a decision to make, I get that. But if you are going to *think* about allowing me to partner with Chase, I want you to weigh the odds knowing one of your major concerns is a nonissue." She opened her eyes wide for dramatic emphasis. "We've already established neither of us has a social life." Offering half a grin, she added, "What's another ten minutes?"

Sara didn't argue her logic, and as they walked through the building to the kennel area, Izzy tried to figure exactly how she was going to accomplish the task at hand. Eighty pounds of solid muscle was going to be a challenge for her slim five-three build. Truthfully, she hadn't a clue how to approach it. But inside she was calm. Chase seemed to bring out her inner zen, and as she walked, she realized she wasn't remotely worried.

By the time they reached him, Chase was already on all fours, doing a tiny prance at Izzy's presence. She smiled big for him, giving him a fantastic greeting when Sara pressed the button to lift the cage.

"Give us a minute," she said to Sara.

Sara stepped to the side arching her eyebrows in unspoken amusement, affording them space.

Izzy bent down in front of Chase like she'd done the very first time they'd met. She held his face and touched his head, looking over at Sara as she whispered words of encouragement in his ear. Finally, she stood up. "Okay, we're ready."

Sara closed the gap between them and watched intently as Izzy stroked his back lightly, speaking to him as she rubbed his fur. "Okay, stand up, buddy." She guided his body with her hands, looping one under his belly and using the other to support his chest. She lifted him swiftly and kept him pressed to her body for half a minute rotating slowly from side to side, illustrating her range of motion before returning him gently to the ground.

"Sit."

On her command, Chase sat down and waited for what might come next. Since this completed her agenda, she bent down and petted his head, a simple thanks for his willing compliance. She darted her glance up to check Sara's reaction, pleased to find her smiling, palms up in surrender.

"How can I argue with that?"

Izzy smiled so big she felt her dimples pop on both sides.

"I think you just got yourself a partner, Isabel Marquez."

"Oh my God. Are you serious?" She didn't even try to contain her excitement. "Because I could pick him up?" she squealed, still reeling at the turn of events.

"Well, the fact you cared enough to come to me and were clearly willing to fight for him didn't hurt either." Izzy thought she heard a kind of pride in Sara's voice. "Plus, you two do have a sweet bond." Her smile was gorgeous and genuine, and Izzy had to hold back from reaching forward and hugging her in appreciation. Instead she poured her excitement into Chase, rubbing his head as she updated him.

"Hear that, big guy?" He looked right at her as she spoke. "We're going to be partners. You and me."

His bark was surely a reaction to her excited voice, but the timing was perfect and she crouched a little, her hands on her thighs, jutting her face out. Chase balanced on his haunches with one paw on her knee, and he leaned up and kissed her cheek. When she looked over, Sara was shaking her head through a smile, and Izzy saw real joy in her expression.

"Thank you, Sara." Izzy almost stuttered as she spoke Sara's name aloud for the first time. She talked over it hoping it wasn't noticeable. "I won't let you down. I promise."

"I know." Sara ushered Chase back to his kennel. "I meant what I said before. Chase is spectacular. Smart, social, obedient, loyal. His play drive is unmatched. Truly." Powering the gate down, she went on, "But with that come a few idiosyncrasies."

"Right." Izzy nodded, following Sara back into the main section of the building.

"What I mean is…this whole first week has been very… mundane." She stuffed her hands in her pockets. "Even the free play has been kind of controlled," she said. "Once we start doing real explosive detection training, it requires a lot more focus. Chase can do it—I've no doubt about that. He wouldn't be here if he couldn't." Reaching her office door, she paused and leaned against the frame. "He'll need more outlets. Ways to burn off his energy. Both physical and mental. Otherwise he'll develop bad habits."

"Like darting after chipmunks."

"Exactly."

Izzy was busy trying to memorize everything Sara was saying, and it must've showed.

"Quit stressing. You've got this." Sara rubbed her arm supportively. "Anyway, I'll help you."

"You will?"

"Of course." She reached for her phone from her back pocket. "Give me your number. There's some good websites you should check out. I'll text you the info."

"Thank you so much."

Sara smiled as she thumbed Izzy's number into her phone. "This is me texting you right now. Feel free to pick my brain anytime, day or night."

"How about right now?" Izzy held her breath as she floated the invitation she hadn't at all planned on extending. She went with it in spite of her nerves. "Grab a drink with me at the pub in town?" She raised her eyebrows hoping it made her seem casual. "We can talk dogs, training, all the good stuff," she added.

"Tempting, but…" Sara looked at her watch.

Izzy was fueled by excitement. "Come on." She lifted one shoulder up slightly. "I just got my first ever K-9 dog. Celebrate with me."

Behind them, Sara's desk phone rang. "I should get that." She reached forward and gave Izzy's shoulder a small squeeze. "Congratulations." Her face wore an expression Izzy couldn't quite figure as she backed away. "Rain check, okay?"

She should have been disappointed at Sara's polite rejection. But she just felt too damn good. Chase was going to be her partner. And Sara had talked to her, she'd looked at her—for Christ's sake, she'd even touched her. A lot, actually. She bit her lip at the thought as she started up her truck. She rolled down the window and let the warm breeze wash over her as she jacked up the music, completely content to replay the last hour in her mind as she sped home.

CHAPTER SIX

S ara stood at the front door a good few seconds, debating whether she should ring the bell or just walk in. It was an odd feeling, having lived the majority of her teenage years under this very roof. Just as she was about to knock—an even compromise in her mind—Alyssa pulled the door open.

"I was so happy when my parents told me you were coming." Before she could even respond, Sara was inside, her old friend's arms around her. "I haven't seen you in forever."

"That's what happens when you move clear across town."

"Ha. That's rich, coming from someone who lives practically at the Canadian border."

Sara enjoyed that they could slip right back into a spirited back and forth even though it had been ages since they'd seen one another. She squeezed Alyssa tight before stepping from her embrace. "Where's the birthday boy?" she asked, shaking a small superhero-themed gift bag in front of her.

"You didn't have to get him anything, Sara." Alyssa took the gift and placed it on the table. "But thank you."

"And disappoint a four-year-old on his birthday?" She put on a fake look of horror. "It's bad enough I'm crashing his party."

Alyssa whacked her arm lightly. "Please. Hannah and I are convinced Mom and Dad would trade either one of us for you in a heartbeat." With her corny joke she let out a high-pitched cackle Sara'd almost forgotten about. For a split second she fell all the way back into the past, a fourteen-year-old orphan graciously given shelter by her high school besties and their parents.

Her smile was bittersweet over the memory. Life with the Dixons had been wonderful despite the tragic circumstance that brought on the makeshift arrangement. Sara had been devastated at the loss of her mother, but John and Rose Dixon were kind people. They'd made her feel comfortable in their home and let her bring along Lucky, the German shepherd rescue no one else was willing to consider. Alyssa and Hannah were good friends and they'd stayed close even as their interests diverged over the years.

Sometimes when she thought about it, she wondered how different life might be if she'd never come to live with them. If they hadn't rescued her, if she'd been forced to stay with her Aunt Maureen and Uncle Jim, who were nice people but wanted no part of her dog. The Dixons saved her from that fate, and then John had introduced her to a career she loved, one she'd likely never have found without his influence.

The birthday boy charged through the living room followed by his crying baby sister. Alyssa scooped her up handily, shaking a bottle as she headed to the kitchen.

"Is your dad around?" Sara asked over the jingle of a toy xylophone.

Alyssa pointed with her chin, popping open the microwave. "On the deck."

Sliding open the glass door, Sara walked outside, enjoying the sound of quiet and the feel of the late day breeze as it hit her. "Hey, boss man," she said.

"Can't get enough of me, huh?" he teased, offering her a beer from the cooler.

She took it from him even though she wasn't at all sure she wanted a drink. "Who's talking to you?" She reached down and gave John's partner Duncan a good scratch on the head. "I'm here for this guy."

"Same difference." He took the Adirondack next to her. "You saw us both two hours ago."

Sara picked up a tennis ball and whipped it across the yard, then watched Duncan scamper after it with glee. She needed a service dog of her own. It had been too long. "Three," she corrected.

"Huh?"

"It's been closer to three hours."

"Get anything done after I left for the day?"

"I scheduled all the re-certs for next month."

"That's good."

The cold lager felt good as she swallowed a long sip. "I decided to partner Chase and Izzy together." She watched Duncan lope back over. She felt John's eyes on her, turned, and could almost see him process her decision.

"I think that's the right call." He rubbed his mustache, a habit she knew meant he was thinking hard. "I know you had some concerns, but I think it's a good match."

"I hope so." She said it almost under her breath, her uncertainty coming through against her will.

"She reminds me of you, ya know."

His statement was matter-of-fact, and Sara squinted in the sun, wondering if she had the heart to tell him that the tough, feminine vibe he was picking up on was nothing more than his own gaydar at play.

But before she could say anything, he explained, "She's a natural. Like you." He brushed a wayward flower petal from the flat wooden arm of his chair. "When I saw you that first time with Lucky." His eyelids dropped closed as he fell into the memory. "That dog was tough as nails and you handled her like a pro." He picked at his soggy, peeling beer label. "I knew right then you were special." With his thumb he pushed the label back in place. "Izzy has no experience. No training. But man, does she have the knack."

Sara wanted to believe him, but she worried her emotions influenced her objectivity. "You think so?"

"Come on, Sara." His expression was pure disbelief. "You see what I see. Chase is a great dog, but he's not easy," he said with an even expression. "He's big and smart and has so much drive. He likes to chase things. His name is fucking perfect." He laughed at the irony, knowing the true source of his moniker.

"You're just highlighting all my concerns, you know."

"But, Izzy, from day one"—he shook his head and his tone signaled awe—"she had him under control." He poked her arm with his meaty index finger. "That's my point." Draining the last of his beer, he stood up to snag another. "Not to rub it in, but I would like to mention I did say I had a good feeling about her right off, even if her path to us was less than traditional."

"Speaking of…" Sara twisted her drink in her hands. "Nicole called me earlier."

"Oh, yeah?" He shook the ice chips off the dark brown bottle he pulled from the cooler, then offered it to Sara first but opening it for himself when she declined. "What's new with her?"

"I didn't really ask. I was too busy railing into her for not telling me about Izzy."

"What'd she say?"

Sara shrugged. "That it was an oversight. She figured you told me. It was last minute." She ticked her head from side to side as she enumerated the excuses. "A bunch of things. All weak."

"Did she apologize?"

"She did. And capitalizing on her guilt, I took the opportunity to try to get some real info out of her."

"About?"

"I asked her who Izzy's connection is." Not knowing was starting to make her a little twitchy, and she wasn't sure why. "It's just so unusual the way it all went down. I guess I'm still trying to figure out how she ended up in K-9."

"And?" He started prepping the grill.

Sara frowned a little thinking about it. "Nicole said she got a call from a ranking officer at the NYPD she's close with, saying it was a must. She didn't give me any other details." She watched Duncan entertain himself in the yard. "Honestly, I got the impression she didn't know too much."

"Hmm." Smoke rose from the barbecue grate as he cleaned it with a wire brush. "Why don't you just ask Izzy?" He adjusted the burners, holding his hand a few inches above the flame to assess the heat. "She seems like a good egg. I bet she'd be straight with you."

"It hardly matters, anyway," she responded, brushing his suggestion off as she focused on a blue jay a few yards away.

"How's Nicole otherwise?" He swallowed a hefty sip of his beverage. "How are things with the two of you these days?"

She wasn't sure what he was asking. Even though she never talked about their breakup, she and Nicole hadn't been a couple in years. In fact, they'd been platonic for a while now, aside from the minor hiccup a month ago when they ended up in Nicole's bed. But John had no way of knowing about that.

"Things are fine. I guess." She didn't even try to hide how thrown she was by the question.

"I only ask because I know you went to DC recently." Yeah, he read her like a book. "And I saw your truck parked outside her house last week. Was she in town?" He mimed driving a golf ball deep with his spatula.

"Keeping tabs on me, boss?" She was kidding and she knew he knew it.

"Her house is around the block." He shrugged in playful defense. "Your car is very distinctive. Primarily because it belonged to me less than a year ago."

She laughed in response. "I love that truck. I don't know why you wanted to get rid of it so badly."

"I use the work car so much I wasn't putting any miles on it. Rose didn't like it. She complained it was too big for her."

Sara shook her head, the theory unfathomable to her. She adored every inch of the black Dodge Ram 1500 she'd inherited for a bargain price. It was perfect for the rugged terrain near the trails by her house, and she felt invincible behind the wheel of the sturdy pickup on a daily basis.

"You didn't answer my question, by the way." John interrupted her train of thought. When she looked at him, her face must've revealed she'd forgotten the question entirely. He jutted his chin forward. "You and Nicole. Everything good?"

She took a long sip of her drink. "Things are fine. The same." She hoped her easy tone reassured him. "She asked me to go by her place the other day to let a service guy in. Her gas meter needed to be read." She reached down to pet Duncan, who'd settled into a lazy sprawl by her side. "I don't know why she doesn't put that house on the market already."

"I heard a rumor she might be coming back up north."

The thought piqued her interest, but not because she sought to rekindle their romance. The gossip was intriguing but sort of annoying at the same time. Why was she getting all Nicole's info secondhand from John?

"I thought maybe"—he paused stumbling over his words—"you two might be getting back together." He blushed a little, having obviously misread her silence.

Sara was moved by the effort he was making, even if it was way off the mark. "No." She smiled sincerely so he would know it was all good. "That ship has sailed," she said, focusing her attention on Duncan so he wouldn't see hesitation in her face. "It's fine, though. We're better off as friends." She wondered at the truth of her own statement. When Duncan rolled on his side, she rubbed his belly. "What I need is a dog," she said, showering the pup with affection. "Isn't that right, Dunc?"

"I hate to be the one to tell you this," John said, interrupting the love session with phony chagrin. "What you need is a girlfriend."

Sara couldn't contain her laughter. "Where is this coming from?" she asked, marveling at the direction their conversation had taken.

"I'm only half kidding," he said through his own broad smile. Getting a touch serious he added, "Look, Sara. I worry about you." He scratched his five o'clock shadow. "I can't help it." He rearranged his barbecue tools for the umpteenth time. "Can you blame me? I mean, you've been single a while now. And, Christ, you moved an hour and a half away from civilization. Up to the boonies in Shandaken or whatever it's called."

"Phoenicia. And it's thoroughly civilized. Also, quaint and beautiful," she added, still beaming at his obvious concern. "Honestly, lately"—she swirled the last few sips at the bottom of her beer—"I practically live in the dorms these days anyway." She wondered if that bolstered her argument or his.

"The point I'm trying to make here"—John blew right past her comment—"is you need to get out there. Go on...apps." He fisted his hand repeatedly as though grasping for the right terminology. "Or whatever they're called. Find a match," he finished, throwing air quotes around the word.

Sara wiped tears of laughter from the corners of her eyes. "Are you drunk?" she asked through hysterics.

"Shut up, you." He pointed the long neck of his beer bottle at her in a fake kind of scolding. "I'm not drunk." He shuffled back and forth. "I'm a dad and I'm your friend."

Sara pointed one finger straight into the air. "Also, technically, my boss." She wiggled her eyebrows playfully. "Which makes this conversation super weird and possibly reportable," she added in good fun.

"Stop it, I'm being serious." He put his drink down and looked right at her. "If your mother was alive she'd be saying the same things. Nudging you, I mean."

Sara huffed out a small thoughtful laugh, idly wondering if he was right.

"Hey. I'm being a parent. We nudge, we nag. It's kind of our job." He tapped the grill with the flat end of the tongs. "When we see our kids stuck in a rut, we push them. Like it or not, you're part of this family, kid."

They weren't huggers, but Sara couldn't help being moved by his sentiment. She met his eyes and gave him a heartfelt smile, hoping it conveyed a fraction of the gratitude she felt at his concern. "I'll take it under advisement."

"That's all I ask."

Thankfully Rose broke up the heavy moment by passing through the sliders with a tray of marinated skewers in need of grilling. Sara jumped up to pitch in and gave her a hearty hello. The remainder of the night was light and fun, filled with good food and great people, old stories and tons of laughs. But when she zipped along the highway to her home in rural New York, one conversation echoed in her mind.

John was right. It had been too long. She needed to get back out into the dating world—she'd given herself the exact same lecture just the other day. But even as she considered it abstractly, the image of one person raced to the forefront of her mind.

At first, Sara pictured her in the environment she saw her in daily: the training field, the classroom, even the cafeteria. But then the daydream took on a life of its own, moving them seamlessly to her on-campus quarters, her lovely house in the quiet woods. There was no denying who she wanted.

As the suburban streetlights faded in the distance, the sounds of traffic giving way to crickets chirping in the trees, she welcomed the fantasy. Because that's all it was. She wasn't going to allow herself to act on it. Not in real life. One of these days she'd buckle down, create a profile, Tinder away. But for now, she indulged herself a small departure from reality, letting Izzy Marquez occupy her mind as she walked through the front door of her house, changed out of her clothes, and slipped under the covers, the solace of sleep pleasantly eluding her for hours.

Chapter Seven

I zzy was already pouring her second cup of coffee when she saw her phone light up on the kitchen island a few feet away. She looked at Chase, who perked up at the sound of the notification.

"Saturday morning. That's going to be Elena." She gave him her full attention when she spoke. "We talk a lot. And you're going to meet her tomorrow. Isn't that exciting?" Maybe it was weird that she was explaining this level of detail to Chase, but it was only his second day in her house and she wanted him to know he belonged here. That meant knowing about her sister and her family and being part of their weekly gatherings.

Chase's mouth dropped open into his familiar smile as though he understood at least the sentiment of her words. "You're going to love her." She petted his head sweetly as she walked toward her cell. "And she is going to go crazy for you. They all are." Izzy smiled to herself because she knew it was the truth. Her eyes still on Chase, she reached for her phone, ready to snap a pic of his gorgeous face to send to her sis, but froze when she saw it was Sara's name illuminating her screen, not Elena's.

Before she even opened the text, a second message came through. Izzy thumbed out her passcode in anticipation.

Good morning. Sara had punctuated the greeting with a smiley face before asking, *Is it too early?*

There were more bubbles, but Izzy raced to respond. She didn't want a third message to come without Sara knowing she was fully awake and available. *Not at all*, she typed. *I'm already on my second cup of coffee.* Was that stupid? She hit Send before she could overthink it.

How did Chase do? Sara asked.

Of course. Sara was checking in on Chase since last night was his first away from the kennel, his first night in his new home. If there was a part of her that was bummed the message wasn't strictly personal in nature, it was overshadowed by how much Sara clearly loved her dogs. Even though the check-in was on Chase's behalf, Izzy melted just the same.

He did great.

She thought about the night as a whole. Chase had been eager to explore his new digs, and he seemed happy enough with her modest house, although she wondered how she would even know if he wasn't. *I think,* she added, owning her slight fear. *How would I know?* She hit Send before realizing that depending on how it was interpreted, her last statement could come off rude. She tried again. *Sorry. I mean, are there signs I should be looking out for, to know if he's sad or depressed or something?*

LOL, no. There was a short pause before another message popped. *Chase is a great dog. I'm sure he's fine. And trust me, you would know if there was an issue.*

Whew!

There was silence for almost a minute and Izzy wondered if their exchange was done, but then more bubbles appeared.

Tell me about the night.

Izzy felt her heart rate speed up and she wondered if Sara was following up with all her classmates to this degree. God, she hoped that wasn't the case. Izzy wanted it to be just her. It was foolish and ridiculous and surely missing the point of the program, but every time Sara Wright looked in her direction, she felt a charge through her whole body. She ached to get to know her better. She longed for her undivided attention. And, for the moment at least, she had it.

We got home around four. Chase was great in the car. He didn't seem to mind the drive one bit. I picked the music, though. She dropped in the laughing emoji.

Good. It's important to let him know who's in charge. Sara answered with a wink of her own and Izzy smiled, seeing she was lighthearted enough to play along.

Seriously, though, when we got home I took him through the house first. Just showed him the rooms, explained the setup. Then we went for a walk through the neighborhood. I also took him around the yard but didn't let him roam free yet.

Probably a good move.

We dipped into the woods behind my house for a bit because I knew he was dying to see what was going on there. I wanted him to be comfortable with his surroundings, plus I wanted him to get a good workout in. Then we played for a bit. Both outside and in the house. I figured I should tire him out, so he'd sleep. I knew the excitement of something new would rev him up, so I tried to burn some of that off. I thought a good night's sleep might be important for setting good habits. She threw in the shrug emoji because she really had no idea if she'd done anything right at all.

Smart. Sara's answer was one word. But it was a good word, right?

Yeah? she typed back.

You have great instincts.

I have a great teacher. She almost hit Send but thought better of it. It was the truth, but she deleted it anyway. It was too forward and she knew her intention was flirtatious. She needed to get ahold of herself. Taking a deep breath, she replaced the sentence with a bland and professional *Thank you.* She didn't want to seem ungrateful.

So now, the real question. Did YOU get any sleep?

Izzy laughed out loud and Chase tilted his head at her. "She's got me figured out, buddy," she said as she typed her response.

LOL. I was up a lot at first. I was worried about him! She hoped her emotion came through as concern, not paranoia. *Once I realized he was off in dreamland, I fell out too.*

Did he stay with you in your room?

Izzy walked over to the area just outside her bedroom where there was a small nook that was bordered by her linen closet on one side, her bedroom wall on the other. She'd always found it to be the oddest layout because there were six or seven feet of dead space.

But once she brought Chase home, she realized it was the perfect spot to turn into a cozy corner for him. Close enough to her, but still a space of his own. She snapped a picture of his bed and cropped it so a few of his toys were in the frame. She posted the pic onto their text thread with the caption: *I set this small area up for him just outside my bedroom.*

Aww. That looks comfy.

He seemed happy there.

Perfect.

I didn't know if there was a right or wrong place for him to sleep. Like, with me in my room or out in the living room, etc. I actually had no clue, lol. I should have texted you.

You did great. And there's no right or wrong answer. You have to do what feels right for you and for him.

Izzy knew it was pathetic but she was enjoying the back and forth and she didn't want it to end. She tried hard to come up with something to say but blanked. Thankfully Sara was still typing.

For what it's worth, I think it's good Chase has his own little sleep spot.

Oh, yeah?

You know, you two will spend a lot of time together. Working, training. More than if he was simply your pet. It's good to have some boundaries. You gave him a place where he can decompress. And I'm sure there are times where you might appreciate some privacy too. She capped it off with the winking emoji.

Izzy almost dropped her phone. Was she reading too far into the words, or did Sara just make reference to her love life? Maybe she was overanalyzing.

Sara's next text: *What do you have planned for today?*

Sara was obviously more coherent than she was. At least this was an easy one.

More of the same. A small hike, get my boy acquainted with the neighborhood. Play. Nothing crazy. You?

Some yard work. Errands. Research.

Research, as in work? Sure, she was fishing to keep the

conversation going, but she was also genuinely curious. *On a weekend?* she added, hoping to keep it light.

Ha! Yes. But I love my job, so it never feels like work. There was a pause, more bubbles. *I'll do my chores today and then tonight I'll light a fire, put on some music, maybe have a glass of wine. It won't be so bad.*

It actually sounds lovely. Was that too much? Screw it, she sent it anyway.

Sara answered with the smiley face that was kind of blushing, and Izzy wondered if she was.

I should let you get back to your day. I'm glad you had a good first night. Give that pup a kiss for me.

Izzy wanted more, but knew she had to let it go. *Ok, bye!* She fired off the message, playing it cool. Turning to Chase, she channeled her optimism. "I don't know about you, pal, but she texted us first thing on a Saturday morning. I'm going to take that as a sign we were on her mind. And I, for one, am hella excited about that. Should we celebrate with a walk?"

Chase hopped to his feet, ever ready for action.

"That's my boy." Izzy smiled right at him as she downed her coffee and grabbed the leash.

❖

Izzy spent the rest of the weekend half wondering what Sara was doing and resisting the urge to contact her. She made it all the way through dessert at her parents' Sunday evening, when she was about to send a pic of Chase looking unbelievably sweet as he sat perfectly behaved at her side. Before she could compose a message, a new text from Sara came through. Thankfully her nephew had everyone's attention and no one commented on the huge smile that she knew spread across her face. The message was a link to an article on training tips and techniques, with the tag *Thought you might find this interesting.*

Izzy responded right away. *I'm at my parents' but will definitely check it out when I get home. Thank you!* She sent the shot of Chase for good measure.

That face. Sara followed with a heart emoji and Izzy used all her willpower to remind herself it was about Chase. *See you both tomorrow.* Sara's final text left no room for banter, so Izzy just smiled, already counting down the hours in her mind.

❖

"Teams one, three, and five, you're with Agent Hayes. Two, four, six, and seven, with me," Agent Gilmartin called out, glancing at a Post-it for reference. "Eight through ten, you guys are with Dixon. The rest of you get Sara."

Izzy felt her spirit sink, the same as it had each time the daily assignments were called out. By the middle of week three Izzy knew the routine. Mornings were filled with agility exercises, obedience, and skills training. The afternoons were devoted to developing techniques specific to K-9 as the cops and agents practiced their new roles through classroom instruction and practical exercises. Training was more intense but it was also more rewarding, not to mention loads of fun.

Izzy and Chase were inseparable, and as the human half of team seven, Izzy's only complaint was that she rarely got the chance to work directly with Sara. While the staff juggled the groups around to work with each other and different trainers, it seemed her assignment never sent her in Sara's direction.

Maybe it was for the best, she reasoned to herself, although when she broke the thought down, it made little sense to her. Why would she be denied the opportunity to work with the best instructor on staff? At times she wondered if her separation was by design. But that didn't resonate either. In fact, she had an open line of communication with Sara. Their texts the previous weekend proved it. But wait, was that the reason? Did Sara feel she was too social and was pulling away?

Izzy pushed the negative thoughts right from her mind, focusing instead on getting into the zone as she walked over to station one. Dubbed baggage claim by her classmates, this was the area where canines and their handlers learned the proper methods to search all kinds of bags. Luggage, backpacks, purses, and briefcases were set up in varying arrays: alone in the field, coupled together with other household items, shrink-wrapped simulating a cargo delivery. The dogs didn't need to learn how to smell, of course, but there was an art to knowing where to sniff: along the seams of a suitcase, underneath a pallet where the vapors that are heavier than air settled.

Chase was the master. He never missed, and Izzy was beginning to learn the feel of his body, the subtle tension in his muscles, the delicate tweak of his ears the moment before he would sit down, using a passive alert to indicate the presence of bomb-making materials. Each success garnered massive praise from Izzy and some well-earned time with his favorite toy, an eight-inch jute tug as tough and strong as he was.

Every single day at the facility Izzy's confidence grew exponentially. She was self-assured and calm, and despite her initial fears of not belonging, she found herself every bit as qualified as her classmates. And she picked up on something special right away. Like the dogs, the handlers had a certain motivation, a drive which almost felt like a calling. There was no competition among them, just united desire to learn from each other so they might all succeed. And while the group members couldn't be more different in some ways—coming from different parts of the country and representing various agencies—they had a natural synergy. Already Izzy knew she'd made true friends in Mark, Jen, and Ryan. The four of them were something of a clique, trading tips and pointers during breaks and telling war stories every day at lunch in the campus cafeteria.

They were all laughing their heads off as they left the corner table they shared with a crew of federal recruits in agent-training over at the north side of the facility. Izzy led the way to the door walking backward so she could focus on Ryan, who was continuing an embarrassing anecdote about his rookie year on the force. A Florida native, he loved giving the lowdown about the craziness at the sheriff's department he and Jen worked for. He was a natural storyteller and great at delivering self-deprecating punch lines and had the gang in stitches daily.

Izzy was holding her stomach and getting her breath back as she turned for the door and nearly bumped into Sara, who was on her way in.

"Whoa," Sara said with an easy smile, her hands finding Izzy's hips to stop her forward momentum.

To keep herself from falling, Izzy reached up, and her hand brushed over Sara's breast. "Oh my God. I'm so sorry."

"No worries." Sara's small chuckle was forgiving but Izzy saw her blush and divert her eyes as she moved past the group. Her friends didn't seem to notice anything out of the ordinary, and Ryan yammered away without missing a beat. But Izzy tuned out and suddenly wished she'd left her wallet or her sweatshirt inside, something to give her an excuse to go back, find Sara, and strike up a conversation. It was ridiculous and she knew it, but on the spot she couldn't help herself.

"Hey guys, I'll catch up with you in a bit." She tweaked her head back toward the café. "I left something inside," she lied. Booking back to the lunch hall, she rushed through the doors and wondered what the hell she was going to say when she saw Sara. A couple of ideas swirled through her head and she rehearsed them as she hung around for a solid few minutes, fake looking for a lost item and even purchasing a coffee to justify more time. Sara never showed. Somehow, she'd missed her.

CHAPTER EIGHT

A week passed, and by the following Friday, Izzy felt like she was getting the hang of her new gig. The drills were becoming rote and the instructors were moving to scenario and tactical exercises. Izzy was a model student, paying full attention, even if she did always scan for Sara's whereabouts. She often saw her observing from afar or giving a handler a tip here and there. Unfortunately, Izzy'd received most of her individual attention from Hayes. He was a nice guy, but she missed the rapport she had with Sara. Maybe she'd text her over the upcoming weekend. She could come up with a dog-related question easy enough.

Izzy considered the plan as she browsed the cafeteria lunch options. Nothing appealed today. But it was no big, her usual lunch crew was scattered anyway, and she wanted something light she could grab on the go. Settling on a strawberry yogurt, she made her way to the register, adding a banana at the last minute before heading to the plastic cutlery baskets.

"That's a light lunch." Sara's voice was lively and sweet behind her at the condiment counter. Izzy turned, ready with a quick response, but Sara's frothy pink beverage distracted her.

"What is that?" Her mouth watered from sheer jealously.

Sara couldn't contain her smile as she reached for a straw, sliding the paper wrapper off with one hand and slipping it through the plastic lid. "This is a fruit smoothie." She took a small sip, her perfect lips curled at the edges.

"But where?" Izzy looked around for the source, truly baffled at her oversight.

"Uh-uh." Sara handed a plastic spoon to Izzy. "Courtesy of my buddy Doug. In the kitchen."

Izzy fake frowned. "Well, that's no fair."

"Membership has its privileges." Sara added a guiltless shrug as they ambled through the seating area.

Izzy opened her mouth to talk but a peppy blonde brushed her shoulder as she passed. "Hi, Izzy." She looked shy as she spoke. "You coming to sit?" Holding her lunch tray, she gestured with her chin. "We're by the window today."

"Oh, thanks," Izzy responded. "I'm going to head back to class today. I'll catch up with you next time."

The girl's face registered obvious disappointment even though she smiled. "Have a great weekend."

"Yeah, you too." Izzy waved with her banana.

Sara stopped walking and glanced back and forth between Izzy and the blonde. "Who's that?" she asked, her lyrical tone implying a connection that wasn't there.

"That's Jackie. She's in training to be an air marshal." Izzy made light of it, even though she suspected Jackie had a crush on her. "We all sit together sometimes. Me, Jen, Mark, Ryan, and some of the recruits." She hoped her explanation proved there was nothing between them.

"Don't let me stop you." Sara held both hands up in surrender.

"No, no." Izzy shook her head. "It's just me today. I'd rather talk to you." She pushed the door open and stepped aside, holding it ajar for Sara. "I haven't seen you around much." She slid the banana and plastic spoon in the cargo pocket of her pants. "I mean, I see you in class and, you know, practical exercises." It sounded ridiculous hearing herself say it. She checked Sara's expression and saw she was smiling slightly as she nursed her drink. Izzy took a deep breath, determined to not sound like an idiot. "How are you?" she asked, hoping to start over.

"I'm good." Sara rolled her shoulders and tossed her hair in the light breeze. She couldn't have looked any sexier if she tried. Izzy had no idea what to say next.

"You're doing really well. Not that I'm at all surprised." Sara looked right at her and she hoped the unexpected praise hadn't made her blush. "I'm sure you know that, but in case you don't, we all think you're doing great." Sara bumped her shoulder playfully. "You feel good about things?"

"Yeah, sure."

"How's Chase doing at home?"

"Fantastic, actually." Izzy couldn't keep her smile hidden when she talked about Chase. She was still wrapping her head around the truth he was her dog. "He's adjusting really well, I think." She drew a lazy circle on the foil cover of her yogurt. "I'm working with him on a few things at night."

"Like what?"

Sara's interest seemed genuine and Izzy wanted to share, if only to get her opinion. "You know, because I'm so near the park and the woods I get a ton of wildlife. Squirrels, birds, rabbits."

"And? How's our rascal doing with constant temptation?"

"Okay." Izzy reflected on their impromptu training session last Sunday. "We're making progress. He's getting there."

Sara swirled her drink a little. "What's your approach?"

"Nothing special. Off-leash work. Positive reinforcement," she said with a definitive nod. "I bought him a Kong that he's obsessed with. I use that as a reward." She flipped her container of yogurt in the air, catching it after one rotation. "He goes crazy for it. It's a good motivator."

"Smart." Sara stopped in her tracks and Izzy stopped with her, waiting to see what was up. Sara used her drink to point right at her. "This is why you're the best."

"What?"

"The idea that you broke out a different toy for this type of coaching. Not falling back on the jute. I know that's your go-to in class." Izzy bit the inside of her cheek, hiding her bliss at the realization Sara'd been paying attention to her after all. "You have fantastic instincts. You can't teach that." Sara's expression told her she was impressed, but there was something else there she couldn't put her finger on.

"Thanks," Izzy said, mesmerized by the way the sun highlighted the dark blue rim around Sara's hazel eyes. How had she missed that before?

"Do you have any questions for me?" Sara held her arms up and spun in a circle. "I'm all yours."

If only, Izzy thought. Fueled by nothing but good vibes and courage, Izzy cocked her head to the side. "I might have a question."

"Oh, yeah?" Sara faced her and took a long sip of her fruity beverage. "What's on your mind?"

"I guess I was wondering if, you know, maybe…" Izzy shifted her yogurt from hand to hand, feeling her heart pound at what she was about to do. "I don't know, maybe you wanted to go out sometime." She lifted her shoulders high, hoping her nerves played as cute instead of desperate. "Get a drink, maybe dinner…"

Sara's expression revealed absolute surprise at the invitation. She licked her lips and ran her delicate fingers along the condensation on her plastic cup. "Izzy," she started. Her tone said everything and Izzy didn't need her to continue, but she did anyway. "You're really sweet. And attractive—"

"So that's a yes?" Izzy's attempt at breaking the tension made the conversation more awkward.

Sara's face twisted with pity and she touched Izzy's arm gently. "I'm sorry."

"It's okay." Swallowing her pride, Izzy tried to keep it light. "I just thought…" She waved a finger between them. "I thought I picked up on something between us. I guess I just misread the situation. Or maybe it's just me." She knew it wasn't just her. "I kind of feel like a jerk now, though," she said, forcing a laugh.

"Please, don't." Sara looked up at the clear blue sky. "Under different circumstances"—she shrugged—"well, things would be different."

Izzy wasn't one to beg, but Sara's statement was so vague she couldn't help herself. "I'm sorry, I don't follow."

Sara huffed out a heavy breath. "The program lasts another few months. But"—she sucked her bottom lip—"after graduation, there's still in-service training. Following a short stint in the field you'll come back so you and Chase can learn basic patrol tactics, that's another nine weeks. And then annual recertification." The explanation made no sense to Izzy, and Sara obviously read the confusion on her face. "We will see each other. A lot, over the course of time."

"Okay."

"You're not hearing what I'm saying."

It was true. Izzy had no idea what Sara was driving at. Even if she was referencing simple fraternization, Sara's excuse failed to make sense. Teacher-student dating rules were based solely on quid pro quo, favoritism, and grading objectivity. Most of those principles carried over to relationships between rank and file, and she supported the theory behind them. In her opinion, this situation didn't fit those categories at all. For starters, she wasn't being graded on this class—she was being trained in the tools needed to do her job effectively. And she'd already been assigned a dog. There was nothing Sara could give her that would constitute any kind of bias. Plus, Izzy knew for a fact outside the additional nine-week patrol training offered at the facility, she was free to conduct her weekly in-service and annual recertification almost anywhere. With so many years in the business, Sara had to know these facts too. Izzy shook her head feeling defeated and bewildered.

"I can see you're not convinced." Sara's voice was warm despite her repeated rejection.

Izzy looked at the tops of the trees in the distance, searching for the right words to convey her feelings over how this was playing out. She let out a small laugh. "I'll be honest. It doesn't really make sense to me." She shrugged and gave a tiny smile. "But I can take no for an answer. It's cool."

"I think you're great." Izzy watched her finger the bright pink straw as she spoke, pleading her case. "And I really like talking to you," she added, unable to maintain eye contact. "I just think it's best if we don't blur the lines."

"Sure."

"If it makes you feel any better, it's not just that you're in the class." Her drink slurped when she sipped it. "I don't date cops as a rule."

"That would be because…"

"I'm trying to maintain a level of professionalism, for one."

"There's a lot of cops who don't go into K-9." Izzy had no idea why she was advocating for anyone other than herself, but she persisted. "Seems somewhat limiting."

"Maybe I don't want to be up at night wondering if my girlfriend is alone on the street getting beat up by some perp or under a pile of rubble, dead at the hands of a terrorist." She shifted her gaze but not before Izzy saw real emotion there.

Whatever nerve she hit, Izzy wanted to spare Sara the pain of the experience she was reliving. "Hey. You don't need to explain yourself to me. We're good."

"Are we?"

"Sure."

"Friends, then?" Sara's forehead crinkled with hope. "I meant what I said. I do like you, Izzy."

This whole exchange was blowing her mind. It was obvious to Izzy that Sara liked her. Maybe just as friends like she was proposing, but everything in her body language suggested more. Every time they shared space, the energy was palpable. And more often than not, Sara avoided being in her presence around other people. Izzy was no fool—she knew that game too. But Sara seemed steadfast in her refusal to explore what might blossom beyond the platonic.

It was in Izzy's very best interests to walk away from this discussion and forge a distance from Sara. Both in the physical and mental spheres. Friendship would only lead to disappointment. She imagined days ahead characterized by unfulfilled fantasies, the dilemma of winning Sara's attention but not her heart. Yet something inside her saw a glimmer. With exposure came opportunity. And maybe Sara would change her mind.

It didn't really matter. Izzy knew regardless of the current conversation, she wanted more time with Sara, not less. If friendship was what was being offered, so be it.

"To friendship," Izzy said, holding her yogurt aloft as a toast to the boundaries. Sara touched the container with the remainder of her drink, nearly empty by now. Her expression was relaxed and gorgeous in the afternoon light. "Although…" Izzy started walking toward the training facility and Sara fell in step beside her. "A real friend would hook me up with a smoothie one of these days."

Sara leaned down to compensate for her height, and her breath was warm in Izzy's ear. "Play your cards right, Officer Marquez, and who knows." Her scent lingered and her frisky attitude sent a shiver up Izzy's spine. This friendship had disaster written all over it.

❖

All day Saturday, Izzy replayed the back and forth with Sara in her head. Even twenty-four hours later, it still made no sense. They made a deal to be friends, but virtually all of their interactions were flirtatious. What the fuck? Rather than losing the entire night to dwelling on it, she impulsively decided to accept the invitation her friends Michelle and Dana had extended weeks ago to attend game night at their house.

Izzy had been thrilled when her friends settled down a few towns away after getting married. She and Michelle had been tight from the first day of police academy, and it was nice to have a pal nearby, even if they didn't see each other much since Dana had the baby. Infant notwithstanding, those ladies loved to throw a party. It didn't hurt that they adored playing matchmaker and stocked their house with every single lesbian in a ten-mile radius.

"What about this top?" Izzy stood in the full-length mirror with Chase by her side watching her as she tried on the fourth shirt. He tilted his head this way and that.

"Still the first one, right?" She watched him lie down, exhausted from the monotony. "I know I'm being weird," she explained, changing again. "But there's gonna be girls at this party, there always are." She pulled on different skinny jeans that were less comfortable but looked better. "And since Sara isn't interested because we're goddamn modern heroes who want to protect the city or some crap like that"—she tilted forty-five degrees to see the fit from behind—"we might as well see what's out there."

Chase followed her to the vanity where she checked her makeup one last time.

"Don't look at me like that," she begged. "I'll be home in a few hours. You have my word." She cupped his chin with her hand. "I just can't spend the whole night in front of the TV fixated on her." She frowned, petting him gently. "It's not healthy." She bent down and planted a kiss on his soft head before heading for the door.

Even though she should be excited, Izzy was anxious at the thought of a houseful of prospects, no matter how abstract they might be. Holding the wine she brought, she strolled the sidewalk, hoping to channel confidence and charm, when an enormous black Dodge Ram 1500 taking up two parking spaces caught her attention. "No fucking way," she said under her breath as she backed up to check the plate. Her pulse raced and her head swirled, a different type of nerves taking over. Sara Wright was here.

At first, Izzy didn't see her in the crowded living room. But then, like a beacon, their eyes met and Izzy watched as Sara's true smile spread across her face. Izzy tracked her as Sara seemed to excuse herself from the small group she was chatting with to come over.

"Hey, stranger," Sara said, lifting her drink in greeting. "Long time, no see."

Michelle came up behind Izzy. "Oh my God, I was just going to introduce you two." She looked from Sara to Izzy. "Do you guys know each other?"

Izzy handed the wine bottle to Michelle. "Hey, you." She hugged her old friend, folding her into their conversation. "Sara's one of my instructors up in Overton."

"Holy shit, you went to K-9? I had no idea."

Izzy shrugged in response. She was about to inquire about

Michelle's career path but Dana pulled her wife away with a childcare issue. Izzy closed her eyes and shook her head, still shocked. "I am surprised to see you here, I have to say."

Sara hitched one eyebrow up. "Because teachers can't have social lives?"

"You're not my teacher," Izzy said through her laugh.

"Eh, debatable." Sara ticked her head to the side. "It's nice to see you too, by the way."

"Did I not say it was nice to see you?" She put her hand over her chest dramatically. "Wherever are my manners?"

Sara's smile spread and her eyes crinkled at the corners. "Come on, let's get you a drink."

They looked around for a second but their hosts were absent, so they made their way to the kitchen to help themselves. Just as Izzy poured herself a glass of wine they heard some commotion in the living room followed by the piercing screams of Michelle and Dana's little girl. A fever had spiked, the moms were concerned, the party was adjourned and postponed. After sincere apologies from the hosts, the gaggle of women dissipated quickly.

"That was kind of a bummer," Izzy said, walking next to Sara in the direction of their cars.

"I know." Sara toed the end of a thin tree branch to the grass at the edge of the sidewalk. "We could get a drink. If you want." Her voice resonated with something Izzy thought was hope.

"We could," she answered, her own response holding a question in its tone.

Sara held on to the bed of her truck relaxing her posture a little. "I mean, friends get drinks, right?"

"I believe they do," Izzy said, nodding for emphasis. "We could head over to Union Street or Main. There's a few places nearby."

"You pick. This is more your territory than mine."

Izzy considered for a second. Wally's on Union Street was a cute little pub, but on a Saturday night there might be live music making it super loud. The same was true for the few other places that came to mind. She wanted to be able to talk to Sara without screaming over a band or a crowd. Without stopping to filter she said, "Want to just head back to my house?" Hearing the implication the invitation carried, she clarified on the spot. "It's just…it would be nice to talk and hear each other. Plus, I hate the thought of Chase all by himself."

"Your house is fine, if you don't mind hosting me."

"Great. I'm only ten minutes from here."

"Should I stop and get anything?" Sara asked. "It feels sort of rude to crash your place empty-handed."

Izzy waved her off. "Not necessary. It's spur of the moment. And I've got plenty to eat and drink there, so we should be all set. You know my address"—she'd almost forgotten Sara knew where she lived from the home visit—"but follow me. These side streets can get weird."

She slipped into the driver's seat of her car, willing herself to remember to keep her cool as she navigated the few miles to her house. This was no big deal. Friends came over, they chatted, they had drinks. It was arguably the definition of friendship. She could do this.

CHAPTER NINE

Any initial awkwardness Sara might have felt at being alone with Izzy in her house was completely diminished by Chase, who demanded attention from both of them the second they arrived. Sara loved seeing him prance around, delighted at his master's return. He was such a sweetie—he even saved some special kisses for her.

Sara rained attention on him right back. "Hey there, big guy. Did you miss me?" She could feel Izzy watching her petting him sweetly.

"I should let him out."

Izzy sounded like she hated to interrupt, but Sara understood and she stood up and answered with a nod of acknowledgment, watching Izzy usher Chase to the back door.

"I'll be right back. Make yourself comfortable," Izzy called over her shoulder.

Minutes later they were on opposite ends of the couch, each armed with a glass of white, Chase perched dutifully by Izzy's feet.

"You never did tell me how you know Michelle and Dana," Izzy said, tucking one leg under the other.

"Oh, that." Sara thought for a moment. "I don't usually go to the parties, but Dana's a friend of a friend, so…" She knew she was being evasive and wondered if that sufficed as an answer.

"So…?" Izzy furrowed her brow, her curiosity clearly unsatisfied. "Come on, friend. Dish."

Sara smiled at Izzy's mild taunt, recognizing the joke in her tone. She could get away without answering, but did she want to? She took a healthy sip of her drink before deciding to open up. "Well, my friend's been on my case about getting back on the dating scene."

"Wait a second." Izzy waved both hands emphatically. "Does your friend know that you went to a party loaded with cops? And that you have serious rules about that?"

"Here we go." Sara readied herself for more good-natured teasing at Izzy's hands. She swallowed her smile knowing she deserved it a little.

"Listen. None of my business." Izzy held her hand up in playful defense. "I'm just saying…Michelle and Dana's parties tend to be law enforcement heavy, with Michelle being five-oh and all." Izzy mimed air quotes around the slang term before feigning disinterest as she pretended to examine her fingernails. "You may just want to rethink your choice of venue."

"Good point." Sara faked consideration as she took a sip of her drink. "In fairness, I was just stopping by to get my friend and her dad off my back."

"Her dad too?" Izzy pressed back into the couch cushion. "This is getting stranger by the second."

Keeping it vague was making it sound weirder than it actually was. Sara tucked a strand of hair behind her ear. "My friend Alyssa works with Dana. Alyssa's dad is John." She waited a beat. "Dixon."

"From school?"

"Yes." Sara caressed the base of her wineglass. "He gave me quite a lecture the other night." She said dramatically, "I guess he's concerned I'll die an old spinster." She placed her drink on the end table and turned serious. "I figured if I went to the party, word would get back to him and he'd relax."

"I didn't realize you all were so close." Izzy's confused expression was enough to make Sara realize she should come clean.

"I should explain," she started. "I lived with them. John and his family. When I was in high school." She looked over her shoulder and grabbed her wineglass but didn't drink from it. "I guess he's,

I mean…not quite a dad to me or anything." She chewed her lip, trying to do justice to their dynamic. "He's something of a parental figure in my life, I suppose." She mused on their relationship for a moment. "Like an uncle, maybe."

"Why?" Izzy grabbed a throw pillow and held it, as though she knew something heavy was about to drop. "Why did you live with them? Can I ask that?"

Sara nodded, bracing herself to talk about her past. "My mother died on 9/11."

"Oh my God. Sara, I had no idea." Izzy reached forward and touched her knee. Sara knew it was only for comfort but it affected her nonetheless. "I'm so sorry," Izzy said.

"Thank you." She brought out her practiced smile. "It's a long time ago now."

"Still." Izzy appeared to hold the pillow tighter. "What about your dad?"

"Oh, I don't have one." Sara relaxed her shoulders. This was the easy part. "My mom used a sperm donor. An anonymous one."

"So, wait." Izzy was visibly shaken. "Your mother died on 9/11 and you had no one?" She looked up at her ceiling, clearly trying to do the math.

"I was fourteen." Sara provided the answer matter-of-factly. She shrugged a little. "It could have been worse."

"I can't imagine how." Izzy's voice was sad and angry at the same time. Sara was well familiar with the reaction.

"I know it sounds tragic. And it was." She sipped her chardonnay, steeling herself. "But we had a lot of good times together, my mom and me." She exhaled heavily, feeling the stress filter out with her breath. "There were a lot of kids who were babies when their parents died that day. I had fourteen amazing years. My mother was my best friend. My hero, without a doubt."

"What was her name?"

"Elizabeth." Sara swallowed hard. Most people didn't ask. She was surprised how emotional she got just saying it out loud.

"Was she…I mean…like, a first responder?" Izzy asked.

Sara was used to the standard line of questioning even if it had been years since she'd spoken about it directly. "She was a financial analyst at Cantor Fitzgerald. Most of the time she worked at the office in White Plains. Sometimes she had meetings in Manhattan." She fought the sting in her throat. All the time in the world wouldn't ease the pain of her loss.

"I'm sorry," Izzy said. "I didn't mean to upset you."

Sara collected herself quickly. "It's fine. Honest." She rolled her shoulders to release the tension. "I just haven't talked about it in a while." She sipped her wine delicately. "Anyway, I had this dog." She laughed out loud at the memory. "Lucky."

"What?" Izzy asked, making no secret of her surprise in the sudden redirection of the conversation.

Sara usually skimmed the story when she spoke about her past. But with Izzy she didn't want to. On the contrary, she felt the desire to give her the details. She turned her whole body to face Izzy, folding her legs up on the couch cushion as she began.

"So, when I was nine, my mom let me get this dog." She ran her finger along the back of the sofa. "I'd gone to the animal shelter with my cousins and my aunt and uncle because they were in the market for a family pet. But all the dogs there were big and barking like crazy. They were horrified." She smiled just thinking about it. "This one German shepherd, she was wild for sure, but she let me pet her." She could still picture it so clearly. "My uncle about had an aneurysm." She paused, allowing herself to indulge in the moment. "That night when I got home, I begged my mom to take me back."

"Lucky," Izzy said, following along as she acknowledged Sara's first dog by name.

"Lucky," Sara echoed. "She was a great dog. I loved her so much." She was wistful and she didn't even care. "But then when my mom died"—she looked over at Izzy hanging on her every word—"my aunt and uncle wanted to take me in. And they were great. God, they still are."

"But they didn't want Lucky?"

"I don't blame them. She was always a little wacky with other people. But I couldn't let her go. She was all I had."

"Of course. So what happened?"

"Alyssa Dixon was my best friend in grammar school and high school. Her family knew my saga. Christ, everyone did." She studied her dark jeans, feeling embarrassed even now at the local publicity an orphaned child created. "They took me in. Lucky included." Sometimes it was still hard for her to believe it all happened, and she knew that was obvious in her tone. "They built a bedroom for me in their basement. It was…" Her heart swelled to think of it even now. "I owe them everything."

"Wow." Izzy let out a long breath. "Just, wow."

"I know." Sara rubbed her index finger over the seam of her pants. "John had been assigned to DHS's training site at Overton. He was just starting to build the K-9 program we have today."

"Looks like he was fortunate too, Sara."

"Hardly." She brushed off Izzy's compliment with a wave. "He's an amazing handler."

"Not like you. Nobody's like you." The words were heavy and laced with something more than accolades. Sara felt her stomach flutter. She could only look in Izzy's deep brown eyes so long before she lost her willpower completely. And she believed in her reasoning from yesterday, didn't she? Silently she assured herself, even though she didn't feel remotely convinced. She just needed to stay strong and remember getting involved with a sexy, young police officer would only lead to distraction at best, heartache at worst. Not to mention days and nights laced with anxiety and fear.

"Anyway, that's my drama," she said, hoping her cheerful delivery would lighten the mood.

"That's some story." Izzy seemed overwhelmed by Sara's past. "I don't even know what to say. My life is completely charmed by comparison."

"Don't do that." She shot Izzy a thoughtful look. "Everyone's life is hard. And easy. No one gets a pass."

"I guess."

Sara saw Izzy's gaze shift to the end table behind her as she spoke.

"I feel pretty blessed, though," Izzy said, pointing at a framed photograph. "That's my family in the picture behind you."

Reaching behind the arm of the sofa, Sara picked it up and examined it as Izzy gave the details. Sara could smell Izzy's light perfume as she leaned into her space to identify each person in the group shot in front of a Christmas tree.

"Those are my parents, Ramon and Maria. My sister Elena, my brother Rick, Abuelo and Abuela," she said, her light pink fingernails touching each person's image as she named them.

Sara smiled, hearing the melodic hint of Spanish come through when Izzy referenced her grandparents. It was sweet and unbelievably sexy and for a split second she heard Izzy's voice in her head, calling her name softly as she begged for more. Sara banished the thought just as quickly, turning to place the picture back in its spot, so Izzy didn't see the blush she knew had crept into her cheeks.

"Do you see them often?" Sara asked, thanking Jesus her voice didn't crack as she spoke.

Izzy scrunched her nose. "Every week. Religiously." She moved back to the end of the couch looking guilty for her good fortune. "I know, cheesy."

"Not at all."

"What can I say?" She reached down to pet Chase. "My family's big on family time."

Sara peeked over at Chase blissed out under Izzy's gentle touch. "Did they meet this guy yet?"

"Of course." Izzy piled the love on her fur baby. "And as predicted, he enchanted them. Isn't that right, buddy?"

Sara was about to ask another question, but the sound of her phone vibrating interrupted her. Nicole texting her on a Saturday night. That was unusual. She ignored it, but not before Izzy saw her distraction.

"Do you need to get that?" Izzy asked. "It's cool," she said, pushing off the couch to stand.

"No, it's fine. She can wait."

Sara watched Izzy pad into the kitchen across the way.

"*She*. The plot thickens," Izzy called over her shoulder as she grabbed the wine from the fridge. Sara didn't think she was asking for an explanation, but she still felt awkward when five more texts and a phone call followed. She silenced them all before she got to thinking something might actually be wrong.

Izzy clearly had picked up the vibe as she waved her hand in what seemed a casual manner. "Don't feel like you can't answer. You can even use my spare room if you want privacy."

"That's not necessary. Let me just see what's going on," Sara mumbled, already scrolling through the messages. "Give me one second here," she added, typing out a quick message to Nicole saying she'd call her in the morning.

With her eyes, Izzy asked if it was okay to top off Sara's wine.

"Just a little," she answered, apologizing again as she finished up her text.

"Everything okay?" Izzy asked as she filled her own glass higher.

Sara nodded into her wine, taking a quick sip. "Yes. Sorry. That was rude."

"Not at all."

Izzy's smile was sweet and forgiving, and Sara felt herself getting lost in the look of her generous lips curving just enough to activate one dimple as she took her seat on the couch. Sara couldn't help but smile as Chase repositioned himself at her feet, and she loved that he followed Izzy everywhere. She was about to comment when her phone lit up again. She leaned her head all the way back in frustration.

"Want to talk about it?" Izzy rubbed her hands together, whether for warmth or in anticipation Sara wasn't sure.

Either way, she knew her response.

"Definitely not."

"Damn," Izzy said, employing full theatrics in her tone. Reaching for her glass and raising it a little she added, "Any woman who's got you this worked up"—she shifted her eyebrows upward—"there's a story there."

Of course, she wasn't wrong. But despite her inner conflict over the situation at hand, Sara was enjoying her time in Izzy's presence too much to allow Nicole into it, in any capacity. Plus, she was still annoyed at her ex's aloof behavior the past few weeks.

"It's a story that's too long to get into. Plus, I've already unloaded enough on you tonight."

Izzy straightened up noticeably. "Now I'm super intrigued," she said. Her voice and eyes were lively and beautiful. Sara forced herself to look away.

"Another time, okay?"

"I'm just teasing," Izzy said kindly. "But since you mention it…" She looked down at Chase asleep on the floor. "I was thinking about taking this guy out tomorrow to do some trail work. I'm curious to see how he does off leash in a different environment. Would you be interested in coming with us?" She gestured to the dog passed out at her feet. "It would mean a lot to Chase. I mean, just look at him. He can barely contain his excitement."

Sara laughed out loud and the noise made Chase lift his head momentarily. "When you put it that way…" She smiled. "I would hate to disappoint him."

They went over details of where to meet up, discussing the best parks and trails for off-leash training. They decided on Arren's Hollow, a midsized national reserve whose border abutted the rear of the training campus, its off-the-beaten-path location a place likely to have limited human traffic, which would enable them to get a good workout for Chase.

For the next long while they talked about work and class, and the time flew so quickly, Sara was shocked when it was almost midnight. She said good-bye, truly bummed at leaving but consoled by the fact they'd see each other again in twelve hours. She didn't have a clue what that meant in terms of the rules she'd laid out for both herself and Izzy, but for a change she decided not to think about it at all.

CHAPTER TEN

Fucking rain. Izzy heard it pummeling her rooftop but pulled the blinds back to validate her fears. A storm this fierce had to pass and sooner rather than later, she hoped, mentally crossing her fingers. As the morning wore on, though, the clouds intensified, and the rain never let up. She trolled multiple weather apps in search of a clear sky ahead, but they all predicted the same doom and gloom. Rain. All. Damn. Day.

Izzy made her coffee and took Chase out in the torrent for his morning walk, holding out hope as the hard rain pelted her face. She wasn't supposed to meet Sara until noon, but at eleven thirty the forecast was still bleak.

Can you believe this weather? Izzy knew she could've sent a one-liner to Sara indicating the simple need to reschedule, but she left her text open-ended, hoping it might lead to some conversation.

I KNOW!

Caps and an exclamation point. Izzy read Sara's strong reaction as a sign she, too, was disheartened by the turn of events. Even though she was alone, Izzy covered half her face, embarrassed that she was analyzing Sara's texts to this level. It was pathetic, but still she agonized over what to say next.

Sara beat her to it, texting, *It's supposed to stay this way all afternoon. Not that I think the rain is a big deal, but I worry the trails might be too messy for our boy.* She punctuated the statement with a sad face.

You're right, Izzy responded, her heart warming at the concern Sara expressed for Chase. She couldn't help noticing the joint possessive she used when she referred to him. It made her swoon. She was completely out of control. *Maybe next weekend will be better*, she typed, hoping to set the wheels in motion to lock in a makeup session.

What will you do with Chase cooped up all day?

Sara's response caught her off guard because she hadn't thought about it at all. Chase still needed a fair amount of exercise and stimulation, and with the rain slated to be heavy most of the day, the thought of outdoor activity seemed unrealistic.

She started typing but deleted it right away because the truth of the matter was she didn't quite know how she was going to entertain him.

Before she could give an answer at all, Sara sent another message: *Why don't you bring him to Overton? All of the agents stay on campus with their dogs. They'll be looking for an outlet too. The gym will be available to do some exercise and train a little.*

Of course that made sense. The agents who were training to be handlers were from various parts of the country. Plus, Jen and Ryan would be there. Izzy knew for a fact they stayed through the weekends instead of traveling back and forth to Florida. But did Sara's mentioning it mean she would be there as well? Izzy was dying to know, but she was too afraid asking would look desperate. Her phone dinged while she weighed the odds.

Unless you don't feel like driving in the weather. I completely get that. Her lack of response must have caused Sara to think she wasn't interested at all. Izzy started typing but Sara was faster. *I know it's not the same as a hike in the woods but I thought we could get some training in.*

Izzy stopped trying to find the right words and spit out what she wanted to know. *Will you be there?*

LOL. I'm here now. I never went home last night. I live far and I'm lazy. She dropped in the shrug emoji. *Plus, we had plans. I remember how excited Chase was…*

Ha! I almost forgot.

What do you think? Feel like driving up here in a monsoon?

I have a truck. It'll be fine.

You have the soccer mom version of an SUV. I have a truck.

Izzy laughed out loud at Sara's playful put-down of her car. Only someone with a Ram 1500 would have the chutzpah to knock the formidable Durango in her driveway. She responded with an eye roll emoji and could almost hear Sara's sweet laugh at the silly exchange. *I need to shower still. Be there around 2. Sound good?*

Perfect.

It sure felt like it.

Chase perked up, recognizing his surroundings the moment they pulled through the entrance gate to the training facility. The roads were a mess and rain was still coming down in a steady stream when Izzy pulled into her parking space. Through the rain they ran to the door, drenched from the short sprint. Izzy was glad she hadn't bothered with her hair—it would have been useless. Even with her rain gear, she was pretty soaked.

Sara came out of her office to greet her. God, she looked amazing. Mastering the couldn't-care-less style, she was sexy as hell in a worn hoodie and casual jeans, strategically ripped and antiqued in all the right spots. They hugged her hips and sculpted her perfect bottom. It was going to be a challenge to keep from staring all day.

"You made it." Sara approached and for a split second there was a slight awkwardness between them. Izzy thought they might hug, but instead Sara bent down to give Chase a quick scratch on the head. "How was the drive?"

"Eh, not great. But okay." Izzy slipped out of her raincoat and Sara took it from her, then hung it over a hook on the back of the door.

"Let's go to the gym. A bunch of folks are there already."

Izzy felt her heart sink a little at the realization that they'd have company right away. She heard the other dogs barking in the distance and felt Chase's energy peak as they got closer.

"That's right, Chase. We're going to see your friends."

He pranced and jumped, and Izzy loved that he was somehow able to discern this was different from a regular day at school. They got to the gym and hung out with Jen and Ryan, Mark, and a few other agents and their pups. The day was filled with a mix of free play and organized exercises, training, and games to entertain and educate the dogs and their humans. And even though Izzy'd had regrets about sharing Sara with her colleagues, Sara seemed to give the majority of her attention to her and Chase. She worked with them individually and spent time chatting one-on-one with her while they trained. Izzy's pulse more than fluttered when Sara used a hand over hand technique to demonstrate a neat way to wind the leash around her palm, ensuring control but allowing for slack.

What might have been a dull afternoon at her house instead zipped by amid a blur of barks and commands, stories, jokes, and easy conversation with her classmates and the new friend she was so quickly falling for.

She was enjoying Sara and Chase as they sat on the floor with Jen and Tempe when Ryan approached.

"Mark and I were just talking about heading into town and grabbing Mexican for dinner. You ladies in?"

"Sure." Jen's response was quick. Izzy wasn't the only one crushing. She was pretty sure Jen would follow Mark into the pit of hell and back.

Izzy felt Sara's eyes on her. "What do you think, Iz?" She touched Izzy's arm lightly. "You're the one with a drive ahead of you."

She would have stayed all night if it meant this much attention from Sara. She tried to sound casual. "A girl does have to eat, right?"

"Let's go." Sara hopped up, brushing off the back of her jeans as she stood. They gathered their things and returned the dogs to the kennel area before they headed to Sara's office to grab their jackets. "Come with me," Sara said as she pulled a rain parka over her shoulders. "There's no sense in us taking two separate cars."

"Great." Izzy smiled, elated with how this day was progressing.

The ride to the restaurant was quick, but Izzy indulged herself for the short trip, basking in Sara's scent as she rode shotgun in the pristine cab of her enormous pickup. "*Star Wars* fan?" she asked, eyeing a small Lego R2-D2 keychain hanging from the air vent.

"You know it." Sara made a turn onto a side street in the small town. "R2's my guy." She cast a quick look at Izzy. "What about you, who's your favorite?"

Izzy shrugged. "Don't have one really. I saw one of the movies. Maybe two," she added, pausing to think about it. "Definitely not all of them."

Sara brought her truck to a dramatic halt. "That, Isabel, is a disgrace." She shook her head. "I consider it my duty to fix such a travesty." She pounded her fist on the steering wheel in emphasis, as though she'd accepted an assignment. Izzy laughed out loud, but inside her pulse raced at the invitation Sara was off-handedly floating. To her knowledge there were at least six *Star Wars* episodes, maybe more, and whatever Sara's motive, her idle suggestion implied more time together. Izzy focused her attention on the windshield wipers swooping across the glass as she tried to tamp down her excitement.

When they entered the restaurant together, Izzy was thrilled to see that even though the other three had arrived first, the seating arrangement had Mark and Ryan on one side of a six-top, Jen on the other. Her heart did a ridiculous happy dance knowing she was going to be able to sit next to Sara.

As they perused the menu, the party of five fell into an easy conversation about the class curriculum and a few upcoming field trips on the agenda. Izzy tried not to make too much of her knee brushing against Sara's under the table. Even though the touch was subtle, Sara didn't move an inch. There was plenty of legroom, but Izzy took the risk and kept her leg there, savoring the heat from their mild contact as it spread up her thigh to her center.

Ryan drove the conversation by asking a slew of questions about New York City, and Izzy was happy to answer them, but she had to try hard to stay on point when Sara's phone on the table lit up with a flurry of texts. *Nicole*, the name read. Izzy wondered if it was the same woman from last night.

Even as Sara dismissed the messages routinely, they kept coming. "Wow, whoever Nicole is, she's really blowing up your phone there, Sara," Ryan said over his iced tea. At least she wasn't the only one distracted by the interruption. On cue a call came in. "Better answer that," he added with a hearty chuckle.

"Hello." Sara leaned back in her chair as she answered, the move giving her little privacy. Jen tried to steer the group conversation back on track and Mark joined right in, but Izzy couldn't keep from paying attention to Sara next to her. Her entire body language changed as she spoke into the phone. She sat upright and rigid as she whispered, "Can it wait? I'm in the middle of something right now." Her voice was even and low, but apparently Nicole was not one to be put off. "You're where?" Sara barked loudly, clearly surprised by the response her suggestion garnered. "Fine," she said, giving in after several long seconds of listening to Nicole on the other end of the line. Izzy could tell Sara was frustrated—she figured they all could. But when Sara looked at her watch and uttered, "I'll be there in twenty minutes," Izzy's spirit bottomed out and she doubted her colleagues were similarly affected.

Ending the call, Sara glanced around the table, her eyes breezing over Izzy as part of the crew. "I'm sorry, gang. I have to deal with something," she said. "Can you get a ride back with these guys?" She faced Izzy but didn't make eye contact. It was hardly a question, and Sara barely waited for Izzy's response before she was out the door into the dreary evening.

Later that evening, when Izzy returned to the facility to collect Chase, she looked for Sara's truck but didn't see it anywhere. Her desire to know what was going on was somewhat pitiful. After all, on the surface, nothing drastic had occurred. Her friend, Sara, had gotten a call during a group dinner and had to leave unexpectedly. It wasn't awful or earth shattering. But deep down Izzy knew there was something more going on between them. Even if they didn't acknowledge it directly, the day had been defined by knowing looks and soft touches. She wasn't imagining it. In her mind, she was owed something of an explanation, and she floundered around her house all night waiting for a call or a text, but nothing came.

CHAPTER ELEVEN

Five minutes. It didn't seem like an unreasonable request. Five minutes alone with Sara. Fuck, she'd even settle for three. Izzy needed just enough time to read her face, assess her body language, determine what the hell was going on. Since she skipped out Sunday evening, Izzy hadn't heard a peep from Sara. She'd barely even seen her at school. She was absent from morning agility, and when Izzy finally spotted her, she was on the sidelines standing next to a tall redhead, talking nonstop as they watched the training together. Izzy witnessed a repeat of nearly the same situation when she eyed Sara on the catwalk above the gymnasium with the redhead, watching keenly as the class did scent work with their partners.

Desperate for attention, Izzy kept her focus on Sara, but was given only a small, thin smile when they made eye contact, as Sara continued to chat with her gorgeous companion whose green eyes stood out even from a distance. Izzy tried not to take it personally. But she wasn't the only one who noticed Sara's cool attitude. In fact, her friends made a point of calling out the entire staff's tense demeanor over the last few days.

Izzy almost caught a break after lunch Wednesday. There were still a few minutes before the afternoon session got under way, and from her seat in class Izzy noticed Sara standing alone by the front desk. She appeared to be reading over something intently, and even though Izzy didn't know what on earth she was going to say, she started over. She only made it as far as the classroom doorway before the mystery redhead was right next to Sara again. Their arms seemed to be touching as they pored over the papers in front of them. Izzy felt her frustration rise to a new level as she pondered the identity of this stranger who'd been foiling her chances for days.

"That's Nicole Vaughn." Jen's voice in her ear made Izzy jump even as she provided the answer to her unspoken question. "She's a real big shot with the Feds. In charge of this whole place." Jen waved her hand in emphasis. "She's here from Washington to—quote-unquote—evaluate the program." Everyone in law enforcement knew program evaluations were always a cover for budget cuts. "That's what's got everyone's panties in a bunch this week."

"How do you know all this?" Izzy knew her voice held both skepticism and envy.

Jen let free a syrupy grin. "Mark told me." Wiggling her eyebrows, she added, "He got the dirt from Gilmartin over beers in town last night. Allegedly there's talk of closing this facility after this session."

"Really?" Izzy wasn't sure why she found it so hard to believe. She knew very little of the federal government and how it operated, but the Overton training center seemed state of the art with its many on-site accoutrements. Her class had been able to train on a real subway car, commuter buses, in buildings that mimicked offices and schools, and that wasn't even accounting for the other side of campus where the recruit agents attended class. Not to mention the cafeteria and dorms. The NYPD would kill for a place like this. She shook her head at the thought.

"Big bad Nicole gets the final say. Dun-dun-dun," Jen added dramatically. Izzy had yet to tear her eyes away from Sara and Nicole still talking at the desk. "Also, rumor has it, Nicole is Sara's ex."

Izzy whipped her head around barely reining in her reaction. "Oh, yeah," she managed to stammer out, hoping it came off like she didn't care.

"That's what I heard." Jen touched Izzy's elbow and steered them back into class. "But you know guys. They always get that shit wrong."

Izzy wondered if her words were meant in comfort, but it

didn't matter. Obviously, Nicole was something to Sara. Whether the future of Homeland Security's training depended on her was the least of her worries. Izzy's concerns lay solely in the personal connection. She already knew Nicole had contacted Sara repeatedly over the weekend and that Sara had abandoned dinner to answer Nicole's call. She tightened her jaw, fighting back the jealousy she felt rising to the surface, one hundred percent sure now was not the time to even ponder why she felt this way.

But even as she lectured herself and tried like hell to channel determination, her focus was off and she knew her distraction was obvious. In the last two days alone, she'd botched an obedience event and nearly missed two indications of low explosive finds by Chase.

By Friday morning the tension that had permeated operations at the facility eased up, coinciding with Jen's update that Nicole had gone back to DC. The entire staff appeared to settle back into their everyday calm. Still, Izzy couldn't seem to get out of her funk.

"Everything in this job, everything in life, I would argue, is situational awareness." Agent Gilmartin stood in front of the class with Jett, his canine partner who demonstrated daily tactics.

"When you're doing a room search, I want you to use the same principles as searching a stationary object. The key is staying sharp, on top of that." He modeled the action with Jett, taking small steps as they entered the room, cutting the pie in tiny triangular pieces. He kept his hand on the butt of the red rubber training gun used for tactical drilling. "You're still a cop. And that means bad guys are gonna want to get you. Sometimes with a bomb, sometimes with a knife or a gun or their bare hands. Stay focused," he lectured through his search. Sniffing like mad, Jett sat down in passive alert in front of a closet in the room. Withdrawing his training weapon, Gilmartin pulled the door open slowly, falling into the ready position, his firearm raised on the target of Agent Hayes wired up as a suicide bomber inside the small space, as the class watching breathed out a quiet collective gasp.

"Look." Gilmartin broke character, waving Hayes forward to join him as he addressed the troops. "The point of this is to remind you that your jobs—just because you got dogs—didn't get any easier." His body took on a fighting stance as he spoke. "It's about the actor as much as the bomb. When you do a room search, whether it's a simple ten-by-ten office or the lobby of Grand Central Station, the principles are the same. You have to know where to direct your dog. He's going to look to you to take the lead. Point, guide, pay attention. Have a plan if your dog hits on something. Look around. Know your surroundings. How populated is the area? Think about crowd control. If you encounter a perp"—he thumbed at Hayes still in his Unabomber getup—are you calling for backup or placing him under arrest first?" He paused, letting the question linger. "I don't expect you to have an answer right now, because honestly, each particular situation will dictate your course of action. But you have to be thinking about these things." He swept his gaze around the room. "You do not want to be figuring this out on the fly, folks."

He clapped Hayes on the back in a kind of dismissal. "We're going to do these room searches using a multitude of different scenarios. I want you to stay sharp." He drummed his temple with two fingers before splitting the class in two groups outside two different confined spaces.

From a regulated distance Izzy watched her colleagues go in and out of the two rooms, and she wondered how the setups differed from each other. Upon completion, students were sent to the main classroom so as not to influence those waiting to go in. The exercise was well thought out and Izzy's heart pounded in anticipation of her turn. She wondered how the skit would unfold, and if there'd be contraband or a perp or both. Would Sara be participating? The thought crept in and she scolded herself for allowing it any attention.

Up next, she rolled her neck trying to stay loose and keep her head in the game.

Just a foot outside the open door, she could see the small space was designed to resemble a hotel room, with a bed and a desk, even a small alcove simulating the space for a bathroom. Her plan was to systematically scan the room counterclockwise. She entered the space with caution, but Chase pulled toward the bed immediately.

She followed his instinct, crossing the center of the floor just as she heard the door to the room close behind her.

"Bang. You're dead, Marquez. Two pops in the back of the head." Agent Reyes, her least favorite instructor, dropped his training weapon by his side. "Izzy, *you* lead." He shook his head at her. "Not the dog." She couldn't help but notice his tone showed disappointment but not condescension as she might have expected considering her rookie error. He leaned in close. "You're better than that, Marquez," he added with a concerned look, shooing her away to send in the next victim.

Izzy spent the rest of the afternoon sulking over her deadly error and the train wreck of a week she'd had. She was looking forward to continuing her pity party in pajamas on her couch comforted by a vat of ice cream. She was already halfway there in her mind when Sara's voice calling her name echoed down the hallway.

"What's going on with you?"

Sara stood in the doorway of her office as though she was waiting for someone, and for a second Izzy wondered if it was her. Her arms were crossed and her gesture bordered on stern when she pointed at her and summoned her over.

Izzy hoisted her gear bag onto her shoulder, shuffling over as she heeded the silent command. Even Chase seemed to hang his head, ready for the lecture that was surely coming. Izzy was in no mood.

"I'm kind of itching to get home. I had a pretty terrible week."

"I know." Sara looked right at her. "I saw that debacle of a room search." She brought her hand to her chin and looked Izzy up and down. "Something's going on with you. You're off your game."

Izzy wanted to scream. Of course something was off. She wanted to yell at Sara for not knowing why she was faltering or for pretending she couldn't figure it out. She was downright furious Sara hadn't bothered to call or text or say anything to her after the connection they'd shared the previous week. First flirting and then not flirting, teasing her and then acting like nothing had gone on between them. If she could have found the appropriate words, she might have said all those things, but she was too stunned to speak at all.

"It's you," Sara said, looking from Izzy to Chase. "Not him." She reached down to pet him and let him bestow a small kiss on her palm. "This dog and his kisses." She rolled her eyes. "Meet me here tomorrow, both of you. Ten sharp. We're going to do some remedial work."

Izzy opened her mouth to respond even though she didn't have a clue what to say. Remediation reeked of failure, two words she bristled at being associated with. Still, a day with Sara might at least give her the opportunity to clear the air.

"Fine." Izzy wound Chase's leash around her hand. "Do I need to bring anything?"

Sara shook her head and smiled. "Just yourself." She nodded at Chase. "And him. I'll take care of the rest."

Izzy wondered which version of Sara would show tomorrow. She almost asked, but her nemesis's approach stopped her thoughts completely.

"You ready?" Nicole Vaughn called out, her heels clicking to a stop right next to Izzy.

Sara dangled her car keys from one finger. "I'm waiting for you."

So much for the rumor Nicole had left town days ago. Izzy couldn't help but wonder where she'd been hiding the last forty-eight hours. And that thought made her nauseous. She just wanted to bolt, but before she could excuse herself, Sara touched her arm, throwing her off again.

"Izzy, this is Nicole Vaughn. She's the director of training for DHS." Sara leaned in and stage-whispered, "Meaning she runs the show here."

"Ma'am." Izzy held out her hand. "It's nice to meet you." She almost gagged at having to be so official toward the woman she was surely losing out to. "Anyway, I should get going." She didn't want to be disrespectful, but she was barely holding it together.

"Hold on," Nicole said. Izzy swallowed hard as Nicole studied her relaxed class attire—an NYPD T-shirt with the signature dark blue cargo pants. "You must be Isabel Marquez. From the NYPD." She nodded in affirmation at her obvious deduction. It took everything for Izzy to keep a straight face. "I know your lieutenant at the Grand Central Command," Nicole said. "Stacey Anderson."

Izzy forced a smile. "Lieutenant Anderson is the best. She's a really good boss," she added, bestowing the highest compliment with the fewest words. It was true. Stacey Anderson was a fantastic supervisor, and not only because she'd called in a favor to hook Izzy up with the coveted K-9 spot. Anderson was honest and fair to all her subordinates on a daily basis. She'd earned respect and Izzy was determined to give it, even in her absence.

"Please tell her I said hello," Nicole said.

"Yes, ma'am," Izzy said, still hating the formality she felt forced to use. She turned to Sara. "About tomorrow," she started, planning to bail on the spot.

Sara shook her head, cutting her off with a firm no. "Ten o'clock, Izzy. No excuses."

Izzy hiked her bag up higher, for the first time realizing her presence tomorrow wasn't a request for a frivolous outing—it was a mandatory session. She wasn't being asked for her company, she was being compelled, in front of the head of training, who was a friend of her boss, no less, and probably about to go on a date with the woman she was seriously crushing on. This day sucked.

She felt the sting in her throat but fought against it until she was in her car and through the gates of the facility, cruising up the ramp to the highway before the first tears fell.

CHAPTER TWELVE

Two granola bars, some water, a new chew toy for Chase. Sara went through her small pack, making sure she had everything she wanted to bring. She went to the storage cabinet in the corner of her office and grabbed a twenty-five-foot lead in case Izzy only brought her standard leash. Sara was hoping to see some off-leash work this morning, but her primary focus was restoring Izzy's confidence, which had wavered in the last week.

Chase raced into her office and Sara squatted to give him a proper hello. "And where is your lovely person?" she asked him.

"I'm right here," Izzy answered, her voice flat and cold as the morning chill.

"Hey." Sara stood. Assessing Izzy's stiff posture, she grabbed both of her shoulders and shook them roughly. "Loosen up. I want to have fun today."

Izzy backed out of her hold. "What's fun about doing extra work because I'm clearly not making the cut?"

Sara stepped away, zipping up her bag. "Relax, Izzy. You're not in trouble."

"Really?" Izzy's eyes were as cold as her voice. "Ordered to the facility on a Saturday. Told I need remedial instruction. Doesn't seem like high praise to me."

"Did you not have coffee?" Sara hoped her teasing response would lighten the mood.

Izzy didn't say a word. She picked up Chase's lead and tucked her hands in the pockets of her jeans. "I hope it's okay I wore street clothes today."

Her voice was full of sass and Sara sighed at her snarky attitude but decided not to engage, hoping the fresh air would turn things around. She grabbed her things and headed for the door, turning Izzy around by the shoulders when she got there. "Come on, grumpy-pants. Let's go."

She led the way out of the building and across the training field to where the thick woods met the campus grounds.

"Where are we going?" Izzy asked.

"These woods are the back of Arren's Hollow." She held some thicket aside for Izzy and Chase to pass through. "We just have to trudge through some of the brush for a minute and we'll pick up a trail." Acorns and pinecones crunched under her boots. "I wanted to take that hike we missed last weekend." She bounced across the forest floor. "And I thought being out here might help you get back on track."

"Great." Izzy's tone was still less than enthusiastic. "So I *am* failing?"

"Are you serious?" Sara cleared a small puddle as she asked the question. One look at Izzy's face and she saw genuine worry. "Izzy, you're the best handler in the class. Hands down." Her words—which were totally the truth—relaxed Izzy immediately, and Sara could almost see the tension drain from her body. Automatically, Chase relaxed by her side. "But something has you rattled lately. What's going on?"

Izzy huffed and looked at the ground but said nothing.

"Come on, Iz. You're completely distracted. Spill already."

"Is the facility closing down?"

The question caught Sara off guard, but she answered it anyway. "No. Why would you think that?"

"That's the rumor around the class. That Nicole Vaughn was here to assess the program and possibly shut it down after this session."

Sara laughed. "Overton is the third largest federal training facility in the country. It's not going anywhere, believe me." She climbed up a few big rocks, using a tree to balance as she hopped down onto the trail. "God," she huffed, "absent the facts, people really will just make stuff up. What else do they say, I wonder?"

"That she's your ex." Izzy didn't move. "Nicole."

"I was being rhetorical," Sara said with a shift of her eyebrows as she pointed them north on the dirt path.

"Is it true?" Izzy's tone held both uncertainty and a hint of sadness, and it killed Sara to realize this might be the real cause of Izzy's stress.

"Yes." She picked up a fallen branch and tossed it to the side. "That part is true."

"And now?" Izzy bent forward and unclipped Chase's leash, allowing him to walk freely next to her.

Sara wasn't really sure what she was being asked. "Now, what?"

"Are you two together now?" Izzy took a tennis ball from her pocket and tossed it a couple of yards away, and they watched Chase snatch it before the second bounce. Izzy let him walk a few feet ahead before calling his name and telling him to wait. He listened and she called him back, taking the ball and rewarding him with love when he returned. "Good boy," she said, turning to Sara, still waiting for her response.

"This?" Sara waited for Izzy to make eye contact. "This is what had you so flustered all week?" She threw up both hands in frustration. "You lose all focus because you're thinking about whether or not my ex-girlfriend and I are back together?"

"Are you?"

Sara clenched her teeth trying to maintain her composure. "No. Not that it matters. But no."

"Is she still here?"

"Where?" Sara joked as she scanned the vacant woods. One look at the heat in Izzy's expression told her this wasn't the time for games. "No," she said evenly. "I drove her to the airport last night. She's back in DC. Is that better?"

Izzy seemed to accept her response but she broke eye contact and started walking. "I think it's pretty shitty you never called or anything after you bolted last weekend."

"I'm sorry." Her apology seemed to fall flat as Izzy walked on briskly. Sara tried to explain. "I got sidetracked helping Nicole while she was here." She took a quick step trying to catch up with Izzy. "She'd been trying to contact me for two days." Izzy was still a half step ahead and Sara grabbed her forearm to get her to stop as she scooted in front to face her. Looking right at her she said, "I never answered her because I was with you just about the whole time."

"Well, I'm sure you made up for it while you were ignoring me all week."

Izzy's sweet brown eyes showed real hurt, and more than anything Sara wanted to make the pain go away. She wanted to pull Izzy into her arms and kiss her over and over, admit she thought about her nonstop, confess to her ridiculous fantasies, her growing feelings that surely couldn't go anywhere. Another thirty seconds and she might have fallen prey to her foolish desires, but Izzy broke the moment, stepping around her.

"So what's the deal?" Izzy's voice was still curt. "I have bosses. And exes." She checked on Chase, who was sniffing the base of the trail. "Neither of them text me nonstop."

"I'm assisting her with a project she's running." Over her shoulder Izzy gave a look that signaled a longer explanation was required. Sara let out a long breath. "Things with Nicole are complicated," she added.

Izzy turned around sporting a blatant I-told-you-so expression, and Sara couldn't help but laugh.

"Not like that. Not anymore." Sara stretched her arms above her head as she thought about what to say. "I've known Nicole a long time," she started. "We haven't been together in ages." She pondered the accuracy of that statement considering her trip to DC in March. "She's my boss. But honestly, she's more than that. We're...friends," she said, knowing the word fell short of adequately defining their relationship. "God, I lived in her house until last year." She made the admission somewhat offhandedly, knowing how ridiculous it sounded.

Picking up the path again, she let her fingers brush Chase's ear as he strode between them. "Nicole has always been good to me, and I suppose I feel a certain indebtedness to her. Even if we're no longer a couple. When she called me the other night, she was locked out." She shrugged. "I have keys."

"Because it's your house too." It was half statement, half question, and Sara could tell Izzy was trying to understand their dynamic.

"I lived there once, yes." She watched Chase investigate a tall weed a few steps ahead. "But it was never my house."

Izzy's eyes held a million questions and Sara decided to save her the trouble.

"After my mother died, I lived with the Dixons, as you know. When I was nineteen I decided to go out on my own. John and his family were great and my time there was a gift. But I never wanted to be a burden. So I moved back to the house where I grew up. It was…" Her voice faded as she searched for the right word.

"I can't even imagine."

"It wasn't unbearable. But there were a lot of memories. Many of them lovely." She looked up at the cloudless sky. "I needed to move forward and it was difficult to do there. I think it set me back. So I sold the house and rented a three-bedroom in town. Not far from here, as a matter of fact." A woodpecker hammered away in the distance. "Lucky had passed by then. I had a new dog. Rocco." Saying his name out loud elicited a string of memories and she smiled, thinking about her early years at the facility. "Rocco worked with me at Overton. We were partners, like Gilmartin and Jett. He was a great dog." She plucked a branch poking out into the clearing and examined the tiny red berries at the tip. "It was great finally having a home and a dog of my own. I felt"—she tossed the branch to the side—"grown-up, I suppose."

"And you were nineteen?"

"I think I was twenty when I moved to the house on Maple Drive. I stayed there until I was twenty-four."

"What happened when you were twenty-four?"

Sara looked down at the tracks her Merrells left in the dirt. "I met Nicole."

"Boom." Izzy used her hands to mimic a rocket taking off. "Lesbian U-Haul."

"Not exactly." Sara chuckled at the well-worn joke. "Nicole is ten years older than I am. She owned a house. I was renting. At some point it just made sense to move there."

"How come you stayed after you two broke up?" Izzy asked. "I mean, if it was her house, why did she leave and you stay? That seems unusual."

Sara thought about the question, trying to figure the most straightforward way to explain her relationship's demise.

"We didn't have this, like, dramatic breakup, Nicole and I."

"What happened, then?" They were at a wide section of trail, and Izzy tossed the tennis ball ten feet and Chase tracked it down. Once he snagged it, she let him get a good distance away before commanding him to stop and calling him back again. "How did you meet? Why did you break up? Tell me your story."

"Really?" Chase nudged Sara's hand with the ball, clearly hoping she would take a turn. She took the tennis ball and handed it over.

When Izzy took it, Sara saw her expression had softened and her shrug held disappointment and forgiveness at the same time.

"I'm pissed you blew me off all week." Izzy touched the fur on Chase's back, getting his attention, then showed him the ball. "Even friends don't do that to each other." She threw the ball again. "There, I said it." She brushed her palms together as if to wipe the slate clean. "We're here now." She did a full three-sixty spin. "It's a gorgeous Saturday morning, this trail is peaceful, thank God I'm still passing the class despite a truly fucked-up week, and Chase is doing well off leash. Let's enjoy it." She bumped Sara's shoulder. "Satisfy my curiosity and tell me about you and Nicole. Start at the beginning." She employed some serious puppy dog eyes as part of her persuasion. "Please?"

"The beginning?"

"You know, tell me how you met and stuff."

"I met Nicole at Overton. She was assigned here after her first promotion above agent."

"Wait a second. Agent?" Izzy stopped in her tracks. She paused, feigning shock as she pretended to puzzle something out. "Isn't that just a fancy word for...*cop*?"

"Don't be a smart-ass," Sara cajoled.

"Me? A smart-ass?" Izzy frowned. "Never. Merely pointing out a minor inconsistency in your dating policy."

"You're forgetting it didn't work out."

"What happened?"

"Nothing crazy. Nicole was always up-front about her career aspirations. She wanted the big time. Executive level management. She climbed a few ranks here, but a field post only yields so many opportunities. The serious promotions involved assignments in other offices. Chicago. Denver. Seattle. Ultimately DC, where she is now."

"So that was it? She just left you here?"

"Of course not." A chipmunk darted onto the trail a few feet away. "She asked me to come with her. And even though I wanted to go, my life was here. I had Rocco and he was getting old—a move anywhere would have been hard on him. Plus the K-9 program was just coming into its own." She felt Chase tense up between them, but he walked on, chewing his tennis ball, all but ignoring the adorable critter. "There was just no way I could leave at that time. John needed me here for the program. He saved my life. I wasn't going to abandon him when this place was just hitting its stride."

"I'm surprised he asked you to stay. If he knew what was going on with you and Nicole."

"He didn't ask me to stay," she corrected. "He would never do anything like that. That doesn't change the fact it was the right thing to do."

Izzy nodded, obviously trying to process all the information, and Sara felt a sudden need to justify her past decisions.

"John and I work really well together. I needed to stay for him and the dogs. That's the bottom line." She pushed her hair off her face feeling defensive of her choices. "It was hardly a sacrifice. I absolutely love my job. I always have, since the very first day." She touched Chase's head for comfort and appreciated the look of affection he gave. "Hey," she said making sure her voice was light. "Can we talk about how this guy just ignored a chipmunk? Right in front of him, no less."

"I was hoping you noticed." There was no mistaking the satisfaction in Izzy's voice. "He's getting very good with his discipline," she said, petting him generously as she spoke. He leaned into Izzy's hand, and Sara loved watching their fierce connection.

"I see that." She rubbed her palm along the center of Izzy's back, hoping the gesture passed as kudos. "He's got you to thank for that."

"He deserves credit too. Right, buddy?" Izzy thumped his muscular body as she spoke to him. "We've been doing walks like this by my house almost every day after school."

"Your dedication shows. Both of yours, actually."

"My week, though." Izzy groaned, covering half her face with one hand.

Sara reached up and pulled her hand away. "Stop. Anyone can have a rough week."

"At least I'm making up for it now," she said with a shrug. "And you can see I'm not a total slacker. Bonus"—she winked— "I'm getting the skinny on your boss slash ex-girlfriend. Not gonna lie. I'm shocked you broke those boundaries." Izzy thumbed at her, the indication pointedly playful. "You, queen of the dating rules and all."

Sara laughed outright at Izzy's brazen humor, and the appreciation of her quick wit garnered one of Izzy's signature smiles, the full dimples adding sweetness to her dark sexy allure.

"Oh my God," Izzy blurted. "She's the reason for all the rules." She narrowed her eyes but her voice stayed good-natured when she added, "I knew I hated her."

"Easy there." Sara matched her spirit. "I'm pretty sure she got you into this program at the last possible second."

"Right." Izzy's voice was low. "Her connection with Lieutenant Anderson."

Sara waited for Izzy to look at her. "I know there's more to that story," she said, all but asking for the details.

"There sure is." Izzy raised her eyebrows in willful defiance of Sara's subtle request. "Patience, Sara," she scolded playfully. "I'm still waiting to hear the end of your saga."

Her saga? Sara was genuinely confused and her look must have shown it because Izzy sighed dramatically.

"You and Nicole," she said. "Tell me the rest."

Sara stuffed her hands in her pockets. "There's not much more to tell."

"That was it? She took a promotion, moved, and it was over?" Izzy scrunched her face up as though she didn't quite believe it.

"We did long distance for a while. It's hard, trying to make a relationship work when you're in two different places." Her attention shifted to a squirrel using the high branches as a jungle gym. "Over time it just kind of fizzled out," she said. God, that sounded pathetic. "Most of the time I think it would have ended anyway. Even if she'd stayed."

"Sounds like you're trying to convince yourself of that."

Sara looked at Izzy and wondered how much truth there was to her observation.

"We were at different points in our lives. I was almost thirty. Nicole was forty." A dark red triangular stone caught her eye and she picked it up to examine it closely. "Age gaps can be tricky like that. Sometimes it makes no difference at all, and then there are phases where the disparity seems insurmountable. In retrospect, I think we were growing apart."

"But you lived in her house until last year? That seems like it could be, I don't know, uncomfortable."

"It wasn't," she said, acknowledging the strange reality of her situation. "We were on and off for a while, so for a long time it felt natural to be there. Even after we broke up, our lives were very intertwined." She knew it sounded like there was more to it, and if she was being honest, there was. More than once she'd expected to get back together with Nicole. It was a truth she rarely admitted to herself, let alone shared with anyone else.

Izzy dribbled the tennis ball, playing with Chase as they hiked. "So let me see if I have this straight." She bounced the ball high and Chase caught it with a leap in the air. "You two dated for years. Had a totally amicable breakup. One that was so easy you stayed close friends over the years, even working together, and you continued to live in her house." She lifted her eyebrows suspiciously. "And in all this time, you never…" She let her sentence dangle, obviously waiting for Sara to fill in the gap.

"We were on and off for a while, I admitted that."

"And since then?" She took the ball from Chase and tossed it back and forth in her hands. "No trips down memory lane? One-offs because you're both gorgeous and single and sleeping under the same roof? Drunken hookups? *Nothing?* I find this hard to believe."

Sara looked at the treetops, pretending to be enraptured. "Is that a bald eagle up there?" She winced in laughter when Izzy chucked the tennis ball at her.

"You're a jerk," Izzy said, slight defeat seeping through her smile. "I knew there was still something going on."

Sara reached down to take the ball from Chase who'd dutifully collected it. "There's not." She couldn't keep from laughing at Izzy's reaction. "Honestly," she said, handing the soggy ball back to Izzy. "I'd be lying if I said there haven't been a couple of moments over the years. And even stretches where I thought we might work things out. But"—she shook her head—"those days are over." It dawned on her that this level of personal information was more than she'd shared with any of her other friends, but Izzy was special. And despite her commitment to mere friendship, she wanted her to know there wasn't anyone else. "Why are we only talking about me?" she asked, turning the question back on Izzy. "When do I get to hear about your skeletons?"

"No skeletons." Izzy's smile was tempered. "Not much of anything to tell, really. I'm single. Available. Looking," she added lightly.

Sara swallowed hard, feeling a pang of desire at Izzy's not-so-subtle inference.

Izzy distracted her with a tiny tap on the back of her hand. "Watch this." They'd reached a section of the trail that intersected with paved blacktop, no doubt used by the forest rangers for park upkeep. Izzy threw the ball as far as she could down the makeshift road and watched Chase bound after it. Before he reached it she called out, "Chase. Stop." Chase stopped immediately, the ball bouncing away as he looked from it back to Izzy. "Come. Come," she repeated, pointing one finger at the ground in front of her. He raced back and sat squarely at her feet.

"You mastered calling him off." Sara was impressed and she wanted Izzy to know it. "Letting the ball go too." She nodded in appreciation of the feat. "That's a huge deal. Particularly out here with all these distractions." She watched as Izzy rewarded Chase with his hard rubber Kong. Chase pranced ahead, rightfully proud as he picked up the trail on the other side of the clearing.

Sara searched for words to convey what she was feeling in this moment. Respect for Izzy's obvious skill as a handler for sure, but woven in with that admiration was pure longing. She seemed suddenly unable to separate Izzy the handler from Izzy the gorgeous woman she thought about nightly. Her feelings were racing toward dangerous and she was hell-bent on keeping herself under control. Still, she needed Izzy to know she was important to her.

"I'm sorry I was distant all week." She watched Chase lope ahead, still chewing his toy. "Forgive me?"

Izzy glanced up, her eyes full of raw emotion. "You know I do," she said, her voice soft as a whisper.

"Izzy, you have to stay focused."

"I know."

Sara stopped walking and Izzy followed suit, turning to face her.

"You were out of it this week and it showed." Sara rubbed her forehead. "It came through in your training. You were sloppy. When you got killed in the simulation—"

She stopped herself from saying any more, all at once realizing this horrific fear was the one thing keeping her from giving in to what she so desperately wanted. Tilting her head all the way back to see the trees reaching for the sky, she let her guard drop for a moment.

"That's exactly the reason this can't happen," she said, wagging a finger between them. "I would never sleep."

Izzy caught her finger and held it with her own. "You worry too much." Her hand grazed over Sara's knuckles and along her fingertips. "I'm careful. And good at my job. And yes, I made a dumb mistake the other day. But it won't happen again. Trust me."

"I do. But God, Izzy…"

They were still sort of holding hands, and Sara's gaze shifted from Izzy's eyes to her mouth and back again. She licked her lips, tossing aside the weeks of excuses, ready to replace them with the rush of pleasure that would surely come with the feel of Izzy's gorgeous full lips against hers. But something ahead of them caught her attention a split second before she made her move, and in an instant her desire was replaced by genuine fear.

Izzy must have read the change in her expression because she spun around immediately.

Chase was ahead of them, bent in a crouched fight position, stiff as a board and ready to spring off his hind legs. He was twenty feet away, halfway between where they stood and a black bear standing upright just off the path.

"Chase, come." Izzy's voice was even. "Come to me."

He took a tiny step backward. "That's it, buddy," Izzy urged him on. "Nice and slow. Come right back to me." He inched his way back, never taking his eyes off the bear. When he reached them, Izzy gripped Sara's hand and guided them slowly backward. Chase's butt pressed up against her leg as he continued the retreat. He was careful and poised and incredibly protective, showing both bravery and acumen.

The second Sara led them through a clearing into the open field, Izzy dropped to her knees and hugged Chase, clearly proud of his success handling the tenuous situation.

"Chase, you are such a good boy!" She scratched his ears and petted his head as she showered him with affection. "I know you lost your favorite toy, but I promise we'll get you a new one." She kissed his head and pressed her cheek against his face. He responded with a huge smile, his tongue drooping out to the side. Sara's heart swelled but she made sure to give them a second before joining the lovefest.

They strolled along regaining their composure, and it took a good few minutes before Izzy expressed her surprise that they were still on the grounds of the training center. Sara explained Arren's Hollow was fully adjacent to campus and the flat path they'd taken was about a quarter mile inland. She also swore she'd never seen a bear in the thousands of times she'd hiked the trails.

"Bears and dogs are actually distant relatives," Sara said, still a bit shaken.

"Is that true, Chase? Was that your cousin?" Izzy asked in an overly cheerful tone, her adrenaline obviously still through the roof. Chase responded with a sharp playful bark, and even though she knew he was just responding to Izzy's enthusiasm, Sara loved that he got in on the conversation.

"Is it too early for a drink?" Izzy asked with a slight laugh. "My heart is still racing."

Sara smiled. "There's an adorable little brunch spot a few miles away, if you're up for it. I don't know about drinks, but I do owe you a meal from last week when I skipped out."

"You owe me nothing," Izzy said. "Let's get this guy set up in his kennel and I'm all yours."

Sara wondered if Izzy's innuendo was intentional or just a figure of speech. After securing Chase, they were almost at Sara's pickup when Jen called out from across the parking lot.

"Hey ladies," she said, sauntering over. She gestured toward Mark, who was standing by the driver's side of his Ford Explorer. "We were just going to grab a bite. You guys want to tag along?"

Sara exchanged a look with Izzy, and she knew they were thinking the same thing. Even though they wanted more alone time, it would be rude to decline the invite. "Sure, why not."

Sara was rewarded with a knowing smile from Izzy at her acceptance on their behalf, and even though lunch was far from a secluded one-on-one, there were laughs and smiles and a million questions from Mark and Jen about their encounter with the bear.

A solid two hours later when they returned to the training compound, their small intimate moment seemed completely distant. Deep down she was dismayed, but Sara couldn't help but wonder if it was for the best.

CHAPTER THIRTEEN

How's things at school?" Elena slid into a cushy lounge chair on the back porch of their parents' house. "Still hot for teacher?"

Izzy leaned her head back against the wooden post of the railing where she sat close enough to keep an eye on Chase and her nephew playing in the grass. The mere mention of Sara made her heart ache, and she wondered what Sara might be doing right now on this warm Saturday evening, the summer weather finally upon them. She was probably in a T-shirt and cutoffs somewhere, enjoying the sunset.

"Completely," Izzy answered, her admission hanging heavy in the space between them. She couldn't lie to her sister—Elena would see through her in a second. She might have downplayed it and avoided the third degree, but something inside her needed to get it out. Two weeks had passed since her bizarrely awesome hike with Sara, a day that had started full of tension but included an almost-kiss, she'd put money on it. There was no arguing Sara had opened up to her, and for a few minutes she'd let her walls down, but then there was a bear, and then their colleagues. And while the afternoon was nice, they'd ended up right back in the friend zone.

She shouldn't complain. In the last week and the one before it, Sara had been attentive to her at school, giving her individual instruction and praise, even chatting her up during class breaks and at lunch. But Izzy could tell she had pulled back again. All of their interactions occurred in the company of others, and even then, Sara avoided eye contact.

"Come back to me, baby sister." Elena touched Izzy's calf with the tip of her pedicured toe.

"Sorry," Izzy said. She took a long sip of the IPA her brother had handed her earlier, the cool beverage helping bring her back to the present.

"Wow." Elena sighed. "Where did you go just now?"

"I'm losing my mind. No big," she said, her mood evening out as she enjoyed another long swallow.

"Because of your instructor?"

"Yes. No. I don't know." She watched Chase tug against the looped end of his rope toy, steering Jack in circles around the yard. Her nine-year-old nephew went crazy when Chase let him win over and over. This dog was a genius. Smart, social, protective. She smiled to herself, every bit the proud parent.

Elena sat upright on the end of the lounge chair. "What's going on? Last you told me you all were doing the friend thing. Give me the latest."

Izzy let out a sigh. "There's nothing really to say. That's it. We're friends, I guess."

"But you want more?"

"Yes," she said emphatically. "The thing is, I know she does too. I'm telling you, I can feel it." She wiped the sweat from her beer bottle. "Elena…" She chewed her lip nervously. "I'm pretty sure we almost kissed a few weeks ago."

"Who almost kissed?" Rick's deep voice surprised them both as he came outside to check on his son.

"Izzy and her teacher." Elena answered, scooting over on her chair to make room for their big brother.

Rick opened his eyes wide. "Your teacher? Isn't that against the rules? I mean, I know you cops think you're above the law and all," he teased. A New York City firefighter, he and Izzy constantly played up the agencies' long-standing rivalry.

"It's not even like that." She shook him off. "She's hardly my teacher. I'm not in the academy. I'm doing specialized training." She thought for a minute. "Like if you were trying out for FDNY marine operations, or something."

"Gotcha." He nodded. "I was just breaking your chops anyway." He turned to peek at his little man rubbing Chase's belly in the distance. "Who's the girl? Woman, I mean." He leaned back on his tanned muscular arms. "I want the dirt on the almost-kiss too."

Izzy smiled, loving that her siblings' interest in her love life was genuine. She tucked one leg under the other and indulged their curiosity, rewinding back to her first day at Overton and bringing them right up to the present, sparing no details about their hike two weeks ago.

"How big was the bear?" Rick asked.

"Men." Elena swatted him. "Who cares about the bear?"

He held both palms up in apology. "My bad."

"The bear was pretty big." Rick had listened to her pour her heart out, so at least she could satisfy his simple curiosity. "I mean, what do I know, I never saw one in person before." She finished her beer and placed the empty bottle next to her. "Anyway, since then all we do is talk shop and she barely looks at me," Izzy said in defeat.

"You think she has commitment issues?" Elena asked.

Izzy shrugged, contemplating the theory. "I don't know." She was about to expound but held her tongue as Jack jogged over and heeded his dad's orders to get cleaned up for dinner. She waited until he was in the house before she spoke. "I actually think she has abandonment issues." Chase sprawled next to her and she petted his soft fur, considering her spur-of-the-moment hypothesis. "Her mom died on 9/11. Her ex left her for a promotion. She has this stupid rule about not dating cops…"

Her brother and sister exchanged a look that was both sympathy and frustration. She adored their support and took a second to appreciate how lucky she was.

Rick broke the silence, saying, "I don't want to minimize her mom's death, or anything she's been through." He leaned forward resting his elbows on his bare knees. "And I know I'm biased and all," he said. "But, Iz, you're a catch. You're pretty and smart. You have a great job. A nice house." He rubbed his hands together. "You have to make her see that you're the real deal. Because you are."

"Rick, I honestly don't know how much more I could do."

"You almost kissed." He pointed right at her. "Don't forget that. And look, if you think there's something there, I guarantee there is. You can't make that stuff up. When you know, you know. Trust yourself."

"Look at you, my big mushy bro." Elena threw her arm across his back, pulling him close for a side-to-side hug as she chided him. She leaned her head on his shoulder but looked right at Izzy. "He's right, though. Even if I'm marginally concerned about his manhood at the moment." He pushed her off playfully as she continued talking. "Don't give up. Keep trying." Elena's tone was full of spirit. "What do you really have to lose?"

"I don't know. Dignity, pride, the one shred of self-respect I have left?"

"Dignity, shmignity." Rick waved her off. "Do you even know how many times I asked Marina out before she agreed to date me?" He thumbed toward the house where his wife was no doubt helping with dinner. "A freaking lot. And then I had to convince her to marry me."

"Text her tonight," Elena said, riding the wave of support. "We're going to eat in ten minutes. You'll be home by nine. See if she wants to meet up for a drink. As friends or whatever. See where it goes."

"She lives like two hours away."

"Even better, maybe she'll have to sleep over." Elena wiggled her eyebrows.

Thankfully, Izzy was spared from responding to her sister's overt suggestion when they were summoned for dinner. For the moment, she ignored Elena's advice, concentrating instead on the simple joy of good food and great company. But hours later in the cozy comfort of her own home, fueled entirely by her siblings' pep talk, Izzy decided to take a small chance.

She let Chase out in the yard and paced the perimeter of her house while he took care of business. In her head, she'd committed to what she was going to do, but she stressed over the wording, changing her mind a thousand times. Once they were inside, she brewed a cup of tea, another stall tactic. Finally, she took a deep breath and went for it, typing out a question she hoped might lead to something more.

Whatever happened to my Star Wars education?

She hit Send and felt her blood pressure skyrocket as she waited for a response. A minute passed, then two, and she thought about googling whether there was a way to retract a text message once it was sent. Her hands were sweating and she burned her tongue on her tea, jerking quickly when a response appeared.

Hey, you. Izzy melted at Sara's familiar greeting. The gray bubbles followed. Sara was typing more. Her heart beat faster with every second. *Are you so bored that you'd even watch Star Wars?*

She smiled. *I might be.*

On a Saturday night?

Izzy answered with the shrug emoji.

What? No lesbian parties raging tonight? I hear Westchester County is famous for them.

Ha! Izzy loved that she was referencing their run-in at Michelle and Dana's. She decided to turn it back on Sara. *Wait a second. Are you at a party? Text me the address. Only if there's cute girls there,* she added at the last minute.

The reply was instant: *Funny.*

Serious, she typed back, praying it wasn't too much.

Sadly, I know of zero parties tonight. I'm all by myself up in Phoenicia.

Bummer. At least I have Chase to cuddle me. Izzy rubbed his side and he dropped his chin on her thigh as though he knew he was the center of attention.

Jealous.

The response turned her on even if she wasn't sure whether Sara was envious of Chase or her. It didn't matter. This back and forth was going better than she'd dreamed. It drove her crazy that she was getting the polar opposite of the woman she'd exchanged cool pleasantries with over the last fourteen days, but rather than dwell on that nuance, she chose to enjoy the moment. She dismissed a zillion racy things she could say in response to Sara's comment, opting instead for maturity.

How was your day?

Really nice actually. I went for a long hike this morning. There's awesome trails up here. You would love it.

I'm sure.

Now I'm chilling. A picture came through of a half-drunk glass of red wine, Sara's soft square fingertips holding the stem. Izzy blew it up, examining the rustic-modern furnishings in the background. *How about you?*

I just got back from dinner with the fam.

Nice.

Me and Chase were sitting here looking for a movie, and then I remembered this unfulfilled promise made to me weeks ago. Something about righting a wrong. Correcting a cinematic injustice…

You are 100% right. I owe it to you and to the film industry to fix this massive flaw. Name the time and place.

Izzy's heart was going a mile a minute. *Tomorrow. My house.* She smiled at her bravery for putting it out there. Now the only question was whether this would actually happen. There were bubbles for a solid minute before Sara's answer came through.

Damn, Izzy. I can't tomorrow. I'm sorry.

Her spirit sank as she wondered if Sara really had a conflict or if her retreat was a reaction to the plan's tangibility.

As if she knew what Izzy was thinking another message popped: *I have to go to DC tomorrow. I'm actually going to miss class Monday and Tuesday.* She punctuated it with a frown.

Izzy had no idea how to respond. She was sure this trip was work related, but it undoubtedly meant time with Nicole Vaughn. She resisted the temptation to ask for details, hoping playing it cool would work in her favor.

Sara rewarded her instantly. *How about next weekend? Mini-marathon. I'll hook us up with the first two installments, you provide the food. Deal?*

Now I have to feed you too? What next?

God, she hoped Sara knew she was kidding. Text messages were tough where tone was concerned.

I guess you'll just have to tell me what else I can do to make this experience worth your while.

Izzy was too stunned to respond. This was beyond flirting and Sara had to know it.

Although... Sara's follow-up hung there for a second. *Star Wars is fantastic. You may be left wondering what you can do to repay me for bestowing this life-changing gift on you.*

Oh, brother. Izzy added an eye roll emoji. *Let's see if I stay awake through the first movie before you start patting yourself on the back.*

Fair enough.

Izzy was sure Sara's smile matched her own, a hundred miles away. What would happen during the movie event itself remained to be seen. But if their behavior was even half as frisky as this text exchange, Izzy would count it as a complete success.

CHAPTER FOURTEEN

Monday and Tuesday dragged, and Izzy attributed the grueling pace entirely to Sara's absence. She hated knowing Sara was in the capital doing God knew what with Nicole Vaughn. She tensed at the thought. More than once Sara had said she and Nicole were a thing of the past, but there was something in her body language that seemed uncertain. Perhaps it was simple nostalgia on display, but what if it was doubt? Even an iota of competition was more than Izzy felt capable of handling. And to be measured against a federal agent who'd risen to the level of director seemed completely unfair. That was without even taking Nicole's Hollywood looks into account. With towering elegance, porcelain skin, and wavy red hair that bounced with every step, Nicole Vaughn was the center of the room, no matter where she stood.

Izzy stared at herself in the ladies' room mirror. The reflection didn't lie. She was shorter than the top of the paper towel dispenser, her hair spilling out of her messy bun. She brushed off a few drops of water the overzealous faucet had sprayed on the department patch covering her left breast. Frowning, she realized this was the image she offered Sara every day. While Nicole traipsed around in designer suits, she showed up clad in NYPD standard issue training gear: tactical pants, department tee, boots, duty rig. Not her fault, but still hardly the picture of sophistication.

She cringed inwardly, for the moment accepting defeat in the one-sided battle waging in her mind. Walking back to her seat in the classroom, she reconsidered her evening plans on the spot. Her crew of friends was headed to a small birthday gathering for Jackie, the air marshal trainee. While Izzy had initially declined the invite—things had been somewhat strained since Jackie had asked her out a few weeks back—suddenly heading home and spending the night fixating on her shortcomings was the less appealing option.

Sliding into her classroom seat, she leaned back toward Jen, who was lounging at the desk behind her. "You think it's weird if I go to Jackie's with you guys later?"

"Yay." Jen clapped silently. "I think you should come. Why wouldn't you?"

"I don't know." She hesitated to say more.

"You feel awkward because she asked you out and you said no?"

Izzy had been very careful to keep the incident to herself. "How did you…?"

"Oh, please," Jen waved flippantly. "I have eyes, honey. And intuition." She examined her fresh manicure. "Anyway, y'all seem to be doing okay during lunchtime. Jackie's a sweetheart. I think she'd be fine with you being there."

"Good point." Izzy mused over their easygoing lunch rapport, repeatedly clicking and unclicking the top of her pen. "But promise to hang with me. Don't just sneak out with Mark when no one's looking." She tapped the top of Jen's desk with her pen. "Or at least let me know before you plan your secret escape." Jen's mouth hung open at her straightforward approach and Izzy wiggled her eyebrows in jest. "You're not the only one with intuition."

❖

Three hours later, Izzy stepped out into the warm night, one hundred percent satisfied with having attended the shindig. There was good company and halfway decent pizza—for upstate, anyway. Jackie seemed not at all bothered by her presence and Izzy was relieved there'd been no awkwardness between them. Now, she just had to collect her dog and get through the last few hours before sleep.

More important, tomorrow her countdown would be over and Sara would be back at training. Izzy crossed her fingers they might pick up their spirited conversation from the other night. But even if they didn't, and she got reserved Instructor Sara, which was highly probable, Izzy still felt inner peace knowing she'd get to see her gorgeous face. And when she was eventually lucky enough to be granted a look into Sara's lovely eyes, she would know there was something more between them, whether Sara chose to admit it or not.

She swung her keys around her index finger as she passed the residential parking lot near the dorms where she knew Sara often parked when she stayed at the facility. Her heart jumped a little when she saw the black Dodge Ram backed into a space in the corner. Izzy stopped walking and looked up at the housing quarters, realizing she had no idea which unit was Sara's. Against her better judgment, she reached for her phone and went for it anyway.

Hey. What housing unit is yours? I'm on campus and would love to say hi.

Sara's response was quick: *I'm in my office.*

Up for a visitor?

Absolutely.

Great. I'll stop by on my way to get Chase.

Sara answered with a smiley face and it was all Izzy could do to keep from sprinting the rest of the way.

Sara could barely focus on her busywork as she waited for Izzy's arrival. Still she jumped when Izzy knocked lightly on the glass wall of her office.

"Hi." Izzy's voice was bright and cheerful and Sara spun her chair away from the computer to face her.

"Come in," she said, with a happy wave.

"What's this? Overtime?" Izzy asked with a slight nod at the screen.

"Ha," Sara answered. "I wish. Government consultants do not get overtime," she added with a grin.

"Just burning the midnight oil for free?" Izzy's delicate hand grazed the top of the chair across from her desk. "That's dedication."

"How was the party?" Sara asked.

Izzy raised her eyebrows, seeming confused and impressed by Sara's knowledge of her whereabouts.

"Fine, fun," she answered, turning back to examine a photo of Sara and John surrounded by a crew of work dogs. "How'd you know where I was?"

Feeling guilty at being caught, Sara zoned in on the papers on her desk, separating the documents into three separate piles. "When you work with investigators as long as I have, you pick a few things up here and there." She grabbed a set of manila folders and wrote headings on each of the tabs. "Also, I found Chase in the kennel. I grilled him." She snapped her fingers crisply. "He gave you up in a second."

"Now I know you're full of it." Izzy shook her head. "Chase would never betray me."

"You seem awfully certain of that."

"You and I both know that dog is as loyal as they come." Izzy's voice dripped with confidence.

"Damn." Sara smiled, stacking up her folders. "I guess I'll have to tell you the truth then."

Sara felt the change throughout her whole body. She knew she was flirting and she didn't care. For the last seventy-two hours Izzy had more than dominated her thoughts, both when she was awake and when she slept. She was tired of fighting it.

"The truth is, I saw your car when I got back a little while ago. I asked around. Heard about the party." Fingering the edge of the files as she avoided eye contact, she tried to sound endearing. "Once I realized Chase was here, I knew you'd have to come back sooner or later to pick him up." She met Izzy's gaze. She wanted her to know she'd been waiting to see her.

"Why didn't you text me you were here?" Izzy asked.

"I didn't want to take you away from your friends." Sara glanced at the work on her desk. "I had a few things to do here anyway."

"Couldn't wait until tomorrow?" Izzy pushed.

Sara walked to the cabinet next to where Izzy stood. She slid the three thin folders into the top drawer. They were so close that when her forearm grazed Izzy's it sent a chill up her body from the skin-to-skin contact, giving her arms goose bumps from wrist to shoulder. She closed the file cabinet drawer, and the loud rumble echoed in the silence between them.

"I wanted to see you." Sara kept her gaze on the floor.

"I wanted to see you too." Izzy touched Sara's wrist with the tip of her finger. "I hated that you weren't here for two days."

"Yeah?" Sara heard her own longing come out loud and clear.

Izzy pouted. "Chase missed you."

"He did, huh?" Sara smiled.

With her thumb and forefinger Izzy demonstrated the tiniest measure. "Just a little."

"I missed him too," she said, hearing the desire in her voice betray her attempt at banter. She turned to her side, half leaning against the cool metal cabinet, suddenly face-to-face with Izzy, their bodies inches apart. She reached forward and ran her fingers along Izzy's smooth forearm. "I thought about you." She carefully caressed Izzy's soft skin, still unable to make eye contact. "While I was gone."

"All I do is think about you." Izzy's hands found hers and she laced their fingers together. "You can't keep doing this to me," she said, her voice low and husky. "Flirting and getting my hopes up and then completely ignoring me. It's torture."

Sara pressed her lips to Izzy's forehead.

"Your rules are ludicrous and archaic."

"I know." Sara moved her lips along the side of Izzy's gorgeous face, dropping baby kisses.

"You like me. I know you do. I can feel it when we talk and text. I see it when you look at me."

Sara stopped when Izzy reached both of her hands into her hair and pulled her face back just an inch, staring deep into her eyes and seeming to search for proof.

"Shh," Sara whispered. "I do." She leaned in and closed her eyes. "Of course, I do." Her mouth found Izzy's sumptuous full lips and she sank into them, feeling herself melt as she kissed her softly, sweetly, over and over, until their lips parted and their tongues met in the middle. Sara pulled Izzy closer so their bodies touched, deepening the kiss, not even caring that she was breaking all her rules. Suddenly every minute leading up to this moment was nothing but wasted time. Izzy's mouth was lush and divine and Sara heard her making adorable tiny moans with each swirl of their tongues. She ran her hand over Izzy's face, stroking the soft skin of her cheek and down her neck, indulging in this moment she'd fantasized about hundreds of times.

"Wow." Izzy seemed almost breathless when she broke them apart, wrapping her arms around Sara's neck and burying her face in her shoulder. "Just, wow."

Sara knew what she was feeling. Her own body tingled everywhere, her pulse racing beyond her control. She hadn't felt like this in…well, maybe ever. She held Izzy gently, kissing her cheek in response. "I know." She dropped her gaze, feeling sheepish at being so emotional. Without overthinking it, she located Izzy's hands and backed them both away from the file cabinet across the few feet of her office until she reached her desk. Perching against the front of it, she lost a few inches and was almost Izzy's height. She had moved them so they could talk, maybe process what was happening here, but once she looked into Izzy's beautiful dark brown eyes, she forgot everything she might say and instead guided her forward, the need to kiss her again immediate.

Izzy didn't protest. She rested her arms across Sara's shoulders and leaned all the way in, giving herself over completely. They kissed for a good long time, fully swept up in the moment.

Minutes passed, maybe more. "I need to go home," Izzy finally said between soft kisses, her hands pressed against Sara's chest.

Sara stole another kiss. "I know you do." She reached for Izzy's hand and held it. "Your poor dog must be going crazy in the back."

"I'll fill him in on the ride," Izzy said.

Sara laughed, completely believing Izzy would give him the play-by-play. "I'm sure you will."

They walked through the hall holding hands, and Sara took a moment to appreciate it, knowing they wouldn't be able to be this open tomorrow.

As if Izzy was tuned in to her thoughts, she leaned in close, squeezing her palm as she pressed against Sara's body. "You're not going to wig out tonight and pretend none of this happened tomorrow, are you?" she asked.

Sara faced her as she reached for her ID card to access the kennel area. Pausing for a second, she cupped Izzy's face. "No. I promise you," she added, making real eye contact. She gave her a tiny kiss before holding the door open so Izzy could pass through first. "I do think we should be a little discreet," she added, hoping the comment didn't make her sound insensitive.

She watched Izzy nod once, then explained, "There's only a few weeks of training left, not that there's any code preventing this"—she gestured between them—"but still."

Izzy pressed the button to raise the barrier separating Chase from them. She rubbed his head and his neck before looking at Sara. "Are you saying you want to put this on hold until the end of class?"

"Not at all." Sara touched the small of her back. "I'm just suggesting we keep it quiet. Not advertise it, you know?" Sara bent down to pet Chase, so she could see Izzy's reaction. "Look, if people find out, so be it," she said, as Izzy fastened Chase's leash and collar with practiced ease. "I just thought it might be better if we stayed professional during the school day. Is that okay?"

"Yes." Izzy's expression told her she was in agreement with the logic. "I'm with you," she said giving the subtlest tug on the end of Chase's lead. "I just wanted to make sure you weren't backing out already."

"I'm not." She reached for Izzy's hand. "I'm in this. For real."

"Thank God." Izzy let out a sigh that was pure relief as she laced their fingers together. "Because if you were all meh now, after that kiss…" She fanned herself playfully. "I might not recover."

Sara felt herself blush at the tiny compliment, more than a little pleased to know the effect she had on Izzy. "So what now?" Sara asked, the newness of their courtship suddenly upon her.

"Now I go home."

As they walked through the building, Chase strode between them, and when Sara dropped Izzy's hand to hold the main door, he turned, seeming to wait for her to accompany them.

"I'm coming, big guy. Hold your horses."

She let the door click shut behind her, and before she could reach for Izzy's hand on her own, Chase nudged it with his snout, positively aggressive in his desire to match it with Izzy's. Sara laughed out loud.

"Oh, you think this is all your doing?" she said right to him.

His pant was a smile and he kissed her palm in response, ducking his head underneath their interlaced fingers to steal some gratuitous head rubs as they walked to the car, where Izzy opened the door for him to climb in, then tossed the slack of his leash in after him.

Sara followed Izzy's eyes to the gravel parking lot beneath them and watched as she nudged the edge of her shoe.

She bit her lower lip and Sara stared at it, swollen and wet, full and inviting. She brought her thumb up and touched it delicately. Izzy opened her mouth ever so slightly in response, the kiss she placed on the pad of her finger the promise of something so much more. Sara didn't want her to leave. She was dying to ask Izzy to secure Chase back in the kennel for the night, beg her for even a paltry few hours in her campus suite where she could hold her and kiss her, live out every last fantasy she'd imagined since the first moment in this very parking lot.

"This is where we met," Sara said. The realization took her by surprise and she reached for Izzy's other hand, drawing her closer. In the dark night, she saw something of a smile play at her gorgeous mouth. "I knew right then you were trouble."

"Pft." Izzy leaned back against the body of her car, taking Sara with her. "You thought I was an idiot that day."

Sara laughed at being called out so many weeks later. "No." She dropped a kiss on her lips. "I thought you were...beautiful. And sexy." She moved her hands to Izzy's hips and guided her lips across her face leaving kisses everywhere. "Maybe slightly ditzy," she whispered in her ear.

Izzy pretended to push her away. "You're a jerk."

Sara hugged her closer. "But only that first day," she said with a laugh. She met Izzy's eyes, becoming serious. "After that, I was..." She got caught up in her own sentiment and didn't want to overdo it. She dropped the sentence completely and leaned forward, finishing her heavy thought with action. At the end of the searing kiss, she backed away, still holding Izzy's hand until the distance was too vast and she had to let go.

"Text me when you get home, okay?" Sara called out in the space between them, watching as Izzy nodded agreement and climbed into her truck, started the engine, and drove away into the night.

CHAPTER FIFTEEN

"Doug, can I bother you for two today?" Sara held up two fingers and smiled big at his easy nod. She loved that he asked for no explanation, just gave a simple nod and reached for more strawberries. She leaned against the industrial kitchen counter, trying to stay out of the way of the busy lunch crew. Grabbing her phone, she checked the time: 11:40. She shot off a hurried text to Izzy.

Have lunch with me?

There was a long pause before Izzy's answer appeared: *Um... okay?*

They had never eaten together during school hours and Sara knew her offer seemed to buck her own request for discretion. She could almost hear Izzy's confusion pinging from cell tower to cell tower.

Meet me on the trail in Arren's Hollow. The one we hiked with Chase a few weeks ago.

When Izzy agreed, Sara detailed the best place to access the path, describing the most precise markers she could think of. Fifteen minutes later, she stood in a small clearing, next to an oversized boulder, holding both smoothies.

"You got me a shake." Izzy's tone was soft and lyrical as she swept over the brush and met Sara in the middle of the wide dirt path.

"I did." She leaned forward and kissed Izzy before handing over the drink. "It's the perfect day for one of these." She looked around them, acknowledging the eighty-degree heat from the shade of the woods. "I hoped I could steal you for at least a few minutes."

"You were a no-show during training this morning." Izzy took a sip of her drink. "Busy?" Her voice had a kind of doubt in it, and more than anything, Sara wanted to put her mind at ease.

"Come here," she said, taking Izzy's hand and pulling her close. She kissed her softly for a good long minute. Their faces were only inches apart as she whispered, "Hi." She brushed her lips over Izzy's. "I conducted three annual certifications this morning." Leaning back against the huge rock behind them, she added, "Ones that were not on the schedule." She rolled her eyes dramatically. "Damn NYPD officers think if they just show up, the world will stop for them."

"As it should." Izzy's nod was playful in defense of her brethren in blue.

"Cops." Sara shook her head, still teasing. "You're all the same."

Izzy stepped into Sara's space, her body so close Sara felt the thick nylon duty belt press against her abdomen. "I think, Instructor Wright"—her lips grazed Sara's neck—"in due time, you'll see I am very different from the three people you dealt with earlier."

"Is that right?"

"Mm-hmm," Izzy purred in her ear, kissing the soft spot just below it.

Sara found her way back to her mouth and kissed her again. Caught up in the moment, she turned them around, leaning into Izzy. Her hands moved along Izzy's cotton T-shirt, over the soft curve of her breast, making her yearn for more. Breaking apart to catch her breath, she touched her forehead to Izzy's. "You cannot do that to me." Her breath came out tempered, her voice raspy as she spoke. "Not here," she added with a slight laugh.

"Me?" Izzy countered dramatically. "This is *your* clandestine rendezvous." Sara felt Izzy's hands slip alongside her waist and give a tiny squeeze before Izzy glanced back to assess the rock behind her and hoist herself onto it. She patted the space next to her. "Sit with me."

Sara complied and for the next few minutes they talked about the day, the beautiful weather, their delicious fruit smoothies.

"Can we go out to dinner tomorrow night?" Sara asked, hearing unexpected nerves in her own delivery.

"I wish." Izzy ducked her face into a ray of sunlight sneaking through the trees.

Sara pretended to remove a knife from her heart. "Ouch."

"I have dinner with my family tomorrow." Izzy grabbed her hand away from her chest and explained. "We usually try for the weekend, but my brother is working Saturday and Sunday." Izzy still held her hand, and Sara felt tingles all through her body when Izzy lazily matched their fingertips up. "I didn't want to give up Friday, so tomorrow's family night."

"Don't tell me." Sara squeezed her hand in response. "Your brother's a cop too?" She stared at the clear sky above them. "And your dad and grandfather. Right?"

"No, smarty-pants." Izzy used their clasped hands to whack her thigh. "Rick is a fireman." Taking her hand away, she folded her arms across her chest and levied no-nonsense sass directly at her. "My dad drives a truck for UPS. Abuelo is a butcher. They came here from Cuba when my dad was six." She used three fingers to poke Sara's shoulder, the gesture clearly indicating she wasn't really upset by Sara's assumption. "Don't go thinking I'm some spoiled third-generation cop getting good details because I have family connections." She was teasing but Sara heard truth behind her defensiveness.

"I didn't. I don't," she answered seriously. "I was honestly just kidding." She touched Izzy's uniform pants. "For so many people, law enforcement is in their family." She traced lazy circles on the blended polyester fabric covering Izzy's thigh. "Wait a second. You said you were keeping Friday clear. What's going on?" Sara asked.

Izzy let out a long sigh. "I was wondering when you were going to bite." She took a long sip of her drink. "I was hoping after class on Friday"—she licked her full lips, making them shine—"you'd come to my house and teach me about Luke and Laura. Get my *Star Wars* on."

"Oh boy." Sara slapped her forehead, hopping off the rock. "Leia. Luke and Leia," she corrected with a mock sigh as she turned to lift Izzy down. "This may take all weekend."

Izzy let go a salacious smile. "If you're lucky."

❖

Class dismissed early on Friday and Izzy was happy for the extra time. Not that she needed to do much before Sara arrived at six, but she liked taking her time getting ready.

She took a long hot shower, in no rush as she shampooed, conditioned, and shaved—just in case. Methodically lotioning everywhere, her skin felt soft and smooth and she wondered if Sara's touch would be gentle or needy or both. She had to stop her mind from getting ahead of her. Sara was so reserved—she might want to take things super slow and that would be just fine, she lectured herself. Just because she'd been fantasizing about this for months did not mean Sara was on the same timeline. She closed her eyes and took a deep, measured breath, reminding herself to appreciate the fact they'd finally reached this level and not to sabotage things by pushing for more than Sara might be ready for.

Taking a full minute to center herself and relax, she looked in her closet for clothes to match the occasion, ultimately selecting black leggings and a trendy T-shirt that was tight enough to show her curves. The mirror told her it was casual and sexy, the perfect combo for an at-home movie night.

For the next half hour, she flitted about her kitchen, wiping the spotless countertops a trillion times until Chase hopped up on all fours and started his telltale dance. She looked out the window and saw Sara's truck just making the turn onto her street.

"You are good," she said praising his early detection skills. As the car moved down the road, he let out a few excited whines, peppering his enthusiasm with welcoming yips and barks. "Be cool, Chase. Be cool." Izzy followed him to the door where he was already pacing in eager semicircles. "We don't have to tell her how excited we are that she's here. Rein it in, okay, buddy?" she pleaded. But he responded by pawing the door, and she couldn't help giving in to his excitement. She opened the storm door and watched him bound to the truck, practically assaulting Sara with wet kisses as she climbed out of the driver's seat.

"Sorry about that," Izzy said, letting them both in the house at the same time. "He really couldn't wait to say hi."

"He's a sweetie," Sara said. She held aloft a bottle of pinot and a bag of gourmet chili popcorn. "I brought snacks." She dug into her bag and pulled out a stuffed chipmunk toy, squeaking it between her fingers. "This is for you," she said, looking at Chase and tossing it a foot away to watch him dive after it.

"Thank you," Izzy said on behalf of both of them, leaning up to kiss Sara on the cheek. She smiled at Chase pawing and chewing the squeaker toy. "He's going to annihilate that in about one second," she said with a proud laugh.

"I'd say he's earned it," Sara said.

"Here, let me take these," Izzy said taking the wine and the popcorn and placing both on the kitchen island. She turned to the far cabinet and had to reach for two wineglasses on the top shelf.

"Let me help you." Sara's lithe body was inches from hers as she easily reached the third shelf.

Izzy turned around and touched her hands to Sara's bare forearms, caressing all the way up to the short sleeves of her super-soft, flawlessly antiqued V-neck. "Show-off."

Sara answered with a perfect smile. "You're welcome," she said, wasting no time before she leaned forward and planted a kiss on her lips before taking a step back and resting against the island.

Opening a drawer to retrieve the wine opener, Izzy stole a glance at Sara's loosely fitted gray T-shirt touting Baltimore's Inner Harbor. It was probably store-bought vintage with factory-applied wear, but damn, it looked good. Knowing the location's proximity to Washington, DC, Izzy almost asked if she'd visited, but when Sara tucked her hand in her pockets, her jeans dipped down revealing the black edge of her panties just above the low-slung waistline. It was everything Izzy could do to ignore the heat she felt surge through her and form words.

"So I have a little confession," she started, avoiding eye contact.

"Wait. Don't tell me." Sara looked positively impish. "You've actually seen all the *Star Wars* movies and this"—she circled one finger in the air—"is all just a ploy to get into my pants?"

Izzy guffawed. Great, classy! Her face was surely bright red at her motive being called to the forefront, but she didn't even care. "What's gotten into you tonight?" she asked, pouring them each a wine.

"I'm just teasing you." Sara reached for her hand and pulled her in front of her, wrapping her hands around her waist. "What did you want to tell me?"

Izzy took a sip of the dry white wine before placing it on the counter. "Ah, that." She brushed her hands across the tops of Sara's shoulders delicately. "Remember how you were going to change my life with these movies? And in return I was going to feed you?" She waited for Sara to nod acknowledgment while toying with the neckline of her shirt and letting her fingertip graze the skin just under it. "See, I don't cook. Like, at all." Sara seemed about to speak, but Izzy covered her lips with one finger. "But..." She hoped her coy act was coming off cute. "I have these amazing leftovers from yesterday. Paella my abuela made. Plantanos. Some salad too."

"Spanish?"

"Cuban, actually. Do you like it?" She made an *eek* face, a little nervous she'd put all her eggs in this one basket. "We can order takeout if you want. I should have asked you first."

Sara's smile was positively delightful. "I've never had Cuban food." She linked her hands at the small of Izzy's back, the slight move forcing them infinitely closer. "I'm excited to try it."

"If you don't like it, we'll order anything you want."

"Stop. It's going to be great. I'm sure." She bent down and stole another kiss, before she leaned back to reach her oversized bag. "For my contribution, I brought these." She pulled out a huge box set collector's edition of the *Star Wars* saga.

"Wow, DVDs. Hard-core."

"If you don't have a DVD player, we can stream it from my Amazon account."

"Just how obsessed are you?"

Nothing about Sara's confident body language suggested she might be the least bit embarrassed about her dedication. "Look, you never know when you'll need a fix. I like to be prepared."

"You're cute." Izzy hooked Sara's pinkie with her finger and guided them into the living room. As they sat on the couch sipping their wine, she watched Sara spread out the discs on the coffee table.

"So there's some debate over where to start because there's the original three movies and then the prequels and the sequels," she started. "Some people theorize for continuity's sake you should start at Episode One and continue through in order."

"But...?" Izzy said with a smile.

"I'm a purist." Sara shrugged. "I say we watch them in the order of their release, so you get the full experience."

"I definitely want the full experience," she said, locking eyes with Sara, her tone loaded with innuendo.

Sara didn't miss it. Her eyes grew heavy with passion and she leaned forward and kissed Izzy softly and deeply. "I'm sorry," she uttered, pulling back, a bit breathless from the spontaneity of the action.

"Never be sorry for kissing me like that." Izzy draped her arms over Sara's shoulders and smiled against her cheek. "Put this movie on and educate me already."

About twenty minutes in, Izzy made them plates and they ate in the living room, watching the plot unfold. Izzy loved that Sara plied her with little tidbits of filmmaking lore dating back to the original production of the movies as they ate and watched.

"This food is amazing," Sara whispered under Darth Vader's breathy threats.

Izzy smiled, popping the last sweet plantain onto Sara's plate, then wiping her hands with a napkin. Sara speared it with her fork, bit half, and held the other side aloft for Izzy to finish. It was an adorably cute, totally couple-y gesture. It made her swoon. Was she being ridiculous?

At the conclusion of the final scene, she gave the film its due praise before she admitted that she'd skipped Chase's nighttime walk in order to see the end uninterrupted.

"Do you want to take him now?" Sara asked, standing from the couch.

Izzy hesitated, unsure quite how to play this. Chase needed a walk, but she didn't want Sara to leave just yet. "We'll be fast. As soon as he does his thing"—she snapped her fingers, causing Chase to look right at her—"I'll come right back." She saw something in Sara's eyes, and fearing the worst, she blurted out, "Don't leave. Please."

Sara's smile was unbelievably sexy and she practically crooned, "I'm not leaving." She reached for her shoes. "I'm coming with you."

Just like that they seemed to slip into girlfriend-land, taking their time with the walk, allowing Chase to smell every fire hydrant along the way. Suddenly there was no urgency, and when Sara reached for her hand as they strolled the deserted suburban streets, it seemed the most natural thing in the world. They talked about school, the other handlers, the beautiful warm night around them, letting their conversation lead them right back to her comfy sofa.

"I never asked if you liked the movie," Sara said, still holding her hand.

"I did." Izzy smiled in response. "Not as much as the company."

"Oh yeah, huh?" Sara's voice sounded laid-back but the look on her face when she leaned her head against the back of the couch was anything but casual. Izzy recognized the desire in her eyes—she felt it coursing through her own body. She couldn't take waiting one more second, and she leaned all the way forward, kissing Sara so thoroughly she thought she might die if Sara didn't take her right here and now.

CHAPTER SIXTEEN

C ome." Izzy's voice was soft in her ear.
They had been making out on the couch for what felt like forever, and even though Izzy's body language seemed to scream for more, Sara didn't want to make any assumptions about taking things to the next level. For that reason alone, she'd been careful to keep her hands from drifting beneath Izzy's shirt, even though her prominent nipples were begging for her touch.

"Let's go inside," Izzy rasped, virtually reading her mind.

One look at her flushed face and dark eyes told Sara everything she needed to know. Izzy was ready. Faced with the moment of opportunity, Sara was more nervous than she wanted to admit, and she could only muster a small nod in response to Izzy's request.

Wordlessly, she stood up and took Izzy's hand, allowing herself to be guided down the hall. If Izzy had any nerves over what was surely about to happen, they didn't show as she casually flipped off light switches along the way. Just outside her bedroom, Izzy pointed Chase toward his bed tucked in an alcove and handed him a stuffed dinosaur to snuggle as he cozied in. "Night, buddy," she said, bending down to touch his head.

Inside Izzy's lovely bedroom Sara recognized the faint scent of vanilla and lavender. She watched Izzy cross the room and turn on a small corner lamp, but barely moved at all from the doorway.

"Are you okay?" Izzy asked, her voice husky as she met her in the center of the room.

Sara drew in her breath as Izzy wove their fingertips together and dotted a trail of delicate kisses down her neck. She felt her body tense up, and Izzy must have noticed because she continued lightly brushing her lips over her jawline up to her ear.

"Relax, Sara," she said sweetly.

It was as though Izzy knew she needed both reassurance and calming as she backed them up to her bed.

"It's just me," Izzy whispered, kissing her face gently and taking Sara's hands in hers, guiding them under her shirt and upward.

Sara cupped Izzy's full breasts, running her thumbs slowly over her taut nipples and savoring Izzy's reaction as she pressed herself against Sara's hands. Sara felt herself throb in anticipation and she almost lost her breath at the sensation. She lifted Izzy's shirt over her head, finding her mouth and kissing her as their bodies perfectly synched. Sara felt Izzy's soft hands graze along her belly under her tee, exploring her tingling skin then unclasping her bra, until it was off her body and added to the growing heap of discarded clothing on the floor.

As Izzy drew down the bedcovers, Sara tugged off her own jeans, sliding between the cool sheets and leaning back to stare at Izzy's perfect curves as she slipped out of her leggings and crawled in beside her. When Izzy reached across Sara toward the end table light, Sara held her there caressing her back as she guided her face close to kiss her.

The kiss was soft and sweet until Sara's desire took over. Running her hands through Izzy's thick dark hair, Sara kissed her greedily, loving the feel of Izzy's tongue against hers. The lace of Izzy's bra tickled her own naked breasts, so she dispensed with it, finally able to enjoy her perfect erect nipples against the palms of her hands. She rolled over, taking Izzy with her, her hips pressing into Izzy's, and kissed her way down to each breast, feeling Izzy's nipples grow tighter in her mouth.

"God, you are beautiful," she whispered in the moonlight.

Izzy answered her with a sweltering kiss as she spread her legs wider so Sara could slide between them. Sara struggled to keep her breathing even as she kissed her way down Izzy's torso, feeling her muscles quiver with each contact. She was in love with the smooth tan skin of Izzy's soft, sculpted abdomen and the feel of Izzy's hands in her hair as she grazed her lips along her inner thighs. She heard Izzy groan in need and smiled as she inched her way back up her gorgeous body, continuing to tease and nibble the whole way.

"You're torturing me."

She heard raw desire in Izzy's voice and capitalized on it, kissing Izzy's flushed face and her parted lips, her tongue finding Izzy's as she slipped her hand slowly inside her panties. Sliding into Izzy's heat for the first time, Sara's own breath caught in her throat, and she felt her heartbeat quicken in response. "Can I take these off?" she asked.

Izzy gave a small nod, her mouth open, her eyes expectant and heavy. "Yours too." Her voice was low and ragged, but not shy. "I want to feel you against me."

Sara obliged, slipping out of her own panties a mere second after she slid Izzy's down over slim, muscular legs. Sara's breath hitched again as she pressed her naked flesh against Izzy's gorgeous body. They moved together for a moment until she dipped her hand between them, suddenly needing to take control.

Izzy was unbelievably wet and it made Sara yearn for her own release. She slipped one finger inside and stilled a moment, but Izzy's desperate moan said she wanted more. Sara felt her spread wider in invitation, as frantic hands gripped her shoulders in encouragement. She moved gently in and out, watching as Izzy's eyes clouded in pleasure.

"That's it. Right there, just like that." Izzy breathed the words into her hair and it made her thrust harder.

"Fuck," Izzy moaned. "You feel so good," she repeated through short staccato breaths.

Sara felt Izzy's body purring underneath her own, as they found the perfect rhythm. And when Izzy clenched around her fingers, the action made her own insides quake in response.

Being inside Izzy brought a warmth Sara had never experienced. Sure, she'd made love to other women this way—the act itself wasn't new to her. But something in Izzy's voice, her expression, her body, her entire being touched Sara in a way that made it crystal clear this was different. Their connection was passionate and pure, and suddenly everything that had come before it seemed remarkably inconsequential. The feeling overcame her before she was able to wrap her head around the notion. Love was something you were supposed to fall into, recognizing and acknowledging and adjusting to the sensation over time. But suddenly Sara was so far past that plunge, her feelings for Izzy so profound, she knew right then and there she'd somehow slipped into the state without even realizing.

It was at once beautiful beyond words and scarier than she'd ever imagined.

She was brought back into the present by Izzy's touch, and she felt herself throb as Izzy slid her hand between them, innately homing in on Sara's need as she gently eased a finger inside. Her breath caught at the sudden pleasure, and Izzy's gaze locked with hers as she asked, "Is this okay?" But the question seemed a formality. Sara knew her body's response assured her approval. "I want you to come with me," Izzy said softly.

Sara looked deep in those captivating eyes and nodded her head ever so slightly. Her hips bucked as she felt Izzy fill her completely. She pumped faster into Izzy, knowing without a doubt the beginning of Izzy's orgasm would be the catalyst for her own.

"Oh, babe," Izzy breathed out. She bit her bottom lip and Sara felt Izzy's body change, a new cadence taking over. Like practiced magic, the switch flipped inside her own being, her hips moving beyond her control as she rode Izzy's hand until the very last shock wave rolled through her.

Sara leaned forward and buried her face between the pillow and Izzy's lustrous long hair, allowing the tears to trickle from her closed eyes. She only needed a minute to collect herself, but Izzy was too quick. Soft hands tucked her hair behind her ear as Izzy pulled Sara down next to her, cradling her face close.

"Hey, are you okay?" Izzy asked.

Sara heard the sincerity in Izzy's husky voice and realized she sounded stressed at the turn of events.

"I'm fine," Sara reassured her, using both hands to wipe along the top of her cheeks. She waited half a minute but was unable to collect herself. "I'm sorry," she said in a muffled whisper. "I swear this has never happened to me before. I don't know what's going on." She squeezed her eyes shut, forcing away a fresh stream of tears.

"It's okay." Izzy moved closer and brushed away the curtain of long hair that fell between them, letting her hand linger near Sara's face.

Sara somehow felt more naked and exposed, and Izzy seemed to sense her vulnerability.

"Come here," Izzy ordered gently, but Sara turned onto her back, the tears taking a new path along her temples onto the sheets.

"Hey."

Sara pressed her eyes closed, but she felt the mattress move under her as Izzy shifted onto one elbow, pulling Sara's hand away and kissing her damp face delicately.

"It's okay," Izzy said. Her eyes still shut, Sara felt fingertips caress her cheeks and brush over her lips. "Do you want to talk about it?"

Sara heard a weird laugh escape her chest. "I'm completely serious." She opened her eyes and was sure to make real eye contact, so Izzy would know there were no old scars being dug up. "There's nothing to talk about." She found her smile as she kissed the back of Izzy's hand. "That's never ever happened to me." Holding Izzy's hand against her lips she added, "I just got a little overwhelmed, I think." She let out a long breath, hating how vulnerable she felt and that her emotions refused to abate. "I'm sorry," she said finally, wiping away the last of her tears as she shook her head, still in a temporary state of disbelief.

"Do not apologize," Izzy ordered. "The fact that you got so caught up"—she dropped a kiss on her lips—"I think it's sweet. You're sweet," she said, kissing her again. "And that"—she dropped her gaze, appearing almost shy—"was amazing." She drew in her lower lip. "As long as you're not having regrets." The statement hung there for a second as though it was a question that needed answering.

Sara assured her, "No regrets. Ever."

"Thank God." Her smile was warm and beautiful and Sara thought she'd never get tired of seeing the way it lit her whole face. She leaned forward to kiss each dimple, completing the act with a soft kiss on the lips before flopping back on the pillow, her body and soul spent beyond compare.

She smiled as Izzy reached for her arm and wound it around her as she curled into her body. "Please tell me you'll be the big spoon," Izzy said, "because I've been fantasizing about falling asleep in your arms for months."

Sara loved that Izzy made her smile without even trying and she didn't dare protest, instead responding to her demand by cradling her as they both drifted off to sleep.

Snug in her favorite FDNY hoodie, Izzy hovered by the coffeemaker practically counting the beads of liquid as they dripped into the pot. She felt Sara's arms snaking around her waist.

"If this wasn't your house I'd be worried you snuck out on me."

"Good morning." Without turning around, Izzy ran her hand up the side of Sara's face and pulled her down into a kiss. "Chase needed to go out." She swayed lazily in her embrace. "I needed coffee."

"Can I make you breakfast?"

"Definitely." She turned to kiss her in a preemptive kind of thanks. "I was going to suggest a diner, but if you're offering…" A smile spread across her face. "Hey, that's my shirt," she said, eyeing an old NYPD tee from her first precinct. With a downward glance she saw Sara had appropriated some cozy PJ pants too.

"I hope you don't mind," Sara said. She hugged the shirt. "This shirt is so soft."

Mind? Hell, she was thrilled. "I do prefer you out of my clothes." She raised one eyebrow suggestively. "That said, you can wear anything you want." She grabbed two mugs from the cabinet. "And if you're willing to make me breakfast, that shirt is yours."

"Sweet deal," Sara said, swinging into action as she found ingredients to work with.

They ate breakfast alfresco on the back deck, watching Chase play in the yard, darting in and out of his home kennel and sprawling between them as they sipped coffee all morning. Izzy suggested sneaking a walk in before the rain that was sure to come, if the overcast clouds were any indication. Strolling hand in hand through the woods into the park behind her house, the conversation stayed easy and light, and they made it all the way back to the house before the first raindrops fell.

"We made it," Izzy said opening the back door and holding it for Sara and Chase to escape the drizzle. It was barely afternoon, and more than anything Izzy didn't want Sara to leave. "Any chance I can convince you to take me through Episode Two?" she asked, as she filled Chase's water bowl and listened as he lapped at it heartily. "I'm not trying to kidnap you, I swear." She looked over at Sara, delighted to see a graceful smile break across her face. "If you're not up for it, I understand." She rested one hand on her hip, hoping she didn't seem clingy. "It's just"—she gestured toward the window—"this weather is essentially made for a movie marathon. And you did bring the entire series, so…"

"Yes." Sara stepped right into her space, hooking her arms around her waist. She kissed her lips and her face. "I am in no rush to leave." Sara peppered her neck with kisses. "We can watch all the *Star Wars* you want." Izzy followed her gaze as she glanced out the window at the steady rain. "But first, there's something else this weather is perfect for." Sara's lips met hers just long enough for a promise, and then Sara reached for her hands and backed them toward the hall.

Seeing this confident, secure side of Sara emerge excited her beyond words. Without protest, Izzy followed her right into the bedroom where she gave herself over completely, indulging in each tease and touch as Sara took her time exploring every inch of her body. She ached with need and Sara read her perfectly, grazing her lips tenderly across her body until they found her dripping wet center. Her tongue was hot and soft and so greedy that Izzy had to distract herself to hold in her release so she could savor the feeling of Sara's warm mouth on her very core. She lost all concept of time at the feel of Sara's velvet tongue stroking her clit, but the payoff was nothing short of divine as a heavenly orgasm radiated out from her center and cascaded smoothly over her limbs.

Completely sated, Izzy's body brimmed with a mix of euphoria and exhaustion as she sank into the pillow and drifted off to dreamland.

A loud clap of thunder woke her, and Izzy patted the mattress around her, bummed to discover she was alone. The clock said it was only 4:40 in the afternoon even though darkness was settling across her room courtesy of the rain and clouds. Sitting up, she held the sheets against her bare skin and rubbed the sleep from her eyes, then noticed a beam of light spilling from under the bathroom door. The shower was running and she couldn't help but smile realizing Sara was still here.

She tiptoed into the bathroom hoping to surprise Sara, but before she could execute, Sara said, "I hope you don't mind," over the rush of the water. Busted.

"I hope *you* don't mind," Izzy said as she slid open the frosted glass door and stepped in with a grin. Sara welcomed her readily, inching forward to make room. "I'm sorry I passed out," Izzy said kissing the back of her damp shoulder. "Did you nap at all?"

Sara turned to face her, scrunching her nose as she moved to the side to give access to the steady shower stream. "I have a hard time sleeping in the afternoon. Nightmares," she added.

"That sucks."

"It's okay. It was nice just being next to you," she whispered, reaching high and handing Izzy a loofah hanging off the hook of the shower caddy. "I took Chase out, I hope that's okay."

"You didn't have to do that."

"It was no big deal. I wanted to get clothes from my truck anyway." She dropped a soft wet kiss on her lips. "One of the perks of basically living out of my car," she added with an eyebrow raise as she stepped out and grabbed a towel off the rack. "Are we going out to eat or staying in?" she asked with a gorgeous knowing smile.

"You'll stay?" Izzy heard the excitement in her own voice and didn't even care that her absolute enthusiasm showed.

"I know it's not even five, but I'm starving. And…" She let her voice drawl out. "We still have a ton of movies to watch."

"I vote takeout, then. You pick."

Not wanting to miss another minute, Izzy zipped through the shower, smiling at the prospect of a second night together. She loved their easy connection and that they could barely keep their hands off each other. Even as they were getting set up for dinner, Sara seemed to find reasons to touch her—a tiny kiss by the fridge, her hand casually grazing Izzy's bottom as she poured their drinks. The evening was continued perfection as they huddled side by side in comfy clothes at the kitchen island sharing pad thai and spring rolls. Izzy was insanely happy. Even the inevitable barrage of texts from Nicole lighting up Sara's phone wasn't enough to unnerve her.

"Here she is. Saturday night, like clockwork," Izzy teased, hoping Sara knew she was still on the friendly side of jealous. "Don't tell me…" She held her fork up. "She needs you for something."

Sara chuckled, answering Izzy with a peck on the lips before she opened the text.

Izzy watched her read for a second. "So lay it on me. What's the emergency now?"

Putting her phone down, Sara swiveled her stool to face her. Sara held her face and cupped her chin, looking right in her eyes before administering a kiss that started soft and slow but became hard and heavy, somehow evolving into sweet and sexy. Izzy nearly slid off the stool.

"If you leave now, I'm going to kill you."

"I'm not." Sara dropped a kiss on her nose. "I want you to know there's nothing going on." She glanced at her phone. "Nicole's not a threat. I promise." She was clearly waiting for Izzy's acknowledgment and she reached forward tipping Izzy's chin up for eye contact. "You know that, right?"

"I do. I guess." Izzy hated knowing she was coming off as possessive. "Why does she call you all the time?" Great, now she was borderline pathetic. "First she was up here, and now you just got back from being down there. All this to help her with a project?" she asked, knowing she sounded skeptical.

"Nicole just got bumped up a few ranks."

"Another promotion?"

"Well, not a promotion, really. It's more of a lateral move. She was the Director of Training, now she's the Director of Special Programs. Believe it or not, it's a pretty big deal involving a lot more prestige and responsibility," Sara said nonchalantly.

"Okay," Izzy said, trying to understand what any of this had to do with Sara.

"One of her tasks is developing training nationwide."

"How does that not fall under the Director of Training?" Izzy asked.

"Well, before, her division was responsible for administering the training mandates. Now, she's in charge of actually setting protocol." Sara moved some noodles around her plate. "She's been asking me to help her with the K-9 stuff." Her eyes brightened with fervor. "So I've been reviewing federal policies as well as those of some of the local and regional agencies we partner with. Getting her up to speed on trends, training techniques, things like that." She nodded at her phone, appearing almost guilty. "I'm headed down there tomorrow."

"Tomorrow?" Izzy let her head fall against Sara's shoulder. "This is going to be my complete undoing."

"Hey." Sara tucked Izzy's hair behind her ear. "It's just work."

"And there's no one else who can do it," Izzy finished for her, purposely loading her statement with sarcasm. But when she looked up, Sara's expression revealed a truth she wasn't expecting.

In the brief, unguarded moment Izzy could tell Sara enjoyed the extra work. "I'm sorry," she said, reining herself in immediately. "This is what you love." She kissed Sara's biceps. "I know I'm being juvenile, but I just got you and I don't want to lose you to your beautiful, decorated, high-powered ex-girlfriend who practically runs Homeland Security. I can't compete with that."

"Izzy"—Sara turned to face her and placed her hands on the tops of her thighs—"you're not competing with anyone. It's you. I want to be with you. And I finally am." Her smile was soft and Izzy felt herself calming. "Nothing is going to get in the way of that." Sara kissed her. "I do love being part of revamping the training. Not because of Nicole. Although I am grateful for the opportunity." She shrugged a little. "I live for K-9. It's been my sole existence for years. I read articles, stream video, keep up on all the latest tactics, techniques, breeds, bloodlines, you name it. Here and in Europe."

"I get it." Izzy touched her forehead to Sara's, feeling ridiculous and petty. "I'm just being a jealous girlfriend."

"It's flattering." Sara kissed Izzy gently. "But you have nothing to worry about." Izzy met her eyes and relaxed some when Sara reached for her hands and laced their fingers together. "Trust me, okay?" Izzy let Sara tug her off her stool and bring her in close. Sealing her sentiment with a series of kisses that hinted at more, Izzy felt Sara smile against her lips. "Girlfriend, huh?"

"You better be my girlfriend if you're going to run off to DC every weekend." Without letting go of Sara's hand, Izzy spun around, twisting into Sara's embrace and wrapping Sara's perfectly defined forearms around her belly.

She felt Sara hug her tighter in response. "Sounds perfect," Sara said, placing a kiss on the spot just below her ear.

Hours later after dinner was finished and the dishes cleared, they cuddled under the covers, only making it through half of *The Empire Strikes Back* before the need to devour each other took over, and they spent the remainder of the night talking and touching until they finally fell asleep, tangled in each other's embrace. And when Sara left in the morning bound for Washington, DC, her kisses felt lovely, if bittersweet, as Izzy focused on the short few days until they could be together again.

CHAPTER SEVENTEEN

W hat do you hear about Nicole coming back to New York?"
Sara stood in the doorway to John's corner office and
tried to gauge his reaction to her out-of-the-blue question. He took
off his glasses and tossed them onto the stack of papers in front of
him, swiveling in his chair and lacing his fingers behind his head.

"I figured you'd be the one with all the intel on Nicole," he
countered.

"That's just it." She took a small step inside and leaned against
the wall. "She hasn't said boo about it to me."

"Come in." He waved her forward. "Shut the door. Talk to me."

She responded to his gentle request, flopping into his
uncomfortable spare chair and looking out the window as she
searched for the right words. "I don't really know that I have
anything to say," she said, drumming the armrest repeatedly.

"Clearly that's not the case." He picked up his specs and pointed
at her with them, the subtle gesture an overt reference to her agitated
state. "What's this about New York?" he asked, ever the investigator
as he twirled his glasses between his thumb and index finger.

"Nothing. I don't know. A while back you said you heard a
rumor or something." She picked at her short fingernails, avoiding
eye contact. "When I was down in DC, I overheard some guys
saying they heard she was planning on coming back up here."

"But she hasn't mentioned it to you. That's surprising."

She released a heavy, aggravated breath. "We talk about work.
Dogs. Training. Not much else."

He dropped his chin and his look said he didn't believe her, so she elaborated. "Of course we talk about other stuff," she said honestly. "But nothing like that." She met his eyes, gripping the chair as if to brace herself. "She's not transferring here, is she?" she asked, powerless to cover her sincere disbelief over the possibility.

"I heard some scuttlebutt a while back," he offered. "Nothing official." He scratched his chin as though he was considering the percentages. "I wouldn't be shocked, though."

Sara clenched her jaw, knowing the anger she felt at the prospect didn't entirely add up.

"I'm honestly surprised at your reaction." John didn't wait for her to explain herself. "You gals are spending an awful lot of time together these days. You're there. She's here. I figured, you know, things were finally coming together for you." He shrugged. "It's not a crazy assumption."

"We work on program implementation and upgrades. Purchasing. Pedigree. Certifications."

"All things that could be done via phone."

What the hell?

He chuckled at her obvious irritation, putting his hands up in a defensive pose. "I'm just pointing out the facts."

She closed her eyes, trying for composure, as she processed his theory.

"Look, Sara." She met his sympathetic gaze, and he leaned forward on his messy desk. "Truthfully I have no clue what Nicole's plans are." He rubbed his stubby mustache. "The fact is, as the Director of Special Programs, she can work almost anywhere. Well, any of the large federal facilities or offices. Which would certainly include Overton. And with our proximity to Manhattan, which is the biggest district office"—he held his hands up in a kind of surrender—"this place sort of makes sense as a front-runner."

He stood up and grabbed sunglasses from his credenza by the window. "Come on," he said, giving her shoulder a squeeze. "Stop stressing. Let's go have some fun with this exercise." He paused, taking a second to look right at her. "If I hear anything at all, I promise you'll be the first to know." He backed out of the doorway, slipping on his shades. "But, Sara, you know her better than anyone. Why don't you just ask?"

There was only one problem with that plan: she was absolutely terrified of the answer.

She reached the practice field still heavy with stress, but one look changed her entire attitude. As soon as her eyes found Izzy among the group of handlers, everything was all right in the world. Sure, her heart pounded and her pulse raced, every moment of their weekend flooding to the surface. But gone were her nerves and agitation. She smiled. Izzy grounded her. As if she could read her mind, Izzy gave her a soft smile, and it hit her so hard Sara had to avert her gaze when a rush of emotion washed over her.

By contrast Izzy was the picture of pure professionalism. Tucked away in a shady spot lined up with her classmates along the exterior of the academic building, she looked primed and ready, all business, with Chase at her side waiting for action.

"Okay, everybody." Sara clapped her hands, hoping to get them pumped for the event. "This is a little practical exercise we like to call *Anything Goes.*" A weed whacker fired up nearby and she nodded in response. "That right there is one of the reasons." On cue a series of pops sounded in the distance, causing the dogs to perk up along with their handlers. "Those are gunshots from your fellow officers in training going through firearms qualifications on the other side of campus." She saw something of a sly smile playing at Izzy's lips, and it warmed her heart to see she'd been missed in the last forty-eight hours they'd been apart. It took everything she had to stay on point.

"Remember your training," she continued. "Stay focused. The guys are going to mix up the scenarios." She glanced over her shoulder toward the backfield. "Sometimes there'll be a bomb, sometimes not. Safety always comes first." She swirled her finger at the ruckus all around. "This is just noise. Don't get rattled. You can handle this. I know it." She was referring to each person, each canine, and she pointed at her heart to express faith in her class. But at the same time, she looked at Izzy and in the moment felt utterly transparent. "Okay, let's go," she said, clearing her throat and clapping it up to divert attention as she signaled Ryan and Jax to kick off the drill.

❖

When they were up, Izzy and Chase sailed through without a hitch, with Chase identifying a high hide from the ground. Sniffing it out, he sat down in passive alert and barked like crazy to make Izzy aware of its presence on the top of a storage bunker. She looked around for something to stand on and found an empty milk crate. She stepped up, holding her phone above her head and activating the camera to make visible verification of the contraband. Together they scored high marks for their find, their communication skills, and improvisation. Milk crate, FTW! With the cycle complete, she and Chase were dismissed for the day, but Izzy headed back to the classroom, taking her time packing up her gear, waiting to see Sara again before she left.

"Hey, are you in a rush to get home today?" Jen's voice from the doorway surprised her.

Izzy almost laughed out loud at the question. "Not at all."

"I was wondering if you'd be willing to work with me for a little bit." Jen stuffed her hands in her pockets. "Chase is always on point." She walked forward holding Tempe's leash tightly. "He never gets it wrong. And you two seem so…connected." She looked between Chase and Izzy and then down at her own pup. "Sometimes I worry about Tempe. We're not clicking lately."

"What happened in the field?"

"Double decoy," she answered with a frown.

"Ooh, that's a tough one." Izzy realized how lucky she'd been to draw a relatively simple high hide. She channeled her best supportive voice. "Don't be too hard on yourself." Making sure her voice stayed even she added, "What did Sara say?"

"Nothing bad." Jen tugged at her ponytail, playing with the ends of her sandy-blond hair. "She told me to stay with it. Not to get bogged down by the near miss."

"See that? You didn't even miss," Izzy reassured her.

"Tempe hesitated. She wanted her reward after the first decoy. Kind of lost focus. Not that I'm blaming her. Once we got the first bad guy, I shut the scenario down in my head. I didn't even see the second perp until he was almost on us."

"That could happen to anyone." Izzy tucked her keys into the side zipper of her backpack, withdrawing her phone and sliding it into her pocket. But she was pretty sure Jen was still stressed—she would be, in her situation—so she smiled and offered her services. "How can we help you?"

"I don't know, really." Jen folded her arms across her chest. "I thought maybe me and Tempe could watch you guys work, get tips." She shrugged.

More than anything, Izzy thought she needed a friend.

"Let's go," she said with a huge smile.

Wasting no time, they headed to the far training area in the back where they'd be sure to be out of the way. For a while they focused on side-by-side obedience work. Knowing Tempe was as play driven as Chase, Izzy told Jen about her system of tiering reward toys—jute, ball, Kong—and mixing in other motivators to keep things fresh. The info seemed to relax her. Perhaps she'd just needed a sounding board and a few new options. After a while, they sat on the grass and let their dogs play, enjoying the warm afternoon sun as their conversation teetered to the personal.

"Are you heading back to Florida for the Fourth?" Izzy asked. With Independence Day falling this Thursday, the school had bestowed a four-day weekend on the handlers, and Izzy knew most of the out-of-towners were heading home.

Jen picked at the blades of grass near her feet as she shook her head. "Staying local."

"On campus?" Izzy couldn't help but wonder how deserted the place would be.

"Actually, I'm headed to Rhode Island." She blushed as she said it.

"Good for you," Izzy responded, adding a shoulder bump. Mark lived in Newport.

"What about you? Are you spending the holiday with Sara?"

Jen asked. Her voice held no judgment but Izzy sputtered anyway. "Don't worry, I won't say anything," Jen reassured her, returning Izzy's playful nudge with one of her own.

"Is it that obvious?"

Jen laughed out loud. "You got it bad, honey," she said, swatting Izzy's forearm. "I wouldn't worry, though—by the looks of it, she does too." Her nod was sincere. "I'm happy for you two."

Izzy was about to delve further into how she'd come by her realization but her phone dinged with a text.

Your car is still here. But I can't find you. A sad face followed.

Back training field, she typed. *With Jen.*

I see you.

Izzy turned her head and saw Sara headed their way with a huge wave and an even bigger smile.

"What's this, extra credit?" Sara said, squatting next to Izzy and Jen on the soft grass.

"I'm freaking out we won't pass certifications." Jen nodded toward her dog. "Today was a hot mess."

"Nah." Sara reached up to pet both dogs, who went crazy for her the instant she sat down. "This girl here"—she rubbed Tempe's neck—"she's just like her namesake. Smart and willing, totally perceptive. A little intense." She added a small thoughtful chuckle. "But an absolute sweetheart. Isn't that right, honey?" She rubbed Tempe vigorously, clearly delighting in the dog's exuberance.

"You knew the officer she's named after?" Jen asked.

"Rob Mullen from Tempe, Arizona," Sara declaimed. Izzy wondered at her spirited, particular response. "That's how he introduced himself. To everyone." Sara shook her head smiling, her expression a mix of fondness and sorrow as she added, "Sweet kid." She pulled a ball out of her pocket and threw it far enough for both dogs to get a good rush. "I trained him a few years ago."

"What happened?" Izzy asked, sort of nervous to hear the answer.

"He was in a car accident on patrol."

Izzy heard sadness in Sara's voice and longed to touch her, provide comfort for the loss she clearly still felt.

"It was just one of those fluky things," Sara said without giving any more details. She took the ball back from Tempe and chucked it again. "You're not going to fail certs," Sara said calmly. "You're right about one thing, though." She leaned toward Jen. "You are freaking out." She pointed at Tempe, who was play fighting Chase for the ball. "Look at her. She's fine." She tapped Jen's shin. "You have to remember, everything you feel comes down that leash to her. You're stressed and she can feel it." She nudged Jen with her shoulder. "Be confident. You're a great handler. She's a great dog. This is all in your head. Now, relax." It sounded like an order and Jen seemed relieved to follow it.

Mark sauntered toward them across the field and Sara was the first to acknowledge him, giving a hearty wave. Izzy followed suit, swallowing her smile at the hilarity of their unspoken foursome.

"Ladies," Mark said. Izzy watched him make subtle eye contact with Jen before he looked at her and Sara. "Jen and I were going to grab a bite. Care to join us?"

Izzy was pretty sure he was just being polite. She might not know how Jen could tell she was hot for Sara, but she was pretty sure Jen and Mark wanted to be alone. Taking pity on them, she declined with a scrunch of her nose. "Thanks anyway."

Mark didn't push. He made casual conversation with Izzy as Jen collected Tempe and thanked both her and Sara for the impromptu training and therapy session.

"Not hungry?" Sara asked, her eyes still on Mark, Jen, and Tempe as they made their way across the field.

Izzy hooked Chase's leash with the toe of her boot, giving half a shrug. "More like I didn't want to share you tonight." She looked up into the late-day sun. "I daresay they feel the same."

"Hey." It was one word, but embedded in the subtext Izzy heard so much more. She watched Sara's body language as she looked at Chase, lying down on his side. "He needs a break."

Covering Izzy's hand with hers, Sara added, "I missed you." Sara put on a serious pout. "I barely saw you all day. Let me take you to dinner." She must've sensed Izzy's reluctance because without waiting for a response she added, "Please?"

Glancing down at her clothes, Izzy frowned. The same boring blue uniform as every other day.

"What's wrong?" Sara asked, clearly picking up on her subtle distress.

"Nothing," she huffed out. "I would just like to look nice for you one of these days."

"Izzy." She paused. "You look amazing every single day."

Even though it was a sweet compliment and obviously sincere, Izzy couldn't help rolling her eyes. She flicked her dark blue tee. "It would be great if you saw me out of this uniform for once."

Sara's smile was demure and brazen at the same time and Izzy shook her head at her unintentional double entendre. "That's not what I meant."

"I know." Sara wrapped her arms around her knees and swayed a little on the grass next to her. "I happen to think you look fantastic in uniform, for what it's worth." She touched the back of Izzy's leg discreetly. "Come on. I know a burger spot a few towns over." Izzy felt her hand slip under the cuff of her pants, the touch of one finger caressing the skin at the back of her calf. "We both need to eat. This place is cute and quaint with good food and a ton of privacy." Sara stood and held both hands out to help Izzy up. Pulling her close she whispered, "I don't know how much longer I can wait to kiss you."

Forty-five minutes later, they sat kitty-corner holding hands under a small angled table nursing their iced teas as they waited for their burgers.

"How was DC?" Izzy asked, hoping she'd mastered keeping the envy out of her tone.

"Fine." Sara rubbed her thigh. "How was class? Did I miss anything good?"

"Dave nearly got bit on the hand being the decoy during bite work yesterday."

"I heard." She rubbed her temples. "I swear to God, I don't know how I'm going to survive this."

Izzy laughed. "What does that mean?"

Sara shook her head as she leaned back in her seat. "When John called and told me someone almost took a bite, right away I worried it was you." She brushed her hair off her face. "I don't know how I'm going to deal when you're back on patrol."

Izzy ran her palm along Sara's thigh. "You're going to trust me. And know that I'm smart and careful. I don't take stupid risks." She felt Sara's hand cover hers. "Because I know I have you waiting for me."

"Promise me. No heroics."

Izzy nodded assurance even though she knew it was a guarantee she couldn't keep.

Sara flashed a skeptical look—she saw right through her. "Did you always want to be a cop?" she asked.

"Always." Izzy fingered the edge of her fork. "Do you know about all the cops who died?" she asked, deflecting the focus from herself and reviving their conversation from earlier. "The ones the dogs are named for, I mean. I was thinking about the guy you mentioned earlier."

"Yes," Sara answered. "But Rob I trained, so that was different." She sounded so sad, Izzy worried she'd made a mistake asking, but then Sara smiled. "Chase, of course you know the story there. Jett, that's Gilmartin's dog, he was named after an army pilot who died in Iraq. Sammy is in honor of P.O. Samantha Burns. She was ambushed responding to a domestic. Shot and killed from the second-story window after a woman falsely reported her boyfriend was beating her. So yeah," she nodded, "I guess you could say I make it a point to know the details."

Izzy was impressed and touched by her thoughtfulness. "That's really something."

"The stories are important." Sara was visibly flustered and took a hasty sip of her drink. "The officers, their legacy…it matters."

"Sara." Izzy could tell her question had sent Sara down a path she hadn't intended. "Look at me." Sara turned and Izzy gently touched her panic-stricken face. "I'm not any of those people." Finding her hand, Izzy held it and waited for eye contact, hoping Sara would see just how much she meant to her.

Sara's expression softened, but only slightly. "Don't you ever get scared?"

"At work?" Izzy stopped to think about it. "God, I'm always so busy, there's no time." She chewed her cheek for a second. "Of course, there are moments that are scary." She shrugged. "But most of the time, I'm giving directions. Telling people the difference between the uptown subway and the crosstown shuttle." She squeezed Sara's hand. "Or, you know, delivering Stanford Wilson's granddaughter in the ladies' room in the middle of the night."

"The senator?"

Izzy smiled in confirmation.

"No way." Sara seemed truly shocked and fumbled her drink, recovering when the waitress arrived with their food just then.

Izzy covered her lips with a finger acknowledging the scandal associated with the situation. As soon as they were alone again, she divulged a little.

"I wasn't sure who knew," Izzy said, taking a bite of her turkey burger. Swallowing quickly, she added, "Judging by the look on your face, this is news to you."

"You're serious?"

"You can't say anything. I'm sworn to secrecy." Izzy reached for the ketchup. "And honestly, I can appreciate that." She shook a small amount from the glass bottle. "Wilson's sixteen-year-old daughter left Oklahoma and ended up like a million other teens—in New York City, alone and terrified. I gather she did not tell anyone she was pregnant before she bolted." She dipped a fry and waited for questions.

"You knew who she was?"

"God, no." Izzy held her fry in the air. "I don't follow politics," she added biting the french fry in half. "But she was hysterical and scared and talking a mile a minute. She spilled her story in about thirty seconds." She wiped her hands on a paper napkin. "She kept saying she wanted her mother. But that baby was coming. No doubt about that." Izzy tucked an errant piece of lettuce back under the bun. "I did what I could. And called my boss right away."

"Did you actually deliver the baby?"

"Yes." She held her burger aloft seeking the best spot to attack. "I was the only person there until an emergency services crew arrived and took over." Man, that was a crazy night, thinking about it now. She placed her burger down. "By the way, the people who showed up were not regular EMS. I have no clue who my boss called, or how far up the chain ascended, but...*boom*." She mimicked an explosion with one hand. "Out of nowhere a special team was on the spot. Along with a bunch of dudes in suits. Maybe it was Secret Service," she wondered aloud. "It was some kind of specialty protective detail for sure." She reached for her drink and took a quick sip. "Anyway, after all the commotion died down, the shift commander called me in his office. I mean, he let me get cleaned up first. Then before I knew it, there were a bunch of big shots on-site. They told me I had to keep everything quiet. I suppose due to Wilson's climbing political aspirations and his far-reaching influence." She fingered her straw. "I would never have said anything anyway. To me, it was never about the senator. That poor girl was terrified. Whatever her father's beliefs about out-of-wedlock babies and how something of this nature might affect his constituency, she deserved the decency of respect and privacy. I couldn't care less about her dad." She crunched into her pickle, savoring the taste before taking a second bite.

"Anyway, during the debriefing, someone in the room asked me if there was a special assignment I wanted." Izzy popped another fry. "I thought they were just making small talk." Her tone echoed her ever-present disbelief at the unlikely turn of events. "I said K-9. I didn't think it was, like, a real question."

Sara laughed.

"I'm telling you this," Izzy said, "not because I think it's okay to betray the promise I made to keep my mouth shut." She reached over and touched Sara's hand. "And I know you weren't serious when you made a comment the other day about my brother and my dad being on the job and hooking me up with special assignments. Of course it's not true anyway, but it's always bothered me, knowing you must wonder how I ended up here. I hate worrying that you think I manipulated my way in. Or called in a favor."

She leaned back in her chair all but admitting defeat.

"I mean, I do realize that's what happened. I got into K-9

through connections. That truth isn't lost on me." She itemized the list on her fingers. "The shift commander, Lieutenant Anderson, your ex-girlfriend." She let out a labored breath. "God, it annoys me that she has a role in this." She fisted her hand and let it drop on the table with a small irritated thud.

Sara covered her hand with hers, effectively deflating her slight anger.

"Izzy, you belong here." Sara paused a second, clearly waiting to gauge Izzy's reaction as she spoke. "I didn't know that story," she said. Izzy knew that was the truth—her shock was honest. "John doesn't know. Neither does Nicole," she offered. "You have my word—I won't tell a soul. Out of respect for you and for Clare Wilson." She offered a small wink at Izzy's surprise she knew the senator's daughter by name. "I do follow politics. I know the huge splash this would have made in the news." She laced their fingers together, obviously choosing her words carefully. "Do not ever think you don't deserve to be here, because you absolutely do." Bringing their intertwined hands to her lips, she kissed the back of Izzy's hand delicately. "As far as I'm concerned, Chase and the citizens of New York owe that young lady a huge thank you." Sara's face flooded with color and she looked down at her half-eaten dinner. "Me too, for that matter." Sara's eyes held so much vulnerability that Izzy thought her own heart might explode. "Without her, who knows when I might've found you?"

Izzy was overjoyed but also overwhelmed, and she couldn't find the words to properly echo Sara's emotion without sounding trite.

It didn't matter, because Sara filled the silence, saying, "I'm sorry I took so long to give in to what I was feeling." Sara looked nervous that she was saying too much but continued anyway. "It was stupid. I was...scared, I think."

"You don't have to be scared with me. I feel what you feel." Izzy was serious and she hoped Sara understood what was in her heart.

Their eyes stayed locked for a few seconds, and Izzy thought Sara was about to say something heavy, but the waitress interrupted to see if they needed a refill on their drinks. They declined but the moment was gone, their attention back on the meal in front of them.

"Do you have plans for the Fourth?" Sara asked, bringing the conversation back to the lighter side.

"Just a barbecue at my parents' on Sunday."

"School is closed Thursday and Friday."

Izzy knew the schedule and knew Sara knew that she knew it. Why was she stating the obvious? She could only hope...

"Spend the weekend with me." Sara spun the salt shaker in her hand, looking slightly shy at her spur-of-the-moment invitation. "There's beautiful trails by my house," she said, as if to sell the offer. "Up in the mountains. It's peaceful and quiet. I would love for you to see it."

"Yes."

"Can we go after class tomorrow?" Sara tucked her hair back behind her ear. "I know I said the weekend, but I guess I meant, you know, more than that."

"You are so unbelievably adorable when you're nervous." Izzy touched her hand. "Do you really think I'm saying no to any of this?" She felt her smile blossom as she spoke. "An extended weekend in the country with you sounds amazing." She let her hand drift up Sara's arm, caressing the tiny raised scars scattered along her smooth skin. Acknowledging them openly for the first time, she asked, "These are bites, aren't they?"

"I've been working with dogs a long time," Sara answered with a small shrug. "Occupational hazard."

"Now whose job is dangerous?" Izzy lifted her eyebrows insinuating the answer to her rhetorical question. "You be careful too."

"Trust me, the dogs are—"

Izzy silenced her with one finger over her lips. "Promise me."

"I promise," Sara whispered.

It was small, the moment, but Izzy knew what she was really asking, and in Sara's simple response she heard a commitment to so much more than safety.

Chapter Eighteen

Whatever Izzy was expecting, it wasn't this.

After an hour and a half of highway, Sara steered them through a small quaint town beyond which they picked up a semipaved road, before guiding the pickup onto a secluded gravel path obscured amidst the towering foliage.

A hundred yards down the rough drive, the trees cleared, and in the center of a lush and green manicured lawn stood a contemporary Cape, bright and fresh and amber hued, bearing a modern Lincoln Log exterior, the color and style a bold and welcome contrast against the rich brown bark of the trees surrounding the property.

"Holy smokes, Sara," Izzy said. She looked over and was rewarded with a shy, proud smile. "Your house is beautiful," she added.

"Don't get too excited. You haven't seen the inside," she said, pulling in front of one half of the two-car garage right next to the porch. "I made sure to come up here last night to tidy up," she said, shifting into park. "Hopefully it passes the test."

"I'm sure it's fine."

"Says the woman whose house is always impeccable."

Izzy laughed, but it was true. She was a neat freak through and through. But after stepping inside Sara's home, she concluded that either Sara was a complete exaggerator, or she'd spent all night cleaning. Her home was modest and beautiful with a rustic elegance that reminded Izzy of luxury log cabins she'd seen on TV. Vaulted ceilings and upgraded furnishings complemented the open plan, yet the house still oozed comfort and charm. She couldn't help picturing herself cozied up with Sara on the corner sectional in front of the stone fireplace, a glass of wine in hand, Chase at their feet, the dead of winter, white and picturesque beyond the warm walls.

Chase nudged at her hand, bringing her back into the moment. He'd bounded out of Sara's truck the second they arrived, and even though he clearly wanted to explore, Izzy made him follow her inside.

"I think he needs to go out, Iz," Sara said, observing his behavior.

"I know." She looked at her weekend bag on the floor. "His leash is still in the car. Let me go grab it."

Sara shook her off, padding through the house to open the back door. "He's free to roam," she said matter-of-factly. "My house is his house."

"You're nice," Izzy said, coming up behind her. "I'm more concerned he'll *explore* to one of your neighbor's homes and mark their property too," she said with an eyebrow raise.

"Doubtful," Sara responded. Izzy loved feeling Sara relax into her body as she spoke. "I'm on ten acres, so no neighbors to speak of, really." She patted Izzy's hand under hers. "Come on, let's get unpacked. We can keep an eye on him from upstairs."

Izzy was busy filling a drawer Sara had graciously cleared for her, when an aged photo on the dresser caught her eye. It was a picture of several women with linked arms laughing their heads off. Izzy zoned in on the woman at the end, a mirror image of Sara with slightly darker hair.

"Oh my God, Sara," she said, lifting the frame to examine it closely. "This is your mother." It couldn't be anyone else, but still her voice held a slight question in its tenor.

"It is." Sara came up behind her and looked over her shoulder. "Those are her college roommates," she offered. "I love this picture. She's so young and happy."

"What does it say on her shirt?" Izzy noticed all the girls had big bold letters printed across their chests.

"*Tish*." Sara's voice dripped with emotion—a touch joyful and nostalgic at the same time. "They all went by these silly nicknames. Bunny, Muffy, LaLa. It was something to do with their sorority, I think." She rubbed her fingers along Izzy's arms. "My mother's name was Elizabeth, but to her friends and family, she was Beth."

Izzy heard something in Sara's voice and she turned to face her just to see the expression in her eyes.

"She had this boyfriend in college. Tim. He called her Lizzie-Tish." She let go a small happy laugh. "Aunt Maureen says he was the love of her life. She would have let him call her anything." She placed the picture back in its place on the bureau. "But she absolutely delighted in his pet name for her."

"What happened with them? Your mom and Tim? Do you know?"

Sara's nod was solemn. "He was in a freak accident their senior year. He'd gone home for the weekend to help his dad with a roofing project." She shrugged, seeming to try to understand it herself. "He lost his footing and fell. Died instantly."

"Oh my God, that's terrible."

"I know," she agreed. "My mother never really got over it, I guess."

"Did she talk about him when you were growing up?"

"Not really. Here and there she mentioned her boyfriend from college. My aunt has filled me in over the years."

Izzy swallowed hard, surprisingly affected by a story that was so long in the past. "Do you think…?" She let her voice trail off. "Forget it," she finished with a shake of her head.

"Tell me." Sara's expression was soft and curious. It made her heart melt.

"This is probably stupid." Izzy touched the faded writing on Sara's shirt. "Do you, like, think they're together now? Your mom and Tim? In heaven, or whatever?"

Sara's arms looped behind her and she watched as Sara drew in her bottom lip and worried it with her teeth. "I don't know." She kissed Izzy's forehead. "I'm not sure what I think happens when we die." She nodded toward the picture behind them. "I have entertained that possibility from time to time, though. It's oddly comforting to me." Some spirit came back into her smile. "Wherever they are, I hope they're happy. And if they're together, bonus." She looked over at the window. "Come on, let's go check on our boy and get dinner going."

It had been a long day with an early start, a full day of school, and the formidable drive to Sara's, so they opted to eat in. Izzy opened a bottle of red and poured them each a generous serving. On her way to keep Sara company at the grill where she was in charge of the filet mignon and grilled veggies, she noticed Sara's phone light up with a text from Nicole. She looked right at Chase.

"Wouldn't be a real date if the other woman wasn't checking in." He tilted his head to the side, her sarcasm clearly lost on him. She booped his nose and gifted him one piece of zucchini, proud of his natural even temper. "You're a better person than I am," she said, petting his head as she stuffed Sara's phone in her back pocket.

"Your other girlfriend is looking for you," she said, handing over the wine and Sara's phone, the playful lilt she tried to inject in her tone barely covering her frustration.

Sara reached for her phone but used it to pull Izzy into a kiss before she read the message. Clicking it off without responding, she placed it to the side of the barbecue grill. "She just wanted to make sure I wasn't alone for the holiday." Sara sounded as though it was meant as a thoughtful gesture, but Izzy saw right through it.

"She wants to spend the Fourth of July with you?"

"Stop." Sara turned their steaks delicately with the tongs. "It's not like you're making it sound."

"Come on, Sara." Izzy brought her wine to her lips and took a small sip. "I'm not that naïve," she said, trying to keep the bitterness from her voice. "And neither are you."

Sara looked into the darkening sky as if searching for something. "I'm not like you, Izzy. I don't have this huge family that begs to see me every weekend." Looking into Sara's eyes, Izzy knew she was being sincere. "Nicole checks in on me. Maybe that doesn't make sense to you and I know you think there's something going on there, but you're wrong."

"I believe there isn't anything going on for you," she said.

"And I guess it's considerate that she cares." She pouted a little, dragging her finger down Sara's biceps. "But you have a girlfriend. She should realize I'll take care of you."

Sara looked away quickly, but there was no mistaking her reaction.

Izzy was stunned, and not in a good way. "She doesn't know about me." Without waiting for Sara to explain she said, "Wait a second, forget about me specifically. Does she know you have a girlfriend at all?"

"It hasn't really come up."

"Fuck, Sara. Are you serious?" Izzy turned to head into the house to process her fury in private, but Sara stopped her.

"I'm sorry. I can see you're upset." She lifted their dinner off the grill. "But you're giving it more credit than it deserves."

"Oh, I am?" She didn't even try to mask her anger. "My whole family knows about you. They can't wait to meet you on Sunday, because I talk about you. A lot." She willed her tears to stay put. "Because I care about you. A lot." Her voice quivered with emotion she wished she could tamp down. She grabbed their drinks and headed into the house, hoping to harness a modicum of self-control.

By the time Sara followed a minute later, Izzy had collected herself and solidified her argument. "If Nicole is truly supportive of you and her motives are as pure as you seem to suggest, she should be happy for you." She doled out silverware as she sat down in the sleek wooden kitchen chair as Sara set their dinner in the center of the table. "Especially since you haven't been together in forever."

Sara's wince was subtle, but Izzy caught it anyway.

"Sara?" She picked up her fork, but stopped short of spearing some squash. "How long has it been, exactly?"

"It's been ages since we dated."

Izzy held her breath. "Is there a *but* here?"

"No." Sara's look was only marginally reassuring. "No," she said again, standing upright next to her own chair, her body rigid as she gripped the smooth wooden frame. "In the interest of full disclosure, I should tell you we were together fairly recently. But it didn't mean anything. Not to me or her," she added defensively.

"Together?" she asked. "As in, you slept with her?" She could not believe this. This was not happening. It took every ounce of her restraint to remain calm.

Sara nodded. "Izzy, it was before I knew you. Back in March sometime." She sounded apologetic, even though they both knew it was ridiculous to expect celibacy before they met. "It was nothing," she said sincerely. "But I'm telling you because I would hate for it to come out later and for you to think I kept it from you."

"Why? How?" she asked before retracting the questions with a wave. "Forget it, I don't want to know."

"It was just something that happened." Sara shook her head, giving an answer even though it wasn't required. "I was drunk, a little lonely." Her tone indicated she knew her explanation was hardly a justification, but she looked remorseful nonetheless. "It had been a very long time since I'd been with anyone," she added, seeming embarrassed at the admission.

"But you two are together all the time now." Izzy heard the distress in her tone and she was sure Sara picked up on it.

"I know," Sara said, walking over to Izzy's chair and crouching beside it. "And I miss you terribly when I'm away. You're all I think about." She reached for Izzy's face and held it. "Nicole and I...it's not like that anymore. Honest."

"How can I trust you?"

Sara's slight smile was gorgeous and pure. "Because you can. Because you should. Because you do." She kissed Izzy delicately on the lips. "I would never do anything to betray you."

Without one iota of proof, Izzy believed her. There was something in her eyes that was too genuine to be dishonest, and it relaxed her to see Sara's feelings were real despite the hard truth she'd just revealed. Still, Izzy bristled a little inside, and after dinner was cleared away she suggested making it an early night.

Sara didn't protest at all and Izzy felt certain her anxiety over the topic of conversation showed, but Sara said nothing as she climbed into bed in loose boxer shorts and an oversized tee. Under the covers, they moved around one another carefully, barely touching, and Izzy hated the distance, but ultimately the drama of the evening took its toll and she drifted off to sleep.

Hours later, halfway in slumber, she turned on her side, instinctively slipping her hand around Sara's waist. Sara answered by covering Izzy's hand with hers and backing into her ever so slightly so their bodies aligned. She laced her fingers through Izzy's and squeezed as though she was attempting to convey the entire depth of her emotion through one single touch. Izzy leaned forward and kissed the cotton shoulder of her tee, still half asleep as she released Sara's hand and found her smooth bare abs. She let her hand drift up to her nipples, knowing how hard they would be before she even touched them. Immediately, Izzy flooded with need.

Even shrouded in sleep, Sara seemed to read her perfectly. In the pitch-black room, Sara turned and faced her, her mouth finding Izzy's in a second, covering it and kissing her deeply. Her moans were deep and hungry, and when Izzy felt her tongue along the roof of her mouth, she slid her hands up Sara's soft muscular back and ripped her shirt over her head. She felt Sara kiss her way down her face and neck greedily, pulling her tank top down and sucking her nipple hard between her teeth. Sara momentarily broke their connection but only to remove Izzy's tank altogether, and Izzy couldn't keep from spreading her legs wide beneath her in response.

"I want you," Sara said against her neck.

Izzy squeezed her eyes closed feeling her heart pound. "I'm yours," she whispered in Sara's ear, tipping her hips upward so Sara could remove her panties.

When Sara entered her, Izzy felt her breath catch and she heard Sara gasp audibly, undoubtedly a reaction to her immeasurable wetness. Sara filled her, and even though she couldn't determine if it was one or two or three fingers, her touch was perfect. She throbbed against Sara's hand, and in that very moment, their eyes locked. Even through the darkness, Izzy saw Sara's whole heart revealed in a look that was at once possessive and passionate.

With her orgasm building, Izzy pulled Sara close, digging her fingers into her back and bucking rhythmically beneath her. Her moans were loud when she came, and she did nothing to suppress them, instead allowing herself to fully revel in the pureness of the moment, selflessly given to her by this woman she was completely in love with.

Izzy felt her heart swell as Sara cradled her from behind, kissing her neck gently and breathing in her ear. Sara's voice was so low and husky it was nearly indecipherable. But when Sara held her close and whispered, "I love you," Izzy heard the words distinctly before falling asleep in her arms, praying to the gods above it wasn't all a dream.

❖

"Nope. This is mine. Get your own." Izzy licked peanut butter from a spoon as she exchanged an unrelenting glance with Chase begging at her side.

"You're mean," Sara said, shuffling down the stairs toward Izzy and Chase in the kitchen. She opened up her cabinets but turned around with a frown. "I got nothing for you, big guy," she said with a sincere pout. Leaning over to give Izzy a good morning kiss, she said, "I could make you a real breakfast you know."

"Sorry." Izzy finished up her tablespoon of sugary protein. "I couldn't wait." She licked her lips and wiggled her eyebrows. "You did quite a number on me last night." She placed the spoon down in the basin with a clink. "I woke up ravenous." She watched Sara continue to rummage through the kitchen cabinets and cupboards. "You do remember last night, right?" she said, mostly kidding.

Sara dropped a look on her that told her she was crazy for asking. She stepped right into her space and her kiss lingered. "Of course, I remember," she said. "All of it," she added seriously, making Izzy wonder if she was referencing her sleepy profession of love.

"Praise Jesus," Izzy said, breaking the moment. "Because if I dreamed all that, I'd be seriously concerned for myself."

Sara dropped a kiss on her nose before bending down to check under the sink. "Nope. Nothing."

"What are you looking for?"

"Dog treats." She held her hands up in surrender. "But honestly, now that I think about it, I've never had a dog here. Hence the lack of treats."

"Hear that, Chase? You're the first." Izzy petted his head lovingly. "Why *don't* you have a dog?" she asked. "I mean John has Duncan, Gilmartin has Jett. Hayes and Reyes have dogs. What's the story?"

Sara started to brew some coffee. "I'm sort of between dogs at the moment." She reached for the cream from the fridge. "After Rocco died...He lived a good long time," she added. "After he passed, I fostered a retired explosives dog, Murphy. I didn't have him for very long. He was at the end of his days too, and for some reason his handler couldn't keep him. I forget the circumstance there," she mused.

Izzy laughed outright and Sara questioned her with a single look.

"I'm only laughing because I think it's ironic you can't remember the circumstances surrounding the handler, but I'm a hundred percent sure you know the details of the person the dog was named after."

Sara's smile was telling and sweet. "J.J. Murphy. He was a twenty-two-year-old soldier killed in action in Afghanistan in 2004."

"See?"

Sara answered with a shrug, but she was clearly flattered by Izzy's obvious respect. "Murph was a good boy," she said with a nod. "Served his country well. Both of them, of course."

"But what about now?" Izzy asked. "You're allowed to have one, right? Even though you're not an agent?"

Sara nodded. "Of course. Rocco was a demo dog."

"Oh, right."

Sara reached high for two coffee mugs, setting them on the counter as she spoke. "The dogs don't know the difference between a real situation and practice." The coffeemaker signaled a completed brew cycle. "Actually, I take that back. I think they can sense the difference. They pick up on it from their handlers. What I mean is"— she poured them each coffee—"a dog used primarily to demonstrate tactics is just as valuable as one working in the field." She retrieved some blueberries and ran them under the faucet. "That was a long explanation," she said making fun of herself. "The answer is yes, I am allowed to have a dog," she finished with a laugh.

"So what gives?" Izzy asked, stirring sugar and cream into her coffee.

Sara placed the blueberries on the breakfast bar. "The truth is…" She inched the bowl of berries forward to Izzy. "God, I haven't told anyone this," she said with a small grin.

Izzy covered her hand in support while she waited to hear what Sara had to say.

"I've been thinking about raising a dog all the way up." Sara's gaze shifted to their hands gently touching. "Usually we get the dogs when they're eighteen to twenty-four months old. They already have basic obedience and olfactory training. We hone that, sharpen it, work the handlers, develop teams." She shrugged. "Thing is, I'm certified in all those areas. Obedience, scent imprinting. I'm a nationally recognized expert in training. I get called to testify all the time for cases that go to trial based on canine detection."

Izzy hung on her words, breaking contact only briefly to snag a few berries.

"My point is I would like to do it myself. Get a puppy and start from a truly clean slate." Sara looked adorably nervous and excited all at once. "I guess I've been holding out for the right time. But I suppose that's sort of now."

"Sara, that's amazing." Izzy leaned forward on her stool so she could reach over and hold Sara's face, bringing their lips together for a kiss. "I think it's a perfect idea."

"We'll see," she said. "Whole grain toast okay?" Sara asked, redirecting the conversation. "I figured I'd pack us a nice lunch for later while we're hiking." She rolled out the pantry where the bread was stored. "But we should eat something a little more substantial than blueberries now."

Izzy noticed how quickly Sara took the spotlight off herself. Leaning against the cushioned back of her stool, she mused on Sara's theory.

"You know," Izzy started, "if you got your own dog"—she drew lazy circles on the top of the granite surface—"you could name it."

"I name a lot of the dogs," Sara countered, clearly not seeing where Izzy was going.

"I mean, you could name it something special."

Sara shook her head, apparently still not following.

Izzy waited until Sara'd popped the bread down into the toaster and was giving Izzy her full attention. "If you raised the puppy from the start and it was yours"—she chewed the inside of her cheek, a little nervous over what she was about to suggest—"you could name it for your mom."

Sara's stunned expression revealed it was a possibility she'd never considered.

"Just hear me out," Izzy said. "Your mother was a hero. She gave her life for this country too. Just because she wasn't a cop or a soldier doesn't diminish the sacrifice she made. It might be nice to honor that. That's all I mean."

The toaster popped and Sara grabbed the bread along with some butter and jam. When she returned to the high counter, her face showed a mix of emotions Izzy couldn't quite put her finger on.

"I don't hate the idea," Sara said. "But it only works if the pup's a girl."

"How's that?" Izzy gave her bread a healthy slather of jam. "You manipulate names all the time. A female dog honoring Rob Mullen is called Tempe." She crunched her toast with satisfaction. "Need I say more?"

"Good point."

"What was your mother's full name?"

"Elizabeth Tucker Wright."

"Betty if it's a girl. Tuck if he's a boy." Izzy held up her hands. "Wait." She paused a full dramatic second. "ET," she declared emphatically, doing a celebratory chair dance at her offering. "I'm good at this. ET is gender neutral and it's cute. I like it."

"You're cute," Sara, said coming around the island to kiss her.

"You're going to do this," Izzy said.

"The dog or the name thing?"

"I was talking about getting the dog. The naming is entirely up to you. I was just putting that out there as a suggestion."

Sara turned Izzy in her chair, so they were face to face. "I meant what I said last night, you know." She looked to the ground seeming almost sheepish before she made real eye contact again. "I love you, Iz." She leaned in for a kiss, but Izzy stopped her, holding her face in her hands.

"Thank God," she said with a sigh of relief as she brought their foreheads together. "Because I love you too."

CHAPTER NINETEEN

The afternoon with Izzy's family was pure enjoyment and the perfect ending to their long weekend together. After three amazing days hiking and talking and learning each other's bodies, it was nice to have a down day, full of delicious food and warm welcomes. Sara was enamored of the easy rapport Izzy shared with both of her siblings, watching them alternate between ribbing one another and singing each other's praises. That relationship was topped only by the affectionate moments she was able to observe between Izzy and her grandmother.

"Sorry about all the Spanish," Izzy explained, settling into the front seat of Sara's car as she arranged containers of leftovers on her lap. "I hope it didn't seem rude, but Abuela is really self-conscious about her English. Particularly in front of new people."

"I didn't think it was rude at all." Sara hoped her tone conveyed the warmth she felt all over. "I actually thought it was sexy." She looked over her shoulder to make sure Chase was secured in the second row of the cab before shifting into gear. "How come you don't talk to me in Spanish?"

"Do you speak Spanish?"

"That's hardly the point," Sara said.

Izzy leaned over to swat her thigh, but Sara caught her hand and held it. "In all seriousness, Iz, your family is amazing. They were unbelievably sweet to me."

"They know how important you are," she said, emphasizing her point by using their joined hands to caress Sara's thigh. "Plus, they should be sweet to you because you are incredibly nice to me." Sara watched her gaze out the window at the suburban landscape. "We drove right by Overton to come here. I know full well you could have dropped me off and chilled out at your place there."

"I wanted to come. Your family is important to you." She activated her turn signal to navigate the side streets. "That makes them important to me. Plus, I'll do almost anything for free food." She wiggled her eyebrows.

"Anything, huh?"

Sara shrugged in playful response.

"Well, that's a tempting offer," Izzy countered. "Care to spend the night at my place to test that theory?"

"What is it you think I wouldn't do for you?" Her voice came out more serious than she intended, but in truth there wasn't anything she could think of that fit those parameters, and she wanted Izzy to know it. At the stoplight, she turned to Izzy to study her face and see if there was anything hovering behind her lighthearted insinuation.

Izzy shook her head. "Nothing," she said, matching Sara's tone. "I think I was just trying for one more night together. It stinks knowing that I have to wait until next weekend to be with you."

"I know. But it's only a little while longer. Then class will be over, and my schedule will ease up a bit. The last few weeks of a session are kind of intense. We want to make sure you're all ready for certifications. Plus, I'd like to finish up my final draft of the K-9 program overhaul in the next few days."

Izzy's confused expression signaled she wasn't entirely following, so Sara clarified. "The project I'm working on with Nicole." Her voice almost cracked when she said her name, and Sara hated herself for it.

"Oh, right," Izzy said breezily. "I just didn't make the connection for a second."

"Normally"—she merged left onto the main thoroughfare— "I would stay another night. I love being with you." She reached over and rubbed her thumb over Izzy's hand. "But it's a big week coming up and I still have some prep work to do for the certs. You understand, right?"

"I do." Izzy sounded bummed, but not deeply upset. Her behavior seemed to support her sentiment with a good-bye that lingered on the edge of sweetness without any pressure at all.

❖

The following day Sara resisted the temptation to sit in on morning agility because she knew it was just an excuse to see Izzy's gorgeous smile. Instead she forced herself to be a grown-up, hunkering down in her office and polishing off the final adjustments to her K-9 project pitch.

She was more than a little proud of herself for sticking to the same regimen all week, and by eleven o'clock Thursday morning, she had a completed proposal. She took a moment to consider the day's schedule to figure Izzy's whereabouts when her phone blew up with a string of texts from John:

Izzy got hurt on the obby.

I'm sending her up to the office with Jen.

It doesn't look too serious but I need you to assess if she should go to medical.

A second passed as she tried to process the fact that Izzy had been injured on the obstacle course.

Another ten seconds went by before a fourth message arrived: *Obviously, if she needs to be treated, please transport and stay until she's all set. Thx.*

She answered John with a quick *10-4* and bolted from her desk just in time to see Izzy and Jen walking into the building.

"What happened?" Sara heard the tension in her voice but couldn't do anything to keep it at bay.

"I'm fine," Izzy said, holding a crumpled paper towel to the side of her face.

"She got hit with some debris," Jen explained. "It was the weirdest thing. We were all just watching, when Dave and Remy went by doing the course pretty fast. They looked great actually, but Remy must've kicked something up and sent it flying in the air." Jen nodded at Izzy. "Poor Izzy didn't even know she was cut until I saw the blood streaming down her face."

"See?" Izzy offered defensively. "How bad can it be when I wasn't even aware it happened?"

"Let me see," Sara said, unable to wait as she began her triage right in the corridor. She pulled Izzy's makeshift bandage away. "Did you feel anything when it happened?"

"Like a sting, I guess," she said.

With two fingers Sara tugged gently on either side of the cut to see if any tissue was visible inside the laceration. "Does this hurt?" she asked.

"Not really." Izzy's big brown eyes were sexy and Sara wanted to hug her, to hold her and protect her forever.

"I think it's just a scratch," Sara said, hearing her own voice relax at the news. She turned to Jen. "You can head back to the course," she said. She just wanted to be alone with Izzy. "Tell Dixon it's minor. No medical necessary." Quickly facing Izzy she added, "Unless you want to go to the medical division or to a hospital. It's obviously your decision." She hadn't moved her hand from where it cupped Izzy's arm. "I'll take you. That's not an issue at all."

"Do you have any medical training?" Izzy said flirtatiously.

Sara loved her spirit even in the face of a small setback. "I was a vet tech in my early twenties," she said, sincerely. If Izzy was inviting her to play doctor, well, it was a game for two, right?

"That'll do." Izzy smiled.

"Come on," Sara said, dismissing Jen with a thankful wave before she faced Izzy. "Let's get you cleaned up."

For some bizarre reason, the first aid kit was stored in the kennel area and secretly Sara was happy for the seclusion. With everyone out in the field training, they had a rare few minutes of privacy. She asked for a second recounting of the incident as she washed out the cut and applied antiseptic, placing a square Band-Aid over Izzy's right cheekbone. When she was bandaged up and completely out of harm's way, Sara leaned in and kissed her.

"This is going to be brutal." She took Izzy's hand and put it over her heart. "Do you feel my heart racing?"

Izzy reached up and touched her face. "I'm fine. It's a scratch." With one finger she lifted Sara's chin so their eyes met.

"This time, sure," Sara said, feeling herself getting overwhelmed with fear. "When I got the text from John that you got hurt—"

"Sara." Izzy held her face softly. "I'm okay. Okay?"

Sara slipped her hands around Izzy's waist and pressed her head against Izzy's forehead, rocking them ever so slightly. "Don't ever get hurt again, okay?"

"Deal," she said, but her voice was a husky whisper.

Sara leaned forward to kiss her again when the door opened behind them.

"I heard there was an injury—" Nicole's affected voice slightly preceded her when she entered and even though Sara and Izzy hadn't actually been kissing, they were still very much in each other's space. Nicole's expression was nothing short of utter shock. "I…I'm sorry," she said, stumbling over her words. Looking from them to the silver door handle where her manicured hand still rested, she let out an audible sigh. "Sorry," she said again, her voice regaining its professional tenor. She closed her eyes and added, in a tone that was positively dismissive, "I can honestly say, I did not see this coming."

Sara felt herself begin to sweat as she watched Nicole purse her lips and flash a fake smile.

"I'm going to assume you're okay, Officer Marquez." She took a half step out of the room before turning back. "A word when you're through here, Sara." Her heels echoed the entire way out, and Sara waited until she was sure Nicole was gone before turning to face Izzy.

"Well, that wasn't awesome." Sara felt her shoulders slump, her annoyance at the situation on display. She met Izzy's eyes, expecting the same reaction, but instead what she saw was fury.

"What is going on here?" Izzy's tone was ice-cold and it threw Sara off.

She stuttered, searching for an answer, confused over the turn of events and what Izzy was implying. She didn't have a clue what to say, but her silence was making it worse and she could see Izzy was on the verge of crying.

"God, Sara," Izzy said. "Just tell me what the fuck is going on."

"Nothing." It sounded weak and she regretted her word choice instantly.

"Oh, nothing. Great. Thanks." Izzy pressed her temples and Sara reached out to comfort her. "Don't." Izzy pulled back and turned away.

"Izzy, why are you so upset? I know it kind of sucks that Nicole saw us. More for me than you, to be honest."

Izzy whipped around. "You don't even get it." Her eyes were red and glassy and full of so much pain.

"Explain it to me, then." She was pleading, but Izzy stepped past her to the door. "Wait," Sara said. "Please. Talk to me."

Izzy stopped and started a few times before giving in. "We have different boundaries, you and me." She let out a long sigh and her chin trembled. It broke Sara's heart to see her insecurity. "I'm not friends with any of my exes. But you are, and that is something I have to adjust to." She looked up at the fluorescent lights. "Nicole is your ex, and your friend, and your boss. Which is…well, it's honestly a lot for me to understand. But I've been trying." She let her face fall into her hands for a moment before she made eye contact again. "But she is also still into you. I don't know how you don't see it. Or maybe you do." Her shrug made it seem like she'd given up.

"Izzy—"

"Sara, you're the one she calls when she's locked out, you're the one she wants to spend holidays with, she's either up here or you're in DC working on her project. I mean, come on."

"It's not like that," she said, but she heard the doubt in her own voice.

"Isn't it, though?" Izzy wiped a stream of tears away. "I hate that I'm saying this."

"So don't." Sara's voice cracked. "Don't say it."

"I have to."

"We can figure this out." She reached for Izzy's hand and held it.

"I know you care about me." Izzy squeezed her hand and Sara felt her throat tighten. "The fact that Nicole has no idea about us, it says a lot." Sara fought back tears as Izzy continued. "Forget that it's me. I can understand you not wanting to tell her you're with someone from the class. But she thinks you're single. Available. I can't make sense of that. Especially after last weekend."

"Iz, I just haven't talked to her yet. I didn't even know she was here."

Izzy's defeated smile told her it didn't matter. The damage was done. "I have to go. I have to get Chase. And go home." She fought hard to swallow a sob and it made Sara's heart bottom out.

"But wait." Sara tipped her head down and a tear fell on the toe of her boot. "What are you saying?"

Izzy dropped her hand and stepped to the door. "I tried really hard to be patient. I have nothing left." Her beautiful face twisted into a knot of agony. "I can't just stand by while you try to figure out what you want. I'm sorry, Sara."

She didn't wait for an answer and Sara didn't have one anyway. She stood completely still, paralyzed by the weight of what was happening as she heard the squeak of Izzy's boots echo down the hallway.

Almost on autopilot, Sara walked out of the facility and into the woods of Arren's Hollow, thoughts of Izzy and Chase and Nicole fighting for space in her brain. She picked up her pace and raced to her favorite boulder, hoisting herself on it as the sun broke through the trees. She was exhausted and crying. She lay back on the warm surface, letting the golden rays touch her face. She wanted to erase the last hour, to make everything better. She was suddenly overwhelmed with the memory of sitting in this very spot with Izzy, weeks ago. Why hadn't she told Nicole about them? It seemed crazy now. Was Izzy right? Was she hedging her bets?

She shook away the thought because it wasn't true. She wanted Izzy. In this moment, she knew it with absolute clarity. She popped up and wiped her tears away, determined to make things right. But by the time Sara walked back to the classroom area, the building was deserted. A quick glance at the practice field reminded her that class had been dismissed for the day. The school routine was the same as it had been in years past. With certifications beginning on Monday, there was no curriculum left to cover. Like always, John had let everyone go early and designated Friday as an optional training day.

She rubbed her face, searching for the way to make things right. She needed to call Izzy, to talk everything through. But as she pulled out her phone, it hit her. There was something else she needed to do first.

❖

"What's with the surprise visit?" Sara stood in the door frame of the dimly lit guest office located in the very back of the building, where Nicole always worked when she was in town.

"I didn't realize I was required to announce my schedule," Nicole answered, not bothering to look up as she pored over her work.

"I just think it's odd." Sara folded her arms across her chest defensively. "We talk all the time. Now all of a sudden, you don't even tell me you'll be here?"

Nicole didn't lift her eyes from the spreadsheet she was studying. "I hardly thought it mattered much." She reached for a fancy pen, sliding it open with a click. "Although my unanswered texts do make more sense now," she added, applying a dramatic signature before giving Sara her attention.

Sara's answer was a shrug, and she knew it didn't suffice, but even though this conversation was a necessity, she was at a loss for words.

"That's it, a shrug?"

"What do you want me to say, Nic?"

"You could have told me you were seeing someone," Nicole responded coolly. "I thought…" She shook her head, seeming genuinely puzzled. "Why didn't you tell me?"

Sara was stunned. "Do we tell each other when we're seeing people now?" Her response was sharper than she intended, but she knew for a fact Nicole had dated other people over the years, and they had never spoken of it.

"I'm not seeing anyone," Nicole barked. "I am busy reorganizing my entire life to be with you."

Sara stepped into the office and shut the door. "Do not make this about me. That's not fair."

"It is about you." Nicole stood up and turned slightly, almost seeming unsure where to go. She swept back her silky red hair with both hands, letting it fall against her shoulders. "What do you think I've been doing here?"

"Honestly, Nicole"—Sara lifted both palms high in frustration—"I have no idea. Are you transferring back to New York?"

"Of course I am."

"And it didn't occur to you that I might be interested in that tiny detail?"

"I thought you knew."

"How? How would I know?"

Nicole looked at the ceiling and let out a somewhat labored breath. "Everybody knows. Come on, Sara. You knew."

"I heard rumors, that's it. You never said a word."

"I couldn't say anything." Nicole's voice matched Sara's frustration as she leaned against the back wall. "Until it was set in stone." Her tone softened. "I didn't want to jinx it."

Sara couldn't believe this was happening. "And is it?"

Nicole answered with a nod. "I came here to tell you in person. I was waiting until I could tell you everything." She looked down, seeming dismayed as she smoothed out her sleek dress pants. "I had hoped we would make some arrangements to see each other last weekend, but you never got back to me, so I delayed my trip until today. Again, I was hoping for a weekend to celebrate together."

Their gazes locked, and for the first time in ages, Sara saw absolute vulnerability behind Nicole's piercing green eyes.

"Nicole," she started, but without anything else to say, her name hung between them.

Nicole came around from behind her desk and her voice was soft when she said, "Why didn't you tell me about her?"

"Come on, Nic. Over the years…be honest. We don't talk about that stuff." Sara felt herself letting out a long, slow breath as she found her civility. "I know for a fact you were dating the Special Agent in Charge of the FBI Denver office for almost two years, and you never once mentioned it." She shrugged. "At least not to me directly."

"There have been other people for you too," Nicole said, as though that justified her silence on the subject.

Sara nodded. "You're right. I dated some, here and there. There's been no one serious, which I expect you know." She shook her head. "My point is we don't really share this stuff with one another. I'm not sure I even understand why," she said, her voice revealing the truth of her uncertainty.

"Because of this." Nicole slowly waved one finger between them, her face serene and sexy. "Us," she said. In the dim light, she seemed hopelessly exposed, unguarded and beautifully bare in her candor. "It always comes back to us."

"Nicole, you've been gone for so long." Her voice was pleading but she didn't really know why. She was happy with Izzy.

"I know." Nicole focused on her heels as she took a step forward. "You're right." She reached for Sara's hand. "But then…March," she said, looking right into Sara's eyes as she referenced their one night together. "You were there. You know what happened."

In all the time that passed since then—the texts, emails, phone calls, and one on one interactions just like this—they'd never once broached the subject of their encounter on that snowy night in March. Sara was stunned.

"God, we never even talked about it," she huffed.

"Because we didn't need to," Nicole responded. She must've read Sara's disbelief because she pressed on. "Sara, after all these years, you need me to tell you how I feel?" She squeezed Sara's hand ever so slightly. "I love you. I always have." She rubbed her thumb over Sara's hand. "And now, finally, the timing is working out."

"Your timing. It's always on your timeline."

"My career is important to me, yes. But don't put this all on me.

I wanted you to come with me when I moved. You stayed here for a dog. Think for a second how that feels."

"I stayed for my job, which I happen to love, and for the only family I've ever really known." Sara waved her arm toward the facility beyond the office walls, making it clear she meant John and the staff, but her dogs too. "You knew what this place meant to me. You left anyway."

"You're right," she said, seeming uncharacteristically embarrassed by the truth. "I wish I had done things differently, although I suppose I only realize that now, after the fact." She was quiet when she turned around to straighten some papers on the desk, and Sara thought she might be nervous. A second passed.

"Whatever the reasons, we waited a long time for this moment. You and me back in the same place again. I'd like to give it a real shot." Nicole looked right at her. "If you're willing."

Sara was blown away by the assumption inherent in Nicole's tone. "I have a girlfriend. Did you miss that?"

"Hard to," she said with a pained smile as she ticked her head in the direction of the kennel area. "I did see the display."

"Yeah, that was…" She was unsure how to explain her atypical public show of affection with Izzy. "Nicole," she started, but Nicole cut her off with a wave of her hand.

"Sara, whatever you have with this girl"—she shook her head dismissively—"it's fine. I understand you have needs, desires. We all do." She averted her eyes glancing at the far wall. "I don't hold it against you for not waiting for me or believing I was coming back to you."

"Christ, Nicole." Sara's voice hit an octave she didn't know she had in her. "I did believe it." She felt the tears starting to build and she hated the thought of letting Nicole see her cry. "For years I waited for you." She tried to keep from yelling. "Years of hoping and waiting and watching you take promotion after promotion with no sign of slowing down."

"I did that for us. For this." Her voice equaled Sara's in both emotion and volume before she stepped away, clearly attempting to regain her composure. "I'm sorry for raising my voice," she said. "I just meant I kept moving up and taking those assignments so that I could have this—the opportunity to write my own ticket. Finally, I'm able to work from anywhere." She let out a long sigh, seeming to release the tension from her entire being. "It would be a shame to waste it because you're swept up in something that's obviously fleeting."

"Excuse me?"

"Oh, come on, Sara." A small snicker escaped her. "How old is she, twenty-five?"

"She's twenty-seven," Sara responded sharply, not sure what age had to do with anything.

"Twenty-five, twenty-seven, same thing," Nicole paused. "In a year she'll take the sergeant's exam. Then lieutenant. Captain, after that. There's no telling how high she'll go. She's a very capable officer and a smart woman." Sara's surprise at the praise must have been written all over her face, because Nicole answered her unspoken question. "I don't endorse just anyone without doing some research of my own."

While Sara reflected on her words, Nicole continued, "My point is, her career is just starting." Her voice was soft and gentle. "We're beyond that." Nicole stepped forward, reaching for her hand again and rubbing it smoothly. "We're ready to settle down and have the future we used to talk about. Sara, I know I must still mean something to you."

In her eyes, Sara saw real emotion, and her heart ached a little. "It's not that simple, Nic. I care about her. A lot."

"Enough to toss aside everything we've sacrificed for?"

Sara didn't even hesitate. "I love her."

Nicole laughed. "I'm sure it seems like love. It always does when everything is new and exciting. But Sara—"

"You're wrong." She registered the look of surprise on Nicole's face at her proclamation. With a shrug she added, "I don't know, maybe you're right and I'm falling prey to the newness and the excitement. But I don't think that's it." She shook her head. "She's all I think about. She has been, for months. Since I met her, really. I tried to talk myself out of it, God, did I try." She almost laughed as she considered the wasted energy. "And yes, she'll probably go for promotions. Why shouldn't she?" She didn't bother to keep her pride in check. "She's a great handler and a great cop. I'll support her every step of the way."

"Ouch."

Sara hated that it sounded like a competition of her past and present feelings and she tried to massage it. "I just mean…I don't know. I want to be with her. Whatever it takes."

"I think you're rushing into things." Nicole folded her arms over her chest. "And in time I think you'll realize this was a mistake."

"Maybe." Sara nodded, even though she didn't agree. It hardly seemed worth arguing over. Not now, when she was finally sure what she wanted. "I should go," she said, turning to leave, but her voice was a whisper and she didn't even wait to hear Nicole's response.

CHAPTER TWENTY

As she walked to her office, Sara contemplated hopping in her truck and heading right to Izzy's house to talk face-to-face. But what if she hadn't gone home? Or worse, what if she didn't want to see her? Her heart told her that wasn't the case, but she decided to play it safe.

Her hands were shaking a little as she scrolled through her phone and selected Izzy's name from her list of favorites. Four rings before it went to voice mail. That was a terrible sign. She ended the call without leaving a message, packed up her things, and headed to her room, resigned to sit it out and wait in her dorm room.

When another hour passed with no word, she tried again.

"Hey." Izzy's voice was hollow and it made Sara's heart sink.

"Hi." Fueled with hope and anticipation, Sara's response was overly upbeat, and she tried desperately to find the right tone even though she had no clue what it was. "I was hoping we could talk."

"I don't think there's anything left to say." Sara heard the sound of water running and dishes clanking in the background.

"How is your face?" she asked, suddenly remembering the morning's injury.

"It's fine. I'm fine."

"Can I come see you?" she blurted out. There was a long moment of silence and Sara couldn't take it. "Please?" she begged.

"Sara."

Sara heard the faucet shut off and she pictured Izzy standing in her kitchen, still in her training gear, Chase close by. She hated that Izzy didn't immediately say yes, echo her need for contact, encourage her to come over, have dinner, spend the night making everything right between them.

"Did you see Nicole?" Izzy asked.

"Yes," she answered honestly. "But it's not what you think."

"I don't even know what I think," she said.

"Izzy—"

"I don't think you know what you want, Sara. When you're with me, honestly, it feels like you're with me. But then Nicole shows up, and I don't know, she has this hold on you. I don't know what to do about that."

"You're right," Sara said. "I don't know that I've ever thought of it that way. But you're right." She weighed the truth of Izzy's words for a split second before coming clean. "I was scared." She hated that it sounded like a pathetic excuse. "The truth is, I've known Nicole, God, for years. She's more than a friend—she's kind of family in a bizarre way. I didn't want to lose that." She sighed, realizing how selfish she'd been. "She's been a constant in my life, in some form or another, forever, it seems." Izzy was completely quiet so she continued. "But then today, when I realized I'd maybe lost you, I don't know, that scared me more. Way more."

"Sara, I just can't spend my life competing for your attention. I want more than that. I deserve more."

"You do, Izzy. I am so sorry I made you feel that it was ever like that. You're who I want. You. I told Nicole that."

"You did?"

"Yes. Just now. I know that doesn't excuse my behavior to this point."

"What did she say?"

Sara paused, wondering how much she should reveal.

"Be honest with me." Izzy had read her silence.

"She's moving back to New York. Nicole's new assignment comes with the option of working from Overton."

"She's moving here for you, isn't she?"

"It doesn't matter, Izzy. I don't want to be with Nicole."

"I knew it."

Sara heard the sadness in Izzy's voice and she wanted to see her, to hold her, to kiss the pain away. To show her where her heart was. "Please let me come there. I need to see you."

"Let's just…" Izzy paused, and Sara felt her heart stop, waiting for her to finish. "Let's just take some time, okay? I'm not in a good place and certifications are next week. I need to get my head on straight."

"Are you coming to class tomorrow?" Sara heard desperation in her tone, but she continued anyway. "It's not mandatory, but we'll be doing some light drills, overview, stuff like that," she said, hoping to sell it.

"No." Izzy's tone said there was no room for negotiation. "I don't think that's a good idea."

Sara wondered if her disappointment could be felt through the phone because Izzy stuttered a little before she spoke again.

"It's not that I don't want to see you. In a way the opposite's true. But I'll see you and I'll forgive you. Immediately. Because I want to be with you. You know that. But I think right now we could both use some distance. To think, and process, and not act purely out of emotion. I know even being near you will make me feel better. It's just, God, I know this is babyish." Izzy paused but clearly wanted to say more, so Sara waited.

"Nicole will be there. Right next to you, like she always is. I know, I know, it's her job," she piped out, obviously frustrated as she exhaled a sound that was half sigh, half groan. "But I can't handle seeing that right now. I think it's better for me if I just avoid that situation altogether."

"I understand." Sara knew it wasn't fair to push, even though she was devastated.

"I have to go," Izzy said, filling the short silence. "We'll talk over the weekend." Sara heard Izzy's voice break before she ended the call with a click, leaving her absolutely no choice in the matter.

❖

Izzy spent the bulk of Saturday in her yard with Chase working on basic commands mixed with some hide-and-seek challenges using his favorite toys. It kept her mind occupied and it forced her to stay in the present. For the last two days, her mind had been in overdrive and she'd barely slept at all. A hundred times she almost caved and called Sara. But she believed in her suggestion to have time apart to separately assess their feelings, didn't she?

Still, she was dying for contact, wondering if Sara missed her or if she'd talked to Nicole again. The thought crept in unwittingly, followed by an even more harrowing fear that perhaps in asking for space, she'd given Sara the gateway to work things out with her ex. She felt nauseous even considering such an outcome. Fighting back her sorrow, she hooked Chase onto his leash, determined that a long hike in Daley Park would burn off the remainder of her dog's energy and settle her own anxiety.

It was a glorious day but the woods did nothing to alleviate her stress. Everything reminded her of Sara. The beautiful blue sky, the lush forest, the rustic trails. Less than half a mile in, she turned around.

"Come on, buddy. Let's go home." Chase followed without protest. "I have to call her," she said. "Even though I don't have a clue what to say."

Chase loped along, seeming to commiserate. He'd barely left her side all weekend.

"It'll be okay," she said, hoping it was the truth.

As if Chase sensed her urgency, he pulled ahead on the leash, and as soon as Izzy could see the edge of her property, she unhooked the lead and let him run free.

She watched him gallop across the yard and race up the steps of the back porch. Her jaw fell open and she couldn't help but smile as Chase pranced in a circle around Sara, who was waiting on the deck.

Even from the distance she could feel the pureness of Sara's actions when she dropped to her knees and rubbed his head and shoulders and back. Izzy felt her heart pound, her body brimming with love and longing as she resisted the urge to run right into her arms.

"I couldn't stay away any longer." Sara stood when Izzy reached the stairs. "I hope it's okay I'm here." She held out her hand and Izzy took it, letting Sara pull her close. "I just missed you."

Izzy sank into the embrace, holding Sara tight, the feel of their bodies together erasing every last doubt she had. Sara wanted her, she knew it. She could feel it. Without a word, she tilted her head up and Sara found her lips. "I love you so much, Izzy." Her voice was desperate between soft kisses. "I can't lose you."

Izzy's kisses were needy in response and, to her surprise, coupled with tears. She felt Sara's fingertips wiping them away, her lips tracing their tracks.

"Please don't cry. I'm so sorry. For everything," she whispered. "It's you I want." Sara leaned back, her eyes meeting Izzy's. "I can work anywhere. I'll get another job if I have to. I don't need to work at Overton."

"Stop." Izzy put one finger over Sara's lips. "Stop." She touched Sara's neck and guided her head down so their foreheads rested together. "I'm glad you're here. I missed you too."

"I was an idiot."

Izzy smiled. "No." A slight laugh escaped her. "I just needed to know this was real for you. Because it is very real for me."

"It is, Izzy. I'll do anything for you. Including leaving Overton—"

"Stop with that." Izzy shook her head. "No one's leaving anything." She kissed Sara before letting her head rest against Sara's chest, delighting in the feel of Sara's arms around her waist. Taking a deep breath, she exhaled with a sigh. They could make everything right. "You love your job," Izzy said calmly. She picked her head up and looked right at Sara. "And I love you." She wiped at her damp cheeks. "And I trust you." Leaning forward, her kiss was delicate and sweet but filled with desire, as she hoped all the love in her heart would be transferred through her actions. She cupped Sara's beautiful face. "We'll make it work. Okay?"

She watched Sara nod slowly, her expression matching Izzy's feelings exactly. In that moment Izzy wondered if there was anything they couldn't overcome. She hooked her arm through Sara's and guided them the few steps to the back door. Chase angled for the lead.

"Nobody forgot about you, big guy," Izzy teased. She touched his head with her free hand. "I'm going to get you a drink," she said to Chase. "And you too, if you want." She squeezed Sara's hand. "But I have to get in the shower. My family will be here in a little bit." At Sara's confused look, Izzy reminded her. "My dad's birthday. Everyone's coming over for dinner. Please stay." Her voice was all hope and Sara smiled.

Forty-five minutes later, Izzy pulled her hair up off her face as she walked into the living room. "Will you help me hang these decorations?"

"Of course." Sara gave Chase one last win at tug-of-war before she stood from the couch.

"Hey, did I miss anything important at school yesterday?"

"No," Sara said as she took the birthday banner and held it high. "The day was completely routine. You missed nothing. We did go over what to expect in certifications," she said offhandedly.

Izzy handed Sara tape. "Can I get a recap? Being in love with the lead instructor has to have some benefit," she teased.

"You're lucky you're cute. The test will comprise an outside area search, a room search, and package identification employing both high and low explosives. Nine out of ten finds must be correctly located for a passing score of ninety percent. Teams will be graded on the dog's ability to identify the contraband and the handler's skill at recognizing the behavior. You're going to ace it." Sara winked.

"You think so?" she asked raising her eyebrows hopefully.

"Absolutely." Sara let out a heavy breath. "I don't know any of the judges this time around," she said. "Not that it matters."

"What do you mean?"

"Judging is always done by an outside panel of three nationally certified officials. But there's rules. None of them can be affiliated with the host agency—DHS, in this case—or any of the participating handlers' agencies. But still, it's kind of a circuit. I judge for other agencies all the time. Usually I know at least one or two of the people that do ours, just because I've worked with them over time."

"Can I just say something?" Izzy said, unable to keep the spirit from her voice.

"Of course. What is it?"

"I'm so happy Nicole can't judge me." She broke into a little happy dance.

"What?" Sara said laughing along with her.

"Don't get me wrong, I'm sure she's judging me right now." She shrugged happily. "Particularly after seeing us the other day." She reached her arms around and hugged Sara from behind. "I'm just thrilled she can't fail me on Monday." She planted a kiss on her shoulder blade. "I was concerned, to be honest."

"Stop," Sara said, but her voice was a little too intense. "You're going to get a hundred. You know it." She turned and squeezed Izzy closer. "I know it too. Plus, Nicole's not even certified in K-9 and she wouldn't do that, even if she was."

"Grrr." Izzy faked annoyance. "Don't ruin my moment by rushing to her defense." She was mostly playing and she placed a frisky kiss on Sara's lips so she would know. "Just let me enjoy my moment of bliss."

"Yes. Absolutely." Sara leaned in close, and Izzy felt her warm breath as she nuzzled her neck. "I love you," Sara whispered softly in her ear.

"You better." Izzy was teasing, but she knew it was true.

As they finished adorning the house with festive birthday balloons, Izzy could barely keep her hands off Sara. What started as small touches quickly escalated, and soon she was straddling Sara on the living room couch.

"We have to stop," she said through a ragged breath. "My parents will be here any minute."

"I know, I know. You're right," Sara grumbled, her lips dancing across the exposed skin along Izzy's collarbone.

Izzy smiled, her fingertips gently scratching against Sara's scalp as she lifted her face to plant an expressive kiss on Sara's lips.

"Later," she said as she hopped up, holding her hands out for Sara to follow her lead. "I promise to make it worth the wait."

❖

"You cleaned up without me." Sara bent down to unclip Chase's leash as she glanced around Izzy's kitchen.

"Of course. You took Chase out. That's only fair."

Sara thought she got the better end of that trade-off.

"There was hardly anything to do," Izzy said, crossing the room to give her dog a nice rub on the head. "I owe you anyway." Sara's face must've shown her confusion at Izzy's statement because Izzy elaborated, "I know it was a long week. And a challenging day." She ran her hand up the center of Sara's back, and Sara felt the touch warming her everywhere. "I love my family. But they are not easy. They grilled you about your job and your family." Izzy kissed her shoulder. "You were an absolute sport. And now you shall be rewarded."

"What?" Sara managed to huff out a laugh with her question, but Izzy didn't respond. She simply took her by the hand and guided her into the candlelit bedroom, the duvet drawn down. "What's all this?" Sara asked. When Izzy answered with a shake of her head, Sara leaned forward to kiss her.

Izzy stopped her. "Tonight, we take our time," she said. Holding up a small tube of massage oil, she looked positively naughty. She slipped off her robe to reveal black lace panties and a matching bra. Sara felt Izzy tug at the hem of her shirt. "Your day, your week..." Sara saw heat in Izzy's eyes as she shook her head back and forth. "I want you to relax. Is that okay?"

Sara was simultaneously touched and turned on. "Izzy." She worried her lip and reached for Izzy's hand. "I just want to be with you."

"And you will." Izzy's smile was sweet and sexy as she guided Sara toward the bed. "Lie down."

Sara listened to the gentle instruction, slipping out of her clothes and between the cool sheets. Her heart pounded when she registered the silky skin of Izzy's thighs straddling her own bare bottom. She felt herself struggling with the urge to flip over and take control, marking Izzy as hers with her mouth, her hands, her heart. But even as she contemplated it, Sara got lost in the feel of Izzy's soft, delicate palms smoothing along her back, between her shoulder blades, and up to the muscles at the base of her neck.

"Oh my God, that feels amazing," she said, restraining herself from moaning under Izzy's touch.

Izzy's hands worked into the most tender areas of her back and Sara couldn't help but wonder how she knew so perfectly where to go.

"Your back is super tight," Izzy said. "I know you had a tense week." She leaned forward to whisper in her ear, and Sara felt her full breasts pressing against her skin. "I feel partially responsible for that."

"Why?" Her voice was muffled by the pillow but her surprise came through.

Izzy sat upright, concentrating on the middle of her back as she spoke. "I know I overreacted the other day." She paused briefly. "When Nicole saw us," she added, some anxiety present in her voice.

Sara hated hearing Izzy blame herself for any part of what had happened with Nicole. Propping up on her elbows, she maneuvered herself so she could turn around without knocking Izzy off. Sara saw a lovely smile spread across Izzy's face as she held her hips in place and settled against the mattress beneath her as she cozied in. She waited for Izzy's stare to reach her eyes.

"Izzy, you didn't overreact." She reached for Izzy's hands and held them. "Honestly. I would have felt the same way if the situation was reversed." She let out a long breath as she considered what to say. "I don't want to talk about Nicole," she said, registering the truth of her words as they came out.

Izzy leaned all the way forward. "Good." When they kissed, Sara felt Izzy's soft tongue fill her mouth, and she moaned gently in response. "I'm not done with your massage yet," Izzy crooned in her ear.

Sara's protest came in the form of a pathetic groan. She was wet and more than ready and didn't know how much more foreplay she could endure. Plus in the forty-eight hours that had elapsed since she'd met with Nicole, one thing had emerged with crystal clarity. It wasn't Nicole she wanted. It was Izzy she thought about nonstop. It was Izzy she hoped for a future with, regardless of how uncertain it might be. She'd known it from the second she'd seen Izzy step out of her cruiser all those months ago, and her desire had only grown over time. The realization made her yearn for Izzy desperately and she didn't want to wait one more second. Sara reached forward, intending to pull Izzy into another long kiss, but Izzy resisted, offering only a smile at the plea as she squeezed more oil into her hands.

"Tell me about graduation," she said, applying slight pressure to the front and top of Sara's shoulders.

"It's...nice," Sara responded, trying to keep her focus as she moved her hips slightly against Izzy's center. "It'll be outside if the weather's good. By the training field. They set up—" Her voice hitched when the center of Izzy's palm brushed her nipples. "You are killing me. You know that."

Izzy laughed. "A little patience, Sara." She licked her full lips carefully, a move Sara was sure was on purpose. "What's the rush?"

Sara whimpered, equally appreciative and frustrated.

"You were saying?" Izzy egged her on.

"I don't even remember." Sara pressed Izzy's hips down as she moved against her deliberately. "What was I saying?"

"You were telling me about Friday's graduation."

Sara couldn't hold in her smirk. "Right. That." Izzy moved off her torso and kneaded her thigh muscles, working all the way down her legs. Seeing she wasn't going to win the battle for control, Sara gave in. She hooked her hands behind her head and relished every second of Izzy's hands massaging her body. "This whole week will be nice and light," she said. "After certifications, which you will ace..." Her voice faded into a sigh as Izzy worked out a spasm in her calf before walking her fingers up her thigh. Her muscles melted into pliable putty under Izzy's touch. Sara couldn't control it when her voice dripped with delighted pleasure. "How do you do that?"

Izzy just smiled and dropped a kiss on her kneecap in response.

Sara shook her head, trying to remember the conversation. "Right, school," she said, trying to concentrate on talking. "After certification finishes, probably Wednesday afternoon, we'll spend the rest of the time just having fun." She heard her voice lift and wondered if it was due to the stress physically leaving her body, the finality of the class session drawing to a close, or the fact that her half-naked girlfriend was inches away. Likely it was the glorious combination of all three. "We always reserve a full four days for certifications, just in case there are any issues or makeups needed, even though there rarely are. In that extra day and a half we'll just do fun stuff. Play drills, have a cookout. It's a good time." She felt Izzy spread her legs wide apart and move between them, and she tried to control her voice. "Do you...I mean...do you want me to move?"

Izzy smiled impishly as she shook her head. "I want you to relax."

She felt the tips of Izzy's oiled fingers gently moving between her thighs as Izzy massaged her gently, the pressure barely there. Her stomach quivered.

"Easy, babe." Izzy placed one hand on her abs and leaned forward to place soft kisses over her belly.

Sara was ready to burst, but she resisted her desire to dominate the situation, instead allowing Izzy to build her up. At the precise moment she thought she wouldn't be able to take one more second, she felt Izzy's tongue on her, at once soft and demanding.

Izzy moaned into her and Sara's breath caught. She wanted to give herself over immediately, but at the same time she wanted this incredible feeling to last forever. It hardly mattered. Under Izzy's touch, her body had a mind of its own, and before she knew it, beyond her control, she bucked wildly, a series of uncharacteristic moans loudly escaping as her orgasm was suddenly upon her.

Several long seconds passed before she was able to talk. "Izzy, that was…" She shook her head, unable to muster adequate praise to match her sentiment.

"Shh." Izzy placed sweet kisses on her chest and neck as she slipped to her side and held her close. "Go to sleep," Izzy whispered, but Sara barely heard it. She was already halfway there, her hand over Izzy's, her back to Izzy's front, their breath rhythmically keeping time as she drifted off, feeling one hundred percent, completely surrounded in love.

CHAPTER TWENTY-ONE

C an we spend the weekend at my place in Phoenicia after graduation?" Sara was packing her bag, reluctant to go back to campus.

Izzy looped her arms around her waist. "On Friday?"

Sara dropped a kiss on her nose. "I know your regular days off will change once you go back on patrol. I'm assuming you don't have every weekend off." It was sort of a question, since she was curious about Izzy's rotating shifts. "I guess I just figured we could take advantage while you're still on a training schedule."

Izzy smiled. "It does fluctuate a lot." She traced the faded wording on Sara's worn tee. "As for next weekend, I know my parents want to do dinner Friday night. As a kind of celebration." She frowned. "I'm sorry. I know they're a lot."

Sara shook her off emphatically. "Stop. I love them. You know that."

"We could go Saturday," Izzy offered. "Or even drive up late Friday night. Would that be okay?"

Sara nodded. In her back pocket she felt her phone buzz but ignored it. "It's nice being there with you."

"It's gorgeous there. Let's count on it." She patted Sara's bottom playfully. "You can check your phone, you know." She doled out another good-natured smack. "Even though we both know who it is." Sara laughed at her eye roll and winced when the caller ID confirmed Izzy's presumption.

"I knew it," Izzy said backing into the kitchen. "Wouldn't be the weekend if she didn't call."

Sara read the text quickly, following Izzy's path. "Hey, Iz," she started. Sara wasn't sure if it was the gravity in her tone or the look on her face but she noticed Izzy stiffen as she spoke.

"What is it?" Izzy asked.

"Nothing." Sara took a step toward her, hoping her closeness would relax Izzy. "She just had a question about funding. For the K-9 program reboot." She slid her phone back into her jeans. "I can recuse myself from that project, you know."

"That's not necessary." Izzy sighed. "Just promise to talk to me. Okay?"

"Always." Sara closed the distance between them. They'd spent the last twenty-four hours talking about everything. Baring their souls to one another by providing missing details from their pasts, but more importantly jointly planning dreams of their future. Sara knew what she wanted and it seemed Izzy did too. And when they were together, talking and touching, everything was better than okay. It was perfect. "I wish I didn't have to go," she said.

"You could stay." Izzy ran her finger over Sara's lips, down her chin, barely grazing the skin on her neck. She felt it everywhere.

"No, I can't." Sara smiled. "And this is exactly why." She reached for Izzy's hand and brought it to her mouth, kissing the tips of her fingers one by one. "Certification starts tomorrow and you need to be well rested. We both know there'll be very little sleep if I stay." She dropped a kiss on her forehead.

"I just wish it was over already."

"You are going to do great. Stop stressing."

"Will you find me and kiss me senseless when I'm done?"

"How about this?" She tipped Izzy's chin up with one finger. "I'm going to watch your test, obviously." Sara kissed her lips softly. "When you get a perfect score, which you will, I'll meet you by the kennel. In the same room where we bandaged you up the other day." She kissed her again, running her thumb over the fading abrasion.

"Promise?" Izzy's voice sounded needy and it made her heart melt.

"You have my word." Sara wrapped her arms around Izzy's soft, compact body. "Get some sleep tonight. That's an order."

"You're not the boss of me," Izzy playfully retorted.

"Oh yes, I am." Sara felt herself beaming. "In this one isolated area"—she nodded in support of her self-righteous claim—"I absolutely am."

❖

K-9 certifications were scheduled out over three days so every team could be granted ample time to complete the course, while factoring in for setup, breaks, judging, and debriefing sessions. By luck of the draw Izzy pulled a high number, which meant if everything went off without a hitch, her test was slated for late Wednesday morning. Even though she was bummed to have to wait around, it wasn't so bad, and the downtime afforded her the ability to hang with her colleagues and their dogs. As a bonus she got to be front and center when Jen and Tempe passed with flying colors.

For two solid days she pep-talked Chase, and even though she was just burning off her own excess nerves, he seemed to understand. When her number was called just before lunch Wednesday, she was one of the two teams remaining.

Her palms were sweaty and her heart raced in her chest.

"Okay, buddy. Here we go." Chase looked at her and immediately her blood pressure stabilized. This dog truly was her personal Xanax.

She was ordered to begin in the field with a stationary detection, then to vehicles, and then room search, finally finishing up conducting an open-area canvass in the back wooded section of campus. Peripherally, she spotted Sara and Nicole watching from the sidelines, but she was too focused to be distracted. She had no idea how much time elapsed, but when all was said and done, she and Chase had successfully indicated the presence of six high-category explosives as well as detecting four low-level explosives.

When she finished she could see John Dixon waiting to congratulate her, but she was too busy raining praise on Chase to hurry over. She rewarded him with his favorite jute tug, their standard toy for work, and couldn't resist squealing as she loved on him, even giving him a sweet hug and kiss before they headed back to debrief.

Izzy was dying to get to the kennel area to see Sara for her split second of promised affection. Even though it seemed the setup time between qualifications was substantial, she knew Sara would want to be on-site with the rest of her staff and the judges just to ensure everything went smoothly for Mark's certification run. She checked her watch to assess how much time she might be able to snag with her.

"Great job, Izzy." John's booming voice right next to her caused her to jump. If he noticed at all, it didn't show as he clapped her on the back. "Listen, kid, I need to talk to you." He sounded serious, and Izzy resisted looking past him to see if Sara was nearby.

"Uh, sure," she said. "Can it wait a few minutes?" She was thoroughly going to pretend she needed to use the facilities just to steal her preplanned meet up with Sara in the kennel storage room.

"Unfortunately, no." He placed his hand on her shoulder as he guided her toward his office. "I just got a call from Lieutenant Anderson at Grand Central."

The hair on the back of her neck stood up. "Is everything okay?" she asked.

A deep exhale preceded his answer. "It seems there's something of a situation down in the city. She didn't get into too many specifics with me, but the bottom line is you're needed there." His voice told her this wasn't a drill. "Even if you didn't just sail through certifications, you'd be going." His uneasy laugh rattled her. "I gather it's an all-hands-on-deck situation."

"Okay," she said, still trying to process the scant information.

"Do whatever you need to do to get ready," he said. "Make sure you have all your gear. Vest, flashlight, service weapon. You have all that with you?"

"Yes, sir."

"Okay. Get on the road and call Anderson. She's waiting to fill you in." He rested both hands on her shoulders, seeming resolute in his concern. "Be safe, Izzy."

Fuck, fuck, fuck, fuck.

What the fuck was going on? She wanted to race to Sara, kiss her, tell her she had to leave, that she would be careful. But there was no time. A quick glance in the field showed no sign of her, and even though Izzy felt sure she knew her location, it seemed there wasn't a moment to spare. Everything in John's voice relayed that she was headed to a bona fide emergency. Minutes could be the difference between life and death. She reached for her cell and typed out a quick text.

Got called into work. Sorry. She punctuated the message with a sad face, knowing her words did little to convey what she was feeling.

Sliding her phone into her pocket, she took one long deep breath, making the subtle shift in her brain from practice to game time. She secured Chase in his place in her truck, then held his chin in her palm.

"You did great, Chase. The best." She looked him right in the eyes. "This is the real deal now, big guy. I know you can handle it." She made a fist for him to bump with his nose and he obliged, adding a small lick to finish it off. "You are my mush." She smiled reassuringly. "Don't worry, your secret's safe with me," she added with a wink before moving to the driver's seat and speeding away, already deep in cop mode as she activated the lights and sirens, zipping along the winding country road.

On the highway she listened as Lieutenant Anderson gave her the lowdown. Grand Central Terminal was on lockdown after someone had called and claimed to have littered the place with explosives. The command was used to getting random, typically unsubstantiated threats, but today while the officers were responding with due diligence, proceeding cautiously to investigate the allegation, a bomb had exploded in the middle of the platform of Metro North's Harlem line. Izzy felt her blood pressure rise at hearing the game-changing piece of information. By sheer miracle the injuries were minor, but it was game on, and Anderson was calling for every single dog and handler available.

Cruising along the FDR Drive, Izzy pictured the layout of the terminal she'd patrolled daily for nearly five years. She knew every inch of the space that was a hub for multiple transit and commuter lines on Manhattan's East Side. There were forty-four platforms and three distinct floors including the vast and iconic main concourse. She felt herself brim with defiance. No one messed with her city, her home. She called over her shoulder to Chase, who rested in the back. "We're going to get this guy. You and me, partner." He gave her one sharp bark in response. It was enough for her to know they were completely in sync.

Even though she was more than eager, Izzy was put on standby the second she arrived, forced to wait her turn in the strategic grid search of the terminal. It could be a long night ahead, and the command staff was keeping a chart and rotating teams on a schedule, trying at all costs to keep everyone as fresh as possible.

Relegated to the sidelines, she reached for her phone to see if Sara had gotten her text. The simple response she saw made her heart swell. *Ilu. Be careful.* By now she'd surely have some of the details of what was happening. Izzy was about to respond, tell her she loved her right back, she was bummed she'd missed their kiss, but Lieutenant Anderson stopped her with a calm order.

"No cell phones, Izzy." She lifted her handheld radio for emphasis. "Radio communication only." The lieutenant frowned. "I'm sure you just want to tell your family you're okay. But the bomb techs and the IT guys have asked us to stay off our phones for the time being."

"Of course, L-T."

She slid her phone back in her pocket. It wasn't her family she was worried about. Even with the terminal closed down, she felt certain her relatives would assume she was safe and sound in training halfway up the state. But Sara would stress, and she longed to ease her nerves.

Izzy lost track of time as she waited her turn, and even though no more explosives had detonated or been uncovered, her sixth sense told her where there was one, there were more. She was pacing the squad area with Chase and a few colleagues when Sergeant Smith walked into the room.

"Marquez, you're up."

He waved her to follow him to the staging area where she was paired with a bomb tech who would trail at a distance in case she and Chase made a find on their assignment to clear the subway platform for the 4-5-6 trains.

Bending down, Izzy thumped Chase's side and whispered confidently in his ear. She knew he was reading her cues and she assured him they were ready.

The terminal had an eerie quiet and she strode briskly with Chase, hoping her swagger would override the inherent dread of what they were possibly about to encounter. A live bomb. Just like the one which had already gone off, obliterating the wall and part of the platform. She shook it off, rolling her shoulders as she approached the landing.

"Okay, Chase, this is it."

Proceeding tentatively, she entered the platform from the north, harnessing her courage. She took in the familiar surroundings: the cement platform, its color somewhere between brown and gray, the faded yellow paint chipped and worn along the edge of the track, the dusky smell of summer and sweat mixing together, layers below street level.

With a flick of her wrist, she ordered Chase to begin seeking along the surface of the interior station wall. Three-quarters of the way down, he picked his head up and Izzy knew right away he was on to something. She read his instinct and guided him toward a post that ran from floor to ceiling, suddenly feeling the familiar tension of his muscles tightening as he moved closer to the middle of the walkway. His ears tweaked, and then, like clockwork, he sat down right in front of the center support beam. Mounted to the post sat the subway emergency intercom system. Izzy looked down at him and he met her with a steady gaze, all but saying *bingo*. Right in front of her face were two circular buttons—red for emergency notification and green to request information. She moved forward slightly and peered into the space between the intercom system and the concrete stanchion. Wedged into the small space was a square brick of... something. She didn't know what it was—she only knew it most definitely didn't belong there.

"Good boy," she said to Chase, keeping her voice spirited and solemn at the same time.

She looked down the open corridor and made eye contact with the bomb technician, nodding once to indicate a positive detection. He returned her nod with one of his own and she reached into her pocket retrieving a Sharpie to mark the spot just in front of the call box on the platform where Chase still sat in passive alert.

A small tug on the end of his leash told Chase to move forward as they continued to search the rest of the platform area. She guided him along the edge of the wall, pointing to the base, as they resumed inspecting the perimeter where they'd left off. They circled down and around the very end and made their way back up to the entrance, tracing the edge of the platform. Again, Chase's body language subtly shifted as he zeroed in on a spot at the border of the tracks, planting his butt firmly on the floor, unwavering in his decision to sit. Izzy looked at the open area around them.

"Where, buddy?" she asked softly.

He pointed his snout straight downward, seeming to examine his own paws, and it hit her immediately.

"If you say so," she answered, retrieving her Maglite from its holder on her duty belt. Squatting down on her hands and knees, she perched over the edge and shined her light, even though it wasn't necessary. Less than a foot from her face, sloppily plastered to the underside of the platform lip, was an exact replica of the makeshift bomb she'd seen moments before stuffed against the support post only a few feet away.

She replaced her light and grabbed her marker. Her hands were shaking even though she felt poised inside. She marked the spot above the device with a giant X and doled out measured praise for her dog. Izzy stood up and searched on, making her way to the mouth of the tunnel and stepping into the terminal. Immediately she showered Chase with affection and rewards, truly proud of his diligent detection.

As a hybrid team of emergency personnel arrived to take control of the scene, Izzy stood back and acknowledged the rush she felt coursing through her body. It was a combination of pride and adrenaline, fear and relief. Mixed in with those powerful emotions was overwhelming love and appreciation for her life, her job, her family, Sara. In barely a split second, she felt the value of life increase a thousandfold. She couldn't wait to call Sara, to see her, touch her, to hold her in her arms forever.

But first she had a job to finish.

CHAPTER TWENTY-TWO

Sara gazed at the sun setting in the distance before checking the clock on her desk: 6:55. It had been hours since she'd heard from Izzy. Earlier in the day she'd gotten a one-line text saying simply, *I love you. I'm safe. I'll call when I can.* Sara was grateful for the update, and she relaxed, if only momentarily, answering the message with a heart in hopes it might convey all of her love and support. A short time later the news reported the situation in Manhattan had begun to settle, as the manhunt for a sole terrorist ended with a standoff culminating in his demise at his own hand.

All told, thirteen explosive devices had been uncovered at Grand Central Terminal. Aside from the bomber, no fatalities had been reported, but during the search two blasts had occurred, the second of which resulted in injuries to first responders on the scene. Sara kept hearing the voice of the local correspondent in her head repeat that dreadful bit of information, and even though she felt certain she would know by now if Izzy was among the wounded, she was still worried beyond belief.

"John said I might find you here."

Nicole's voice startled her and she whipped around to see her ex leaning against the open office door, casually dressed in jeans and a scoop-neck shirt. She looked beautiful and calm, and Sara was envious of her inner peace, the polar opposite of her own state at this very moment.

"I don't want to bother you," Nicole said, nodding with her chin at the pile of papers on Sara's desk.

"I'm not working." Sara gestured dismissively at her computer screen which had slipped into sleep mode. "I just couldn't sit in my room." She closed her eyes briefly. "I thought maybe I could distract myself for a while," she offered.

Nicole's smile was understanding. "That's sort of why I'm here," she said. Sara felt her eyebrows curl in question and she watched Nicole's expression soften in response. "She's fine."

"What?"

"Isabel," she responded. "I have people inside," she offered by way of explanation. "I heard the report of a second explosion resulting in EMS casualties." Her lips were a thin line and she looked at the floor. "I knew you must be a wreck." Nicole appeared to hug herself as she spoke, and Sara wondered what she was bracing to say. "I took the liberty of using my executive privilege to check on your girlfriend." She stumbled slightly over the word but continued, "Sara, she's fine. Completely unscathed. Doing a fantastic job, actually."

Sara couldn't hide her relief as the tension drained from her body and she looked at her phone on the desk. Nicole noticed.

"There's still very little public communication being released. Everyone there is under a gag order. I'm sure she's not able to contact you yet. But I wanted you to know."

"Nic." Sara wiped away a tear she felt forming in spite of her relief. "Thank you. I don't really know what to say. Just, thank you."

"It's obvious how much she means to you." She clasped her hands together. "I think it was the least I could do."

The surprise must have been evident on her face and Nicole appeared to acknowledge it with a heavy sigh as she looked up to the ceiling. "Sara, the other day..." She pushed off the door frame and took a step into the office. "I was surprised. Whether or not I should have been, I was." She shook her head. "And for a few days, I was really wrestling with everything." Nicole looked right at her, her eyes heavy with emotion. "But then I saw the way you look at her." She moved forward and leaned against the file cabinet. "I can't compete with that."

"Nicole—"

"You don't have to say anything. It was incredibly presumptuous of me to assume after all these years—"

"That's the crazy part, though," Sara said, cutting her off. "A year ago"—she shrugged, revealing her own uncertainty—"who knows?" She moved into a half sitting position against the window ledge.

"Once I had the chance to really see you together—" Nicole shook her head. "Well, not together per se, but while she was certifying, I was standing right next to you. I think I heard your heart beating the whole time." A sad kind of laugh escaped her. "I looked over at you—I don't even think you noticed."

Sara opened her mouth to speak but Nicole held a hand up.

"It's okay, Sara. You're in love with her. I see that." She drummed her fingertips on the file cabinet, and the hollow echo filled the small office. "I'm not here to try to talk you out of it or make any predictions about your future together." She hung her head a touch. "I'm embarrassed about my behavior the other day. It was…I don't know…rude, inappropriate, childish. You pick."

"I should have told you about Izzy sooner," Sara said, offering her own impromptu apology.

"I guess we're even, then."

Sara thought she saw Nicole's eyes well up, but in the dim office light it was hard to tell. "So what now?" Sara asked.

"Now"—Nicole pulled the hem of her shirt and straightened it precisely—"I run Special Programs from Seattle." She laughed but Sara heard seriousness in her tone.

"Nicole, you don't have to do that."

"It's for the best, I think."

"I'm not trying to push you out of the job you worked so hard for. We're all adults. I'm sure we'll get through this."

"You're right." Nicole's expression told her the decision was already made. "All the same, I'm going to go anyway." She pushed her hair away from her face and squared her shoulders. "Honestly, I think a fresh start would do me some good. Seattle is a great city. And I have some friends in the regional office," she added. "The past few years I was so caught up in work…it's possible I romanticized parts of our relationship to a certain extent."

Sara nodded agreement, knowing she'd done the exact same thing. It was a truth she didn't realize until she met Izzy, but one that had become obvious since the moment she'd fallen for her.

"Still friends?" Sara asked tentatively.

"We better be. Your K-9 program overhaul is genius. I'm counting on you to help roll it out. If you want. Or you can just be available by phone. Or video. Or not." She stuttered out her explanation. "I don't want you to think I'm being surreptitious or trying to snake you away from Izzy. I'm not. Honest."

"I know." Sara smiled sincerely. "I do know you, Nicole."

"I want you to be happy, Sara. God, no one deserves that more than you."

"That's not true. Everyone deserves it."

"I know. I just meant…" She shook her head. "Izzy seems like a good person. And by all accounts, she's a great cop. She did a phenomenal job yesterday and today." Nicole seemed proud. "That's a testament to you, you know." She brought her steepled fingers to her lips. "I'm just trying to say, I'm happy for you, for whatever it's worth."

"It's worth a lot, actually."

Sara crossed the room and gave her a heartfelt hug, hoping in her embrace Nicole might feel a fraction of the love and friendship they'd shared over the years.

Nicole wrapped her arms tightly around Sara's waist, burying her face in her shoulder. "This girl better be good to you."

Sara was overwhelmed with emotion—the love she felt for Izzy, the fondness she had for Nicole. She held her tightly, acknowledging the end of an era as it bled right into the beginning of the rest of her life.

Hours later, Sara leaned back against the headrest of her pickup, the warm night air filling the cab around her. Even though

Izzy's block was quiet, it was late and she didn't want to alarm the neighbors, so she'd pulled her truck into Izzy's driveway while she waited. She fully intended to move the second Izzy arrived home.

She woke up when she felt a gentle touch on her shoulder.

"Hey." Izzy's smile was warm, her voice soft and husky. "I need to get you keys," she said, ticking her head toward the front door.

"What time is it?" Sara gripped the steering wheel, pulling herself higher in the seat before rubbing the sleep from her eyes.

"Late." Izzy opened the car door, and Chase used the opportunity to hop up and greet Sara with a string of wet kisses. "Hey, don't be a hog," Izzy teased her dog as she nudged him down tenderly. She reached for Sara's hand and helped her out. "It's after midnight. How long have you been here?"

"Not long," she lied. With a shrug she added, "A few hours, maybe."

"I was going to call you when I was leaving, but I looked at the time and thought it was too late. I figured I'd text when I got here just so you'd know I was home, safe and sound."

Sara turned the ignition to close the windows, then slid out and reached for her bag before she shut the door. "I hope it's okay I came. I needed to see you."

In the dark night, Izzy leaned forward and answered her with a kiss. "Of course." Sara ran her hands up Izzy's forearms and felt her skin pebble under the touch. "You are always welcome here. I really am going to get you a key."

Sara could see the fatigue in her eyes, and when she dropped her head squarely on her chest, Sara kissed the top of her hair.

"I would have been here sooner, but even after the terminal was secured, there was a mountain of paperwork." Sara could hear her perk up as she spoke and she looked down at her dog proudly. "Chase here was a star." She met Sara's eyes. "He found not one but two improvised explosive devices."

Sara squatted down to give him due praise. "Is that right, big guy?" she said, petting his head and face lovingly before standing up. "I heard you were quite the hero yourself." She looked right at

Izzy's big brown eyes, feeling herself fall deeper with each passing second.

"John?" Izzy said, seeking the identity of Sara's intel provider.

She swallowed hard, knowing she had to reveal her source. "Nicole."

Izzy nodded, clearly processing the information. Sara didn't want her mind to run amok so she offered up some detail.

"She came by to tell me you were okay." Sara touched the blended fabric of Izzy's uniform shirt, feeling her soft abdomen beneath it. "When the news reported there was an explosion and first responders were injured, I was…well, I was nervous."

"I wanted to call you. I wasn't allowed." Izzy reached for her hand and guided them to the front door. "Also, it was chaos."

"You don't have to explain, Izzy." Sara followed her inside, dropping her bag and pulling her close. "I know what this job is. I've been around it my whole life." She kissed her. "I'm just glad you're okay."

"I'm glad Nicole told you I wasn't hurt. That was kind of her."

Izzy put Chase to bed without protest and Sara melted, seeing how utterly exhausted he was. She didn't want to spend any more time talking about Nicole, but she couldn't resist sharing one other tiny bit of good news.

"She also told me she's moving to Seattle."

Izzy was in the middle of sliding her firearm off her belt, and she stood frozen in the bedroom holding the entire holster in her hands.

"What?" she asked, her voice laced with confusion.

Sara signaled her to put her gun away, and Izzy tucked it safely into the highest drawer of her dresser. Sara didn't even wait for her to turn around. Instead she slipped in behind her, circling her waist with her palms.

"I'm in love with you." She held her ever closer. "She knows it." A small laugh escaped her. "Everyone knows it, I think." Izzy turned in her arms, and she was happy to see her gorgeous face. "There is nothing in this world that will change that. You are the one for me."

"It won't always be like it was today, Sara. And yesterday…" She sighed. "My days are melding together." Sara felt Izzy's hands slide under her shirt just to make skin to skin contact. "I can't believe tomorrow is graduation."

"In a few hours, really."

Izzy looked up at her and her eyes were pleading. "Can we please go straight to Phoenicia right after? I need to be together, just me and you." She rested her arms over Sara's shoulders. "I missed you."

"I thought we had to have dinner with your family. To celebrate, you said."

Izzy hung her head in fake distress. "I'll call them and explain in the morning. They'll understand." Her eyes darted around the room. "Maybe we can just do a quick lunch after the ceremony," she said.

"Whatever you want." Sara smiled right at her. "I mean it," she said with a mild shrug. "I'm game for anything. You're the one who's had a rough few days."

"It won't always be this crazy. I swear."

"Even if it is, I'm never letting you go."

Izzy's smile was lovely and pure. "I love you."

"Promise me one thing." Sara placed a soft kiss on her forehead, moving her lips down over her temple and cheeks, her chin, her beautiful full mouth. "Always come home to me."

"Forever," Izzy said.

Sara smiled at her perfect response. In this small moment, standing in the center of Izzy's bedroom with a lifetime ahead of them, Sara knew what they felt for one another was real and true and perfect. It was forever.

EPILOGUE

One Year Later

"Tish."

Sara called out for her young pup the second she stepped from her back door into the quiet, cool summer morning air. The lack of immediate response meant her rascal was surely off adventuring. She smiled to herself, both elated and relieved to know he wasn't alone. With a small shake of her head she set the two bowls of kibble she was holding on the flat top of the deck railing, calling into the forest of trees from the back porch of the house.

"Tish, Chase," she bellowed, cupping her hands around her mouth so her voice would carry. "Come on, boys."

Squinting, she saw movement in the brush, and a half second later both dogs came barreling out from the line of trees that surrounded the property.

Chase beat his little brother by a good few yards and came to a perfect halt sliding into a seated position, his mouth hanging open in a happy smile. Sara looked from one dog to the other.

"Tish, what's Chase doing that you're not?" she asked playfully.

The six-month old German shepherd mix cocked his head from side to side, joyfully panting from his mad dash.

"Sit, Tish," Sara ordered.

Tish met her stare before checking over Chase's posture and sitting squarely on the ground.

"Good boys. Very good."

Sara reached for their food and placed it on the ground in front of them. "Wait for the command," she said, mostly to Tish. But she barely made him hold out for a second before ordering, "Eat."

Sara ascended the few steps to watch the guys chow down as she leaned against the railing. She swallowed a laugh when Tish popped his snout into Chase's bowl and was just as quickly nosed out.

"What's funny?"

Izzy came up behind Sara and kissed her shoulder.

"Tish just figured he'd maybe sample some of Chase's food. As I'm sure you can imagine, Chase was not having it," she said with a smile.

"You tell him who's boss, Chase."

"Oh, don't worry, he knows."

"And how are the kids this morning?" Izzy asked.

"Just fine." Sara reached behind to usher Izzy in front so she could see for herself. "They were off in the woods," she added with an eye roll.

"Don't helicopter," Izzy scolded impishly.

"Helicopter? Me?" Sara pretended to be annoyed as she squeezed Izzy's waist, causing her to giggle.

Izzy covered her hands and Sara turned her around to get a good look at her gorgeous smile.

"You know Chase won't let him get into any trouble," Izzy said sincerely. "He totally dotes on him. Possibly more than you."

"Their connection is really sweet," Sara echoed.

Izzy turned her head toward their dogs playing together in the open grass. "I can't believe just a few months ago we didn't even know him."

"I know. And already he's such a part of the family. It's like I almost can't remember what it was like without him here."

"I'm glad you waited to find the right dog." Izzy looked over at the puppy holding on to a tennis ball with paws that almost seemed too big for his growing body. He gnawed the hide over and over, letting out a small bark when he bit too hard and the ball rolled away from him. Undeterred, he followed it a few feet, looking over and turning his dark face to one side, seeming to smile at them before he returned to chewing. "He's such a happy little guy," Izzy said.

"My mother would love him," Sara said.

Since naming Tish in her honor, they'd talked quite a bit about Sara's mother—her life and her legacy—and Sara felt the use of her mother's special nickname was the perfect balance of tribute and devotion to her memory. It also made her feel connected to her mom in a way she couldn't quite explain.

"Of course she'd love him," Izzy said. "He's a sweetie." She reached up and kissed Sara's cheek. "And someday, he'll be a great service dog just like his big bro." Over in the distance, Tish fell over his own head into a tumble-sault trying to get the best of Chase's oversized Kong. "All in good time," Izzy added with a laugh.

Sara leaned forward to kiss Izzy. "What time are you two working today?" she asked, slightly nodding toward Chase, who was lounging on the grass in the late morning sun.

"Our tour is two to ten today," Izzy said, looking at her watch. "We should probably get moving soon. It's a hike from up here."

Living together had been a virtually seamless transition, requiring almost no conversation at all. For the last twelve months they'd fully cohabitated, spending the weekdays at Izzy's place in suburban Westchester County and using Sara's home in upstate Phoenicia as their weekend getaway. Sara knew Izzy adored the mountain trails and the quaint little town. Still, she felt guilty, knowing she and Chase had a brutal commute ahead of them today.

"We should have gone home yesterday," Sara said, caressing Izzy's tanned forearms.

Izzy tipped her head back into the warm rays of sunlight just reaching the porch. "Absolutely not." She looked beautiful and pure and completely content. It made Sara's heart swell. "I love it here. You know that." Her eyes sparkled in the sun. "Someday we'll retire here."

"We will, huh?" Sara's answer was a question, even though she knew Izzy was probably right.

Izzy leaned forward and kissed her. "You know we will." She

placed baby kisses all over Sara's face, and Sara felt herself beam at the attention. "The only question is how many dogs we'll have."

"Two." Sara found Izzy's lips. "Always two."

"You sound pretty sure of that."

Sara's eyes shifted to the yard where Chase and Tish were play wrestling. She melted every time Chase lay down and let Tish pounce on him. "I know it's still so new, but I just can't imagine these two without each other."

"Me either," Izzy said. But when Sara looked back, Izzy's eyes were on her, not the dogs.

Sara kissed her before turning Izzy in her arms so they could watch the boys frolic together. "Look at them," she said with a smile.

"Partners in crime," Izzy responded as they got into some mischief with a rope tug.

"They're good boys." Sara held Izzy close, loving the feel of their bodies together. She dropped a decadent kiss on Izzy's cheek and whispered in her ear. "Just partners. Perfect, perfect partners."

About the Author

Maggie Cummings is the author of *Totally Worth It*, *Serious Potential*, and *Definite Possibility*, all part of the Bay West Social trilogy, and the co-authored novel *Against All Odds*. She lives in Staten Island, New York, with her wife, their two children, and their sweet, ancient dog. She works as a police officer in New York City, and is constantly daydreaming about the fictional people who live in her head with the hope of bringing them to life on the page. She loves chick flicks, body switch movies, fanfic, great romances, and fanvids shipping lesbian TV characters. The people who make those are her true heroes. She still mourns the end of *Buffy the Vampire Slayer*, and she has yet to meet a potato chip she didn't immediately fall in love with.

Books Available From Bold Strokes Books

A Chapter on Love by Laney Webber. When Jannika and Lee reunite, their instant connection feels like a gift, but neither is ready for a second chance at love. Will they finally get on the same page when it comes to love? (978-1-163555-366-6)

Drawing Down the Mist by Sheri Lewis Wohl. Everyone thinks Grand Duchess Maria Romanova died in 1918. They were almost right. (978-1-163555-341-3)

Listen by Kris Bryant. Lily Croft is inexplicably drawn to Hope D'Marco, but will she have the courage to confront the consequences of her past and present colliding? (978-1-163555-318-5)

Perfect Partners by Maggie Cummings. Elite police dog trainer Sara Wright has no intention of falling in love with a coworker until Isabel Marquez arrives at Homeland Security's Northeast Regional Training facility, and Sara's good intentions start to falter. (978-1-163555-363-5)

Shut Up and Kiss Me by Julie Cannon. What better way to spend two weeks of hell in paradise than in the company of a hot, sexy woman? (978-1-163555-343-7)

Spencer's Cove by Missouri Vaun. When Foster Owen and Abigail Spencer meet, they uncover a story of lives adrift, loves lost, and true love found. (978-1-163555-171-6)

Unexpected Lightning by Cass Sellars. Lightning strikes once more when Sydney and Parker fight a dangerous stranger who threatens the peace they both desperately want. (978-1-163555-276-8)

Without Pretense by TJ Thomas. After living for decades hiding from the truth, can Ava learn to trust Bianca with her secrets and her heart? (978-1-163555-173-0)

Emily's Art and Soul by Joy Argento. When Emily meets Andi Marino she thinks she's found a new best friend, but Emily doesn't know that Andi is fast falling in love with her. Caught up in exploring her sexuality, will Emily see the only woman she needs is right in front of her? (978-1-163555-355-0)

Escape to Pleasure: Lesbian Travel Erotica, edited by Sandy Lowe and Victoria Villaseñor. Join these award-winning authors as they explore the sensual side of erotic lesbian travel. (978-1-163555-339-0)

Music City Dreamers by Robyn Nyx. Music can bring lovers together. In Music City, it can tear them apart. (978-1-163555-207-2)

Ordinary is Perfect by D. Jackson Leigh. Atlanta marketing superstar Autumn Swan's life derails when she inherits a country home, a child, and a very interesting neighbor. (978-1-163555-280-5)

Royal Court by Jenny Frame. When royal dresser Holly Weaver's passionate personality begins to melt Royal Marine Captain Quincy's icy heart, will Holly be ready for what she exposes beneath? (978-1-163555-290-4)

Strings Attached by Holly Stratimore. Rock star Nikki Razer always gets what she wants, but when she falls for Drew McNally, a music teacher who won't date celebrities, can she convince Drew she's worth the risk? (978-1-163555-347-5)

The Ashford Place by Jean Copeland. When Isabelle Ashford inherits an old house in small-town Connecticut, family secrets, a shocking discovery, and an unexpected romance complicate her plan for a fast profit and a temporary stay. (978-1-163555-316-1)

Treason by Gun Brooke. Zoem Malderyn's existence is a deadly threat to everyone on Gemocon, and Commander Neenja KahSandra must find a way to save the woman she loves from having to make the ultimate sacrifice. (978-1-163555-244-7)

A Wish Upon a Star by Jeannie Levig. Erica Cooper has learned to depend on only herself, but when her new neighbor, Leslie Raymond, befriends Erica's special needs daughter, the walls protecting Erica's heart threaten to crumble. (978-1-163555-274-4)

Answering the Call by Ali Vali. Detective Sept Savoie returns to the streets of New Orleans, as do the dead bodies from ritualistic killings, and she does everything in her power to bring their killers to justice while trying to keep her partner, Keegan Blanchard, safe. (978-1-163555-050-4)